# BLOOD SKY

## MACLACHLAN THRILLER #4

## G. WAYNE TILMAN

WOLFPACK
PUBLISHING
EST 2013

**Blood Sky**
Print Edition
© Copyright 2021 G. Wayne Tilman

Wolfpack Publishing
5130 S. Fort Apache Rd. 215-380
Las Vegas, NV 89148

wolfpackpublishing.com

eBook ISBN  978-1-63977-035-9
Paperback ISBN 9978-1-63977-036-6

# BLOOD SKY

The Air France jet lowered its wheels and its young passengers leaned to see out of the windows as it made final approach to Palma Airport in Mallorca. There was both excitement and noise on the plane. It was full of generally college age Europeans. They were ready to don the tiniest of wisp bikinis and party their hearts out on Mallorca's beaches.

Nisa Faheem and her friend, Adele Martel, grabbed their carry-ons as soon as the plane stopped at the gate. They pushed into the crowded aisle and exited the plane quickly.

A thirty-five-year-old man in work coveralls spotted them and spoke quickly into his sleeve. On the other side of Immigration, two women did the same.

Near the taxi stand, a young man with swarthy skin and a hand full of cards walked up to the two girls and handed each a glossy card with a cover charge waiver for the Shout night club. He was handsome and flirtatious and personalized his delivery of the cards with an invitation to see them tonight.

The two climbed into a taxi and the young man spoke into his wrist microphone. He gave the taxi color and license tag to three surveillance tail vehicles. The taxi moved into heavy traffic and the three vehicles took their positions for the eight-kilometer drive to downtown Palma. Car one "had the eye" three cars back and with the taxi in sight. Car two was in the center lane about ten cars back. Car three ran on a parallel street.

Ten minutes later, the taxi pulled into a luxury hotel. Car two sped up and pulled to the curb as Car one continued past the hotel. A young woman from Car two climbed out and followed the two late teen visitors into the front desk area. She stood close enough to obtain their room number before feigning a phone call and walking away from the check-in line. The trap was set, and the two young women had no clue whatsoever.

Jet lag did not appear to affect wealthy teen females. They moved into their home for a week and went downstairs for either lunch or dinner. They were not really sure which. The dark-haired, plump, rather pouty one picked at her food. The blonde, who looked like a model ate heartily. She trusted her metabolism to keep her slender. So far, so good.

"Adele, where first?" Nisa Faheem asked.

"How about the night club on the cards we were given?" eighteen-year-old Adele Martel responded.

"Sure! It's probably on the beach by all the other clubs. I am ready to get very, very drunk and dance!"

They applied heavy night makeup and dresses of

which neither of their fathers would have approved. Especially Nisa's Jordanian father. The dark-haired Nisa was buxom and had shapely legs. Her middle had always been a source of worry to her, and she had learned to change focal points and dress to minimize it and accentuate her strong points.

Adele had the sense of fashion which seemed genetic to French women. She could take a cheap black dress and some pearls and look like Paris or Rodeo Drive with little else in the way of preparation.

Their hotel was near the night club district. The rather expansive night club district the travel agent had emphasized. It was also near the beach, something Adele loved as much as her tiny bikinis. And something which caused Nisa some image worries. She had already decided to throw modesty to the winds and redirect focus away from her midsection.

The two young ladies walked to the entertainment district. Their destination, the Shout night club, was easy to find by asking anyone. The one they chose to ask had, unbeknownst to them, worked his way into their path even before they asked him.

"I am going to Shout myself," he said.

"Let me show you the way. Allow me to buy your first round of drinks. I am Marcel, by the way," the handsome twenty-five-year-old with a slight French accent said.

He very obviously gravitated to Nisa. Adele wrinkled her nose. *It was usually the other way around*, she thought.

Adele did not waste time worrying about it. Marcel paid their cover charges and Adele walked into a pretty girl's paradise. There appeared to be more handsome young men than women. She would do just fine here. With Nisa already occupied, she had the opportunity to pick and choose without worrying about finding someone for her friend and school roommate.

Marcel bought the first round. By the need for a second round, Adele was working the floor. She had a veritable line of young men waiting to dance with her, buy her a drink, or just stare like puppies. She looked good when she was the age she was pretending to be now. In her twenties, she made a knockout teenager.

Nisa was having the time of her life. She was dancing like a wild woman, her lack of decorum enhanced by the three fruity drinks she had consumed in less than an hour. Marcel left her dancing with an accomplice as he went to the bar for her fourth drink.

He put half the powder from a ketamine capsule into the new cocktail. The boss' order was for her to appear drunk, but not become immobile.

Within a few minutes, Marcel and his back-up dancing associate were leading the "drunk" Nisa off the dance floor.

In the backseat of the waiting car, Marcel, per orders, ripped off Nisa's panties. He groped her. She was only partially aware of what was happening and thought it was all part of a wild night in Palma. She finally passed out on his lap. He thought it was more from the drinks than the drug but could not be sure.

They drove for fifteen minutes. The non-descript ten-year-old Audi pulled into the winding lane of a deserted farmhouse.

Marcel and his associate dragged Nisa out. The

car sped off leaving them near a darkened door. As they propped Nisa up, she vomited all over her dress and shoes.

"Damn! We should have been ready for that."

Inside with the door secured, Marcel ripped her dress off. She lost the shoes being dragged across the floor. They put her in a small bedroom with a new padlock on the door. The room had a bed, a small table, a sink, and a porcelain pot to use as a toilet. The window was covered with boards. A bare bulb in a ceiling fixture provided a small amount of light.

They lifted the naked girl on the bed, facedown and with her head pointed to the side. There were very specific orders to do it this way to reduce the probability of her vomiting then choking to death on it.

The next day, Nisa was refused an aspirin for her headache. She was given a cup of water and a bowl of some sort of oat mush.

Nisa defaulted to her spoiled brat nature and demanded a decent breakfast. A man she had not seen before came in, smacked her several times and then raped her.

Nisa Faheem was scared, sore, and generally pissed off.

*Just wait until my daddy gets these guys!* she thought. Her mood changed and she sobbed herself to sleep.

Marcel received a call from his unknown handler.

"How is the prisoner?"

"She is fine. We have followed instructions to the letter."

"Good. I don't care what you do with her as long

as you don't seriously injure her. Remember, if one of you gets her pregnant, she will be carrying your very identifiable DNA."

"Of course. All possible precautions will be observed," Marcel lied confidently.

The man on the other end hung up.

Marcel took enough cash to bribe a chemist for a couple "morning after" emergency contraceptive pills.

———————

MACLACHLAN ROLLED over and looked at the woman sleeping next to him. She snored softly, almost like a cat's purr. It was not at all bothersome. It was really kind of endearing. Her long blonde hair splayed out on the pillow. She smiled as she slept.

He pulled the sheet part the way up, then stopped just above her waist. She was beautiful. Damn near perfect.

She went silent when the phone buzzed on the bureau across the room.

MacLachlan knew she was awake, though her eyes were not open. She did not bother raising the sheet.

He got up and quietly padded across the yellow pine floors.

"Yes?"

"Slickmeister."

"Okay. Bye."

Only one person called MacLachlan "Slickmeister". Will Grafton, a senior executive in the US Intelligence Community, or USIC. By not uttering another word, Will signaled to call him back on a secure line.

MacLachlan walked into the study off the bedroom. It served as his office when he was in residence at the Florida cracker house on Casey Key.

He picked up an encrypted SAT phone and dialed to an identical phone. The one he called was in Grafton's office in McLean, Virginia. His office was in a complex, while not covert, was very well protected. Protected by some of the best in the business.

"Whazzup?" Grafton answered.

"I don't know. You called me just after dawn on a Saturday morning."

"Guess I did. The Belgian facilitator still there?"

"Yep."

"She within hearing range?" Grafton, a friend and former Defense Intelligence Agency compadre of MacLachlan's asked. Grafton was now one of the top operational executives in the Office of the Director of National Intelligence. The ODNI was the usual way people in the "community" referred to it.

"Pretty much," the intel contractor said.

"Perfectly okay. You can get back to whatever you were doing in a sec. Somebody called looking for assistance today. It was not dawn in their time zone. A bit later. I gave them your name. Stay near this phone for a while. It may be worth your time." He clicked off the connection, leaving the tall former Marine officer perplexed. Grafton loved to leave him hanging, waiting for a shoe to drop somewhere else in the world. MacLachlan could visualize his amused grin. The caller, from the hint Grafton had given him was further east. Eastern Europe? Middle East?

"Assignment?" called a sexy, smoky voice without any accent from the bed.

"Impending assignment. Just a warning about an upcoming call."

"Sound like fun? Need some help?" Anna Visser asked.

"Not a clue. I'll let you know when I get the call and some details."

"Well. We are awake, so you may as well come back here for a few minutes. After, we can have coffee and fruit and decide what else we'll do today," Anna said.

*How could anyone turn such a suggestion down?* MacLachlan thought to himself as he walked back to the bed. Anna's definition of a "few minutes" was more like thirty minutes.

Later, MacLachlan brewed a pot of Black Rifle Coffee Company coffee. It was already rich. He brewed the pot strong. Anna chopped melons, strawberries and bananas. She liberally sprinkled pepitas, or roasted, salted pumpkin seeds, blueberries, and golden raisins on top.

They took the coffee and fruit down the winding lane and across the road to MacLachlan's section of beach. Sitting in the chickee hut, they had breakfast while watching the Gulf waves roll in.

"Beats being on a cold mountaintop in Afghanistan or a back alley in Istanbul," MacLachlan said.

"Yes. No danger here."

"Not now. A hit team dropped in some years ago though."

"How many?"

"More than the fingers on your graceful hand," MacLachlan responded.

"What happened to them?"

"They died. Scattered around the yard."

"Hmmm. That's why you have a 1911 .45 Commander stashed under the tea towel?" she asked.

"Keep your friends close and your gun closer. Better regimen for good health than vitamins."

"How about lovers?"

"Keep them real close, Anna. Real close."

"Mack, when you and Lexi were interrogating me in Monaco it was really serious. Yet you bantered and were warm and humorous. You aren't anymore. Is it her death?"

"It's a lot of things, Anna. You being here helps a lot though."

She wondered if he even knew what was bothering him. Something was and it had to do with someone. It appeared he was not going to talk about it.

They ate the fruit and had second cups of coffee. Anna undid the towel she wore across the road to the beach and walked over the sand into the warm Gulf of Mexico. She swam like an Olympic swimmer, unlike MacLachlan. He could keep up his crawl for miles, but it was painful to watch.

The satellite phone rang. It was either Grafton again or the mysterious caller.

It was the latter. MacLachlan was good at accents. This one was an Afrikaner.

"My name is Schutte. I handle security for a very

wealthy man in Dubai. A family member of his just disappeared. We don't want police involvement.

"I understand you may be able to facilitate finding and recovering the person. Are you interested?"

"I might be, Mr. Schutte. I am a security contractor who usually works on government matters, not a private investigator. I would need to know a lot more to make an assessment which is fair to you and your employer. I realize time is of the essence in these matters. Where can we meet quickly to speak in a lot more detail?" MacLachlan said.

"How about Paris tomorrow? I will text you all the particulars on the rendezvous on this number. You probably will not be able to access them until you arrive at Charles de Gaulle. I will guarantee twenty thousand Euros for the trip, whether you take the assignment or not."

"Okay. I will see you there. Is this the best number to reach you?"

Schutte said it was and hung up.

Anna walked out of the water. Her golden body was dripping Gulf of Mexico onto the sand.

MacLachlan put the phone down and handed her a towel.

She looked at him quizzically.

"A family member of a rich guy in Dubai went missing yesterday. Fancy going to Paris with me? All expenses paid?" he asked.

"We might be able to get a flight out of Miami today," Anna said.

She had done the logistics for an odd pair of assassins since college. She planned their travel, had weapons cached for them, and did the billing. Anna never knew whether they were aware of the money she skimmed off the top, or simply did not care. The male and female shooters lived a modest life. She was a woman who could disappear in a very small group. He looked like a horror movie character. He was a giant with absolutely no moral compass whatsoever... though his platonic partner could kill someone in the middle of a meal and finish eating without a qualm, too.

"Let me get to a computer and put together our travel. Do you want to fly business class or first? Coach sucks crossing the ocean, Mack."

"Business should be fine. It will take us five hours to get parked at the airport and head through security," he said.

They walked quickly up the slight hill from the beach and across the road. A hundred yards down the curving entrance and they entered the house. Anna sat at the Mac Pro in MacLachlan's office.

He called the couple who looked after his house when he was gone and advised them he would be away for an indeterminate amount of time.

While Anna was getting the tickets, MacLachlan opened the large gun safe and removed a metal box. He took out his passport. His *real* passport. Then, he removed a couple thousand in Euros.

"Mack, what's your TSA Pre-Check number?" He told her and heard the printer begin on itinerary and same-day boarding passes.

He went out to the stilted garage and drove the new model Bronco down the ramp, leaving the very special Mustang at home.

Anna was already packed. Paris put her close to her home in Belgium anyway. MacLachlan packed a carry-on. He put his new gun of choice in the hidden locker of the Bronco, and they left.

He drove with the flow of traffic on I-75 South, which was around eighty. They passed the exits for Ft. Myers and Naples. The Interstate crossed the edge of the Everglades.

MacLachlan remembered the Glades portion when it was just a two-lane gravel road known as Alligator Alley. Today, he was glad for the fast lanes of I-75.

He whipped the Bronco into a parking place in the long-term area. MacLachlan and Anna bailed out and rushed to the international gates and made it onto a flight scheduled to leave a bit after two o'clock.

They settled into large leather seats and were offered wine, which both accepted.

MacLachlan covertly assessed every passenger who boarded. No overt threats, though a couple attracted more attention than the rest. Anna observed him and conducted her own assessments.

The large plane lifted off and Anna was asleep on MacLachlan's shoulder within half an hour.

The flight was boring and uneventful. Boring was MacLachlan's favorite kind of flight. They arrived at Charles De Gaulle at eight the next morning.

Once they cleared Immigration, they stopped at a coffee shop and used the Wi-Fi.

There was an email in the clear on MacLachlan's iPhone from Schutte to call when they got in. MacLachlan called immediately.

"Schutte," the phone was answered.

"MacLachlan. We arrived. I have one associate with me. I may bring another over within a day or two, depending on what things look like."

"Good! Can you meet me at Gare du Nord train station at two? I will be carrying a briefcase and have a pink carnation in my jacket lapel."

"Will do. I am six foot one and have short dark hair going gray. I have a blue blazer and dark gray slacks and will be with the most beautiful and dangerous woman in Paris. I'm sure you'll notice her first. See you at two," MacLachlan said as he hung up, intentionally keeping the airtime brief.

"Most beautiful and dangerous woman in Paris? Ha! How about the world?"

MacLachlan grinned at her.

"It's always wise to keep some part of one's capabilities as a surprise," he said.

"Like you being able to speak five languages? Amazing for an American."

"See what I mean? I actually speak several more than five."

She punched him in the arm. It hurt her fist more than his arm.

"What will we do for the next five hours?"

"Let's walk down the street and look for a hotel. We can't just sit on a bench."

They found the Kube Hotel and checked in for one day. MacLachlan shared his reasoning.

"Beyond just our comfort, it will give us a quiet place to meet Schutte and talk. Do you mind checking for flights to Mallorca? I suspect we will be spending the night there. Also, please try to get us a room in Adele's hotel in Palma, the capital. It's on the info sheet Schutte gave us."

"It must be handy having your own logistician traveling with you," she said.

"Indeed. Plus, she will be paid handsomely for her grueling work."

"Oh?"

"Oh, yes. Tax free to any numbered private account you want. I know you have several from the last case."

"Indeed," she responded in kind with a lascivious grin.

At one o'clock, the two walked back down the street to the Gare du Nord train station. Anna ostensibly waited in a double decker tour bus line. MacLachlan crossed the street and walked a couple of blocks in both directions. He noticed a heavy police and military presence. He knew it was from a spate of recent terrorist attacks. MacLachlan considered the lack of border controls in the EU to be a virtual gift to terrorists and criminals. He also realized the proliferation of facial recognition cameras at ports of entry hampered operator activity.

As MacLachlan approached Anna, he saw she had made contact with Schutte. As per their plan, she was chatting until MacLachlan came within her view. She would then begin to walk him back to the nearby hotel.

MacLachlan followed a hundred yards back and did not see any tails. If the young woman had been taken by pros, it appeared to MacLachlan that Schutte did not warrant their surveillance. Or, pro he probably was, had slipped it.

He maintained the distance, getting to the hotel a minute or so behind them. He took the steps rather than the escalator.

MacLachlan heard the door close as he reached the landing for their floor. At the door, he gave a pre-planned distinctive knock and Anna opened it.

"Mr. Schutte, Mack MacLachlan. We've given the room a quick scan and did not find any mics or cameras." Before they sat down, Anna turned on the cold-water faucet for white noise. With the sink within ten feet from the chairs and love seat they were using, it would be an acceptable way to somewhat obliterate their conversation to most types of outside surveillance.

"I believe we are under a serious time constraint. Nisa dropped off the radar around ten o'clock, night before last. She was in the Shout night club in Mallorca. I have photos and her dossier in here. I also included copies of her travel documents, tickets, hotel and credit cards. She was traveling with a French friend from school, Adele Martel. I believe you will find her most cooperative. The two are very close and she wants to help."

"There is also a sheet on her father. While he is extremely careful about his privacy, I thought you would like some background. Once the two of you read it and commit whatever you wish to memory, we will burn it."

"We have not received a ransom call. My sense is Nisa, at seventeen, is a bit old for human trafficking. Quite frankly, she is not pretty or shapely. I think she cruised with her friend, Adele, who served as bait for boys. Anyone who wanted to traffic her as a cleaner would find her devoid of domestic attitude or talents," Schutte said.

Schutte handed Mack and Anna his folder. The first thing they looked at was a color 8 x10 of Nisa. She had an unpleasant look on her face and appeared to be slightly overweight. The professional photographer did an admirable job with the photo but could not hide the smirk.

A similar size photo of Adele showed a potential fashion model. As the two were together and they took Nisa instead, MacLachlan was convinced a targeted kidnapping, not human trafficking, would be the case.

MacLachlan and Anna simultaneously read the tear sheet on the father, Kadar Faheem. He was involved in a number of undertakings. The most interesting to MacLachlan was a pharmaceutical company. He caught Anna's expression, then an almost imperceptible nod. He handed the page back to Schutte, who lit it with a gold lighter and held the burning sheet over the sink. Once the ashes had been flushed by the running water, he resumed his seat.

"Which of these companies should be of the most interest to us?" MacLachlan asked. He was using a standard interrogation probe. Ask a question the answer to which you already know or suspect. Schutte realized what the large operator was doing and grinned at him.

"Yes. The pharmaceutical company would be my first guess, also. Especially since it just won one of the largest drug contracts in history against two other companies. The contract was a five-year guarantee for the whole of the Middle East and Southeast Asia. It covered COVID-19 and any subsequent strains of it. Over the five years, it will add another billion Euros to Kadar Faheem's worth."

He then named the two primary competitors who lost the bid.

"Where is each headquartered?" MacLachlan asked.

"Russia," was the answer. He wrote the names of the two companies and handed the note to MacLachlan.

"I take it Mr. Faheem is Muslim?" Anna asked.

"Actually, he is a Christian, originally from Jordan."

MacLachlan nodded but did not say anything.

"Other than the Russians, please advise us of any other business relationships which have been a cause for concern. Firings of key employees, attempted takeovers, hardhanded moves Mr. Faheem has taken with other competitors?" MacLachlan asked.

"You don't get to be a billionaire by being a nice guy. Corporate skirmishes he has been in and won would fill a book." MacLachlan nodded.

"Are her things still at the hotel with Adele?" Anna asked.

"Yes. Adele, in her innocence, believes Nisa will return. She thinks Nisa just got lucky. I seriously doubt it to be the case. She wants to help, though beyond cursory information, I cannot see how helpful someone I assume to be an eighteen-year-old would be."

"I suspect you are correct, Mr. Schutte," MacLachlan said.

"Here is the promised stipend to cover your trip

and a couple days investigating if you accept. I hope you do. I have known the man who called you for years. He would not risk his reputation by recommending the wrong person."

"Thank you. It was he who originally told me to stop working *in* the government and start working *for* the government. I have been careful since I took his advice. I've been selective over which governments and employers I have represented."

"Give Anna and me a day or so in Mallorca to see what we can find out. I will call you and let you know what we find and whether it's worth our mutual time to take the assignment," MacLachlan said.

"Seems reasonable to me. Call with any news, alright?" Schutte asked.

"Absolutely. And, maybe with a new question or two which crops up during our inquiry. It goes without saying we will learn a lot from any ransom demand.

"The way disappearances like this are solved is with someone studying the security cameras at most businesses and studying street and traffic cameras. Then doing immediate lookup of suspicious vehicle license plates, and informers on the street. Those are things where the police excel over private individuals like us. Are you sure Mr. Faheem would not bring the Spain's Policia Judicial or Interpol in?" MacLachlan asked.

"I suggested what you are asking several times. He is unalterably opposed to it."

"Do you know why?"

"Very rich businessmen are often fanatical over their privacy. They have a carefully controlled public persona, but everything else is hidden. Each tends to have skeletons in his closet he does not want to have Interpol delving into, Mr. MacLachlan. Bring in the Spanish police on a matter like this and Spain's National Central Bureau—its Interpol liaison—will be there before the day is over."

They all shook hands and Schutte left. Anna, unbidden, slipped out the back and rounded the building to watch Schutte's back for tails. She did not see any.

"Impressions?" MacLachlan asked.

"Schutte has an idea of who took the girl and is waiting to see what we think before opening up," Anna said.

"Yes. I believe he does. And he will only tell us what he thinks is the minimum for us to find and exfiltrate the girl. Do you think the Russian mob is behind this? If so, it's going to be a helluva ransom. Or, more likely, Faheem will have to withdraw from the contract to get his daughter back."

"In view of the pharma thing, I do. So, Mack, should we discount human trafficking now?"

"Probably. As Schutte said, she is a bit older than the profile for human trafficking victims at seventeen and does not appear pretty enough to risk the ire of a billionaire father to sell into prostitution. I think we need to get to Mallorca and make contact with the girlfriend right away."

They were in Palma, Mallorca in the afternoon. MacLachlan hailed a taxi, and they went to the hotel and checked in.

Adele's room number was on the information sheet. Anna knocked, but there was no answer. They changed to swimwear and sandals and walked over to the beach.

It took about twenty minutes to find Adele Martel sunning on a hotel towel. Anna approached her.

She spread an identical towel by Adele. Adele looked up and smiled.

"Adele, my name is Anna. A friend and I are here to help you find someone. This is not a place for secure talk. We need you to go back to your room. We are in the same hotel. It is important to speak immediately," Anna said in French.

With a quick, "Oui," Adele rose, folded her towel and walked away. Anna gave her a couple minutes head start to see if anyone followed her. Anyone other than Mack, who was thirty feet behind her.

"Are you police?" Adele asked after the door to her room had closed.

"No, we are private. Nisa's father hired us to find out where she is and return her," MacLachlan said.

"Adele, your help may be crucial to our finding and bringing Nisa back. We will ask a lot of questions. Some won't make any sense, but answer them anyway, okay?" Anna asked.

"Let's start with planning your trip. Who made the reservations for you?" MacLachlan asked.

"Nisa's father's travel desk in one of his companies." Anna wrote it down for Schutte for follow-up on.

"Was anybody particularly interested in either of you on the plane? You both go to college in Paris, right?"

"Right. Nobody on the plane. I kind of thought

the flight attendant was interested in me. But it did not go anywhere."

"What are your and Nisa's preferences?" Anna asked.

"We are both generally straight."

"Generally?"

"Well, you know. Girls like to experiment a little."

"Yes, we do," Anna responded with an engaging smile. MacLachlan's face was as fixed as a marble statue.

"How about once you got off the plane. Anyone pushing in, like trying to see your passport information at Immigration?" MacLachlan asked.

"Everybody was in a hurry to get a drink and to the beach, so yes. Kinda."

"Did anybody show particular interest with you between the airport and the hotel?"

"A dark-haired, good looking guy gave us some advertisement cards for the Shout night club at the taxi stand."

"Did he offer you a ride?" Anna asked.

"No, we took a taxi."

"Was the driver interested in you? Did he ask questions requiring detailed answers?"

"No. We checked in, got some salads for whatever meal it was supposed to be, and dressed for the night club."

"Please describe how both of you dressed. Skin out please," MacLachlan said.

"Are you some sort of perv?" she asked. Her blood ran cold with the stare MacLachlan gave her.

"Adele, every question we ask has a reason. Use

your brain. Shoes, underwear and the like can help us identify a body. They are clues, so answer the questions without any further smartass comments," Anna ordered. Adele reddened.

She described her outfit, including purse and degree of makeup applied.

"Nisa had on a short red dress. It was low-cut. She's proud of her boobs and very conscious about her slightly too-large waistline and hips. She had three-inch heels in red. Wispy thong underwear. Heavier night makeup."

"What color lipstick and eye makeup?" MacLachlan asked.

"Bright red and a muted eye makeup. Not like bright blue or anything. And, Mr. MacLachlan, I apologize. I was caught off guard by your question. It makes my blood run cold to think I may be helping identify my friend's body."

"Adele, we will do everything we can to get her back safe and sound," he said.

"Okay, Adele. How did you get to the club? What happened when you arrived?" Anna asked.

"We had the advertising cards for Shout with us. We picked a good-looking guy and asked for directions. He said he was going there and would buy us our first drinks."

"Please describe him in as much detail as you can remember," Anna asked.

"His name is Marcel. He was not really tall. Nisa is five-two. With really high heels and hair, the two were about the same height. He spoke English to us but had a slight French accent. It was not Parisian."

"Build? Hair and eyes? Clothes? And, then what

after you got in? Did he stick with you?" MacLachlan asked.

"He was slim with brown eyes and curly black hair. He wore a striped short-sleeved shirt open at the collar and dark pants. I don't remember whether black, gray or navy blue."

"Marcel hit it off with Nisa right away. He bought us drinks and after she downed her first one, he asked her to dance. They disappeared in the crowd. We got there at almost ten. By midnight, jet lag set in, and I wanted to leave. I could not find either of them in the club."

"Is it possible you just did not see them?" Anna asked.

"No. Though it was crowded, the club itself is not really large. I even went upstairs to the VIP lounge. They weren't there. The bouncer up there said he had not seen them. While she's not beautiful, Nisa in her red dress with her boobs hanging out would have been memorable. I don't think he would have any reason to lie," Adele said naively.

"Adele, did Nisa have a large amount of money or expensive jewelry with her at the club?" Anna asked.

"No. We agreed to not take more than fifty Euros each. Small bills for snacks and tips. No expensive jewelry or watches either. We actually did not bring anything expensive on the trip, knowing we'd be in clubs or the beach most of the time."

"What do you think happened to Nisa?" MacLachlan asked.

"I thought from the way she and Marcel were dancing, he took her back to wherever he was staying for a one-nighter. By now, I am afraid something bad has happened to her."

"Two last questions for now. Then, we will go through all of Nisa's stuff."

"Okay. But why go through her things? I watch television. Our room is not a crime scene," she said.

"Standard procedure. Helps us flesh out our profile on Nisa. Understand her," MacLachlan said.

"One, was she on any sort of birth-control? And two, are you willing to stay here and help us? We will cover your expenses," MacLachlan said.

"Yes to both. An IUD and of course I'll help. But, why the first question?"

"Sexual assault is not uncommon in kidnappings. If she was on the pill and skipped several, she would not be protected. We would need to apprise private medical authorities very quickly when we get her back," Anna said.

"Okay, here's my suggested plan. Anna, you and Adele go to the five or so hospitals on the island. Use a ruse of you being Adele's big sister and you all cannot account for the whereabouts of her friend, Nisa. See if any Jane Doe's have been checked into the hospital. I will try to talk with some of the people at Shout before they open. I have some time before I can expect to find anyone there, so I will walk the beaches."

"I know the father said no police, but I am wondering if we can stick with the ruse and have either both of you, or just Adele, go to the police department. If nothing else, we will find if any unidentified female bodies have shown up in the past couple days. It's risky, so we need to think about it as an option," MacLachlan said.

"I see the benefit, but I recommend holding the police thing until the end of the day, Mack," Anna said. MacLachlan concurred. He had never worked with Anna as anything but a suspect and was increasingly impressed with her instincts.

He gave Adele a hundred Euros and Anna a thousand.

They went to a shop and bought three matching local "burner" phones and programmed each other's numbers into all three.

"Anna, please explain the finer attributes of a disposable phone to Adele while you are together. Okay, let's check in at two o'clock unless we learn something before then," he said, and they separated.

MacLachlan figured walking the beach would be a waste of time, but he had the late morning and early afternoon to waste anyway.

*I must be getting old,* he thought. *Seeing these kids walking around like zombies and on the beach already drunk makes me wonder where the hell this world is going. Is it worth guys like me fighting to save their freedom?*

In three hours, he did not see anyone who remotely resembled Nisa Faheem.

At two, he called Anna.

"Anything?" he asked.

"No. We have checked four hospitals and no luck at all."

"How about send Adele into the police department to ask about a girlfriend who looks like Nisa, but has a different name? Think she can handle it alone?" he asked.

"I think we have to do it. I'll coach her first," Anna said.

Twenty minutes later, the two women separated a block from the police building on Carrer Son Dameto.

Adele went in and to the reception desk, manned by a sergeant.

"I am worried. My friend and I were at the Shout night club on Thursday. We got separated and I have not been able to find her. She was dancing with a guy named Marcel. Can you tell me if any unidentified teenaged girls have been in accidents, or anything?"

Adele presented as a well-spoken and credible eighteen-year-old. The sergeant checked records and reported no accident victims or bodies matching her description have been reported since Thursday. "Or even before," he added.

He recommended she keep calling her friend and, after another day or so, come in and fill out a missing person report on her. He asked the missing girl's name and description. Adele gave her the fictitious name she and Anna had agreed upon and left.

"Mack? No joy at the police. Sounds like Adele is a natural! There is not really anything which would tie back to Nisa. I guess there could be a police snout working with the Palma police, feeding information to the kidnappers," Anna said, using the British term for "snitch" or informer. MacLachlan had no idea where she had gotten the term, unless she learned it when two British SIS agents were keeping her in custody during her investigation in an assassin case last year.

"Why don't you two do the beaches now? Maybe Adele can spot Marcel."

"Okay we'll go back and change. Then, dinner, another change and the night club. You go in to see the bouncers and we will go in to ostensibly dance?"

"Roger all," MacLachlan said and hung up. He walked out of the immediate tourist area and found a car rental. He chose a ubiquitous white minivan with seating for four. The rear windows were darkened. He considered it perfect. Almost. A supercharger and some Kevlar liners would have made him happier. But such vehicles are difficult to find at normal rental kiosks, he grinned. He drove it to the outskirts of Palma and sought an industrial area. He found exactly what he was looking for. It was a cheap hotel for workers in town for a job. He rented a room for a week. He found a hardware store and bought some long plastic wire ties, a roll of duct tape, and a pair of wire cutters. Returning to downtown, he drove to the club. He found a parking space within half a block of the club. He was sure there would be no parking for blocks by time for the club to open its doors.

They met at dusk and changed for dinner and the club. The two women put on party outfits. MacLachlan wore running shoes, khakis, and a black LA Police Gear polo. With his musculature and short hair, he figured he looked like a bouncer.

*He looks more like what he is,* Anna thought. *An intelligence contractor who was a veteran of combats all over the world. Combats fought on battlefields and in back alleys and high-class casinos. A man I am having fun with. It is a learning experience working with him, too.* She wanted to take advantage of being with MacLachlan for a while, before moving on with her unspoken plan to resume logistics services for a lot of assassins. And, perhaps become one herself, a fact she would withhold from her clients.

MacLachlan told Anna about the van and its location. She had used nondescript vehicles to tail him in Key West. The concept of not using an Aston Martin on ops was quite familiar to her.

"Mack, I have a question," Anna asked as the three were walking to dinner.

"Fire away," he said.

"You are the only person like you who does not have tattoos on your arms. Or, anywhere, actually." The last of the sentence caught Adele's attention and confirmed suspicions she had.

"It is pretty remarkable I did not get the requisite tattoo in the Marines," he said," but my friend Will was definite when he was transitioning me from combat officer to intelligence officer later. He said 'you get a damn tat and it will go on your dossier with every intelligence agency in the world. You can dye your hair, wear a prosthetic nose, whatever. But the tat will be a giveaway and it could get you killed'.

"Will never gave me bad advice. I've stuck with his instructions for years. Periodically, I have used the high-end temporary tattoos as disguises," he added.

"Thanks, just wondering."

"You all are several hours early for the club. Let's get you seated, and you can order some dinner. I will be back after I try the club to see if anyone remem-

bers anything or has a CCTV record. I can eat while
you are having dessert."

They found a nice restaurant and went in. They
were very early for dinner by Spanish standards, so
seating was not a problem.

After a café con leche, MacLachlan left them
ordering and went to the Shout night club.

He approached the security man at the door. The
club had not opened, and he was smoking a Fortuna
cigarette. MacLachlan approached him and spoke in
Spanish.

"Good evening. I'd like to talk with the senior
security man. Are you him?" he asked knowing the
man was not.

"No, Paul is. What do you need with him?"

"A favor. I promised a friend to look for his
wayward daughter. She was here Thursday night and
dropped out of sight. He's afraid she ran off with
some guy she met on the dancefloor. Wouldn't be the
first time she's done it. By a long shot."

The man laughed. Interestingly, after the conversation with Anna about tattoos, a tat was the first
thing MacLachlan noted on the man. It was the
wings, anchor and crown of the Spanish Aeronaval
Forces.

"I see you are SENAN," MacLachlan said. The
man perked up.

"Yes. For twenty years. I was a sargento primero
when I got out."

"Nice!"

"Did you serve?" he asked.

"I did. US Marines. Lebanon and other places.

Usually not very hospitable places," MacLachlan said.

"You sound like you are a Cuban."

"Many of my friends in Miami are Cuban. I speak Spanish with them, so I must have picked up the accent, huh?" MacLachlan responded.

"So. Go into the club and up the steps to the right. If anyone stops you, tell them I sent you. I am Hernando. Paul is Belgian. Former Legion Etrangere. Bigger than you or me, with a shaved head. He will be very hard to miss."

The two men shook, having established their brothers in arms bond, and MacLachlan went in.

Nobody stopped him. He saw a man coming out of the door at the top of the steps. It had to be Paul. He was bald, six-foot-four and about two-hundred fifty pounds. There did not appear to be an ounce of fat on him. He wore a golf shirt like MacLachlan's. It looked like it was painted on.

MacLachlan greeted him in Spanish, saying Hernando had authorized him to come up.

Cops and military men recognize one another with no trouble. Just as Hernando and MacLachlan had. It was stronger with this man. The two recognized one another as equals. Men who had killed and who had faced a variety of enemies day and night.

"I understand you were French Foreign Legion," MacLachlan said.

"I was. Despite your Spanish, you strike me as an American. Special Forces?"

"Yes, America's original special force. The Marine Corps."

"What happens when you say it to a SEAL? Or a Green Beret?" Paul asked.

"Oh, I have said it to both. And yet, here I am." The big man grinned.

"A member of the Legion Etrangere would surely know about the Marines." MacLachlan smiled back.

"Oui," he said, shifting to French. "We do."

"I have a friend who was with the legion. A Spaniard, perhaps. One never knows. His nom de guerre was 'Pirata'. Perhaps you have heard of him?"

"The little terror. I know him well. Where is he now?"

"Living on a Faire in Tahiti with a most beautiful woman. He has shaved his beard and looks almost like a civilian," MacLachlan said.

"Tell him Gran Paul said hello, when you see him."

"I will."

"You came looking for me. What can I do to help you, Messr. Marine?"

"I am Mack MacLachlan. The rather troublesome daughter of a friend came here on Thursday. She apparently met a boy and left before midnight with him. She has not returned to her hotel. The friend fears she has run off with this boy and would like me to find her and bring her home to daddy. I was wondering if I could see the relevant CCTV film for perhaps ten to midnight on Thursday?"

"Has this girl done such a thing before?" Paul asked.

"Yes. My friend could not retrieve her himself as in the past, so he sent me."

"Are you on expenses? It takes time and effort to retrace CCTV film," Paul suggested.

"My friend is a businessman. When you and I were fighting enemies, he was buying his enemies. I believe he would be amenable to a small stipend. Perhaps five hundred Euros for guidance through the film and another thousand for a copy, if we hit pay dirt."

"It sounds equitable to me, Mack. Come to my security room and we will see what we may have."

They went into a cramped security control room. A man in a security uniform sat before a large screen with ten sub-screens on it. MacLachlan immediately picked out the screen for the rear alley from the array.

"Help my friend here to find some information he desires. He will explain everything. Bring him to me when he is done. It is okay for him to have a copy of any film he needs."

MacLachlan passed five hundred in folded Euros to Paul in a handshake as the big man left to prepare the club for its onslaught of rich, drunk, and drugged kids.

It took an hour to find what MacLachlan wanted but find it he did.

Two young men carrying a very drunk or drugged Nisa with one steadying her on each side. They put her into the backseat of an Audi which pulled up when they exited the building. The timing suggested pros. One of the two got in the seat with Nisa and the other came back into the building.

"Hold the film here while I get Paul," MacLachlan asked. He got up and found the big security man and led him back to the screen.

"Paul, this is the boyfriend and the daughter. We don't know where they are, but I bet the second boy who came back into the club does. Could you pass a screen shot around to your men, as well as the servers and bartenders, to see who might be able to identify him? Time may be of the essence," MacLachlan said. Paul nodded, then changed the subject.

"Mack, guess who I just found by way of another friend? Pirata in Tahiti! He sends you his best. He said you met when you were both aiming pistols at one another and mutually decided to not kill each other. He said I can trust you, even though I know you are only telling a sanitized version of the story here."

"Franco, make a copy of this film on a flash drive. And enlarge a screen shot of the car and two boys putting the girl in it. And another enlargement of the second boy coming back into the club. He looks familiar even to me. I believe he is here often."

"MacLachlan, come to my office to sit and have a drink. Franco will bring the items to you there. It is possible the second boy will show up here tonight. If so, you could...er, chat with him."

"I would relish having a conversation with him, Paul. Perhaps in a quiet spot." The big man grinned again. He missed this sort of thing. Missed it a lot.

They went to the office, which was a bit larger than the security room. It was military in its simplicity and sense of order. Paul retrieved a bottle of Glenfiddich scotch and poured a dram in each of two glasses.

"To the Legion," MacLachlan said, holding up his glass. "And, the Corps," Paul returned.

"I am not going to press you for more details, Mack, out of respect for our professions. I suspect the basis is truth and the part you are not telling is irrelevant to the matter at hand. The matter of getting the girl back."

"As in the Legion, missions were shared with crucial information. Superfluous information is just clutter. It is the way men like you and me operate," MacLachlan said, bonding further.

"But, Paul, I do have one female operative in the crowd. She has the missing girl's friend with her." MacLachlan said, "I think she would be hard to recognize except for being a bit older than the rest of the party goers."

Paul nodded. He would have done exactly the same thing, had the tables been turned.

The two men talked. His time there had extended, and he never went back for dinner. MacLachlan knew the club had opened and by now Anna and Adele would be there, working the crowd under the guise of partying.

"Why don't we circulate the dance floor and bars? We might pick up on this kid ourselves. His photo is being distributed to the staff. My entry man at the front has been instructed to allow him in and notify me, but it's possible he may have been too late getting the word," Paul said.

"Sounds like a good idea. I'm up for moving around," MacLachlan said. The two walked down the stairs. MacLachlan, to any casual observer, looked like part of Paul's staff.

MacLachlan and Paul watched as one of his men

made contact with a young man who had made it inside drunk during the opening influx.

They moved in closely to observe. Paul's man approached the young man and asked him to step outside with him. The security man, unlike his boss, was short and wiry. He hardly weighed one hundred forty pounds soaking wet. MacLachlan knew his size meant absolutely nothing and the man proved it as the drunk dropped into a fighting stance.

The security man slipped behind him, picking up his left wrist on the way. He twisted it back in a classic police come-along and guided him out from just behind the drunk's left side. The drunk started to remonstrate, and a quick upturn of his wrist made him think better of it. Sometimes pain can rule a clouded mind, MacLachlan thought from long experience.

"Very nicely and subtlety done!" MacLachlan said to Paul, in the din of the music, laughter and conversations.

"I try to train my men well. Sometimes, several party goers decide to put up a fight, and it is not so subtle. But we end it quickly. The regulars know this. It's first-timers who have to learn the hard way. Mack, it's not always testosterone causing fights. It's about fifty-fifty estrogen, my friend."

"Do you have any female associates trained like the guy we just saw?" MacLachlan asked.

"I have two females and three males on the floor at all times we are open. Personally, I'd rather have to fight the males. My ladies are very serious fighters. One is an ex-cop, one was military. Both are former MMS fighters," Paul said. MacLachlan raised his eyebrows and grinned. He may have some use for Paul in some future op. The man was both tough and a good leader.

"We have a hit on the second guy," Paul said, as he put his phone back into its belt holder. MacLachlan called Anna as he followed Paul from several feet behind.

"Marcel is here. Watch for me," and he killed the call without further details.

It was not difficult moving through the crowd behind Paul's size. As they approached a twenty-five-year-old who was obviously Marcel, they saw a small woman in shorts and a golf shirt like Paul's approach Marcel. She whispered something in his ear and he walked off with her without resisting.

Anna moved up on Marcel's other side with Adele. They flanked out just behind Paul and MacLachlan.

"Yours, I take it?" Paul said.

"Yes."

"Wow," was the security man's response.

Anna tagged along behind Marcel. Again, MacLachlan was amazed at her instinctive tradecraft. She had to have received training somewhere to be this good. They had not been able to learn where when they interrogated her. It was during the case where he and two British operatives met her. The remembrance sent a wave of sadness over him. One of those operatives was gone now. Forever.

The two men followed the small group into a comfortably furnished room used for calming down customers for whatever reason necessary. The door was closed when they arrived, and Paul unlocked it.

"Why am I here?" Marcel was protesting peaceably.

Paul looked at MacLachlan with a "go ahead and take it" nod.

"We have a few questions for you. Adele, is this definitely the man who got the two of you in on Thursday and danced with your friend?" he asked. He intentionally did not use Nisa's name.

"Yes. It is." Smart girl! She did not give away his name, Mack thought to himself.

Marcel looked at Adele for the first time. The professionals could see a spark of recognition. Marcel was trying to hide something.

"What is your name?" MacLachlan asked.

"Paco Ramirez," he said.

"Marcel, what happened to your French accent from Thursday night?" MacLachlan asked in a low, non-threatening voice.

"Are you police?" the young man asked.

"I ask the questions. You answer. Those are the rules," MacLachlan's voice picked up a firm, serious tone, still quiet.

"Anna, would you bring our vehicle up to the alley door?" he asked pleasantly, giving her the keys. She took them and left with Adele.

"Paul, perhaps your associate here could assist Marcel to the rear door while you have the cameras stopped to reload a cassette or something?"

"Yes, it would be prudent to not record for a few minutes," he agreed.

He left, with an envelope containing more than the promised Euros in it. Again, MacLachlan passed it covertly during a handshake. The detainee and female club security officer were facing away.

The officer stopped for a moment, listening to a message in her ear wig.

"We can go now," she said.

She led the way to the rear door. MacLachlan did not bother with a come-along hold. He grasped the man's left wrist in his hand and knew it would be enough to restrain any resistance. Otherwise, MacLachlan thought, *I'll break his damned arm. The intense pain and sound of the crack will suffice to gain his compliance.*

When they reached the door, MacLachlan checked the camera. The active light was off. Good man, Paul! Anna was behind the wheel and Adele hopped out and opened the door. As he suspected would be the case, Paul was not present. MacLachlan thanked the nameless female security operative, got in and Anna took off.

The two women were in the front and MacLachlan sat with Marcel in the rear. Marcel started to protest and MacLachlan elbowed him in the side. He hit him almost hard enough to crack a rib. The Frenchman, or Spaniard, or whatever he was, got the point and shut up.

MacLachlan directed Anna to the hotel.

"Anna, do you two have enough to be able to camp here for the night?"

"Not really. Maybe with a toothbrush, some deodorant and a couple of T-shirts to sleep in we would be," she said. She looked questioningly at Adele who shook her head in agreement. The French woman was now fully engaged in the operation.

"Actually, it might be prudent to go by the rooms

in town and make it plausibly deniable we were there all night, too. You can pick up needed items then," MacLachlan said.

Anna smiled. She loved this spy-type stuff.

Noting he did not ask Marcel if he needed anything, Anna left and took Adele with her. She was not worried about MacLachlan's safety alone with Marcel. She had some concerns about Marcel's longevity though.

---

"SO, HERE'S THE DEAL, MARCEL," MacLachlan began as soon as the women left.

"I am going to ask you some questions. You will answer them truthfully. I have been trained by the very best to detect BS. Lie and it will cause you more pain than you can possibly imagine. You will beg me to kill you. But I won't. I have to find Nisa and return her to her father. If she is okay and you cooperate, I will turn you over to the police. If not, I will turn you over to the father and his terrorist henchmen. They will make me look like your Sunday school teacher.

"Rule one, to repeat, is to tell me the truth. Rule two is to not make noise, scream, or yell for help. If you do, I will cut your testicles off. One at a time. I'm not sure if you will bleed to death or not. It's just a chance I'll have to take."

He held up the wire cutters and clicked the blades together a couple of times. Marcel dry gagged. Nothing came up. Yet.

"Strip to your underwear. Do it now!" MacLachlan ordered. Marcel complied.

MacLachlan had already decided Marcel would take one bed with wrist and ankle restraints, and the two women would share another. He would sleep, more or less, in the stuffed chair. He was in this room because he had requested a room with a bath instead of a shower. He did not like baths, but he needed one for the interview. He was very pleased when they pulled in. It was almost midnight and the rooms on either side were still vacant.

"Marcel, do you want to answer my questions now, man to man? Or would you like what we call 'enhanced interrogation techniques' later once the ladies return?" MacLachlan asked.

"What do you mean 'enhanced'?"

"Waterboarding. Are you familiar with it?"

"Maybe."

"Let me explain. It means, I pour water down your throat until you are willing to truthfully answer my questions. You will gag. You will perhaps drown. Is silence worth going through such an ordeal?"

What Marcel suggested MacLachlan do was physically impossible. MacLachlan wanted to break his nose but decided restraint would be scarier.

"Not nice, Marcel. You just earned another ten minutes of me pouring buckets of water down your throat until you pass out. The question is whether you will ever regain consciousness. It is a horrifying way to die. I am trying to give you every opportunity here and you seem to be resisting me. It's a very dumb policy, this resistance thing."

Marcel began a sarcastic and profane spate of words, but MacLachlan used a bandana to gag him. He got up to struggle and MacLachlan subdued him. The operator did not have to think of the rule "fist only to the soft areas, knife edge hand, elbow, or head to the hard ones". He just smacked him hard on the temple with an open hand. MacLachlan wire-tied his hands behind him and his ankles together.

---

ANNA INSTRUCTED Adele on how to make her room look slept in during the drive to the hotel. They parked the white van several blocks away and walked the remaining distance to the property.

Adele picked up some snacks at the desk and asked if she had any messages. She went to the room and took a shower, leaving damp towels on the floor.

She pulled the covers down and laid on the bed naked and still damp. She tossed and turned as instructed by Anna. The bed appeared to have been slept in. After a few minutes, she donned a T-shirt and shorts with running shoes. She ate a candy bar and left the wrapper on the bedside table. She put the rest of the snacks and several bottles of water in her purse.

Anna also showered.

She called room service and ordered a sandwich tray and four Diet Cokes. She pulled the covers down and air-dried on the bed.

She could hear steps in the hall. There was a knock on the door and she emitted a pair of "Oooh, Oooh" sounds of extreme sexual pleasure before padding to the door.

Anna slid a folded ten Euro note under the door

and said, "We're not dressed. Just leave the tray on the floor outside the door."

She saw the note disappear and heard steps diminishing as the porter walked away. Anna waited a full minute and peeked out the door. The hall was clear, and she stepped out and picked up the tray. She carefully wrapped the sandwiches and put them in a canvas beach bag with the Cokes.

She dressed in more sensible clothes and shoes, picked up a T-shirt and toothbrush for MacLachlan and went to get Adele.

"I don't know for sure what methods Mack is going to use to get Marcel to tell us where Nisa is. But whatever he does is our only chance to get her back. If he uses water boarding, which I suspect, it will be horrible to watch Marcel's terror as he thinks he's going to drown. But you need to know this: I am pretty sure nobody ever died or even suffered permanent harm from the process. It is largely mental. If you want to go sit in the van, it's okay, Adele."

"Thank you. I believe I can take it. I'm fascinated by the way you and Mack have jumped in and pulled out all the stops to save Nisa. I may rethink my career choices. How did you get involved and how long have you worked with Mack?"

"This is the first time we have actually worked together. When we get to know each other better, I will explain our backgrounds," Anna said.

The unsaid story flashed quickly before her mind.

Anna had handled logistics for a very crazy, criminal couple for over fifteen years. Travel, contracts, weapons, and the like. She realized when Mack and his spy friend, Alexis, came for her she had been set up by her employers. Mack killed the male assassin she worked for.

Mack, Alexis, and another British agent negotiated a plea deal for her instead of prison.

Ultimately, the female assassin killed Alexis. In turn, Anna killed her. She would perhaps admit she loved Alexis and Mack and what they did. After shadowing him around the world to keep him safe, she showed up on his beach in Florida a few weeks ago.

"This is our first case together," she said, breaking her silent soliloquy.

"Wow! Where did you learn the skills to do these things?" Adele asked.

"A little from the assassin team. Particularly with respect to how assassins plan and work. I took lots of courses in shooting, fighting, driving, interrogation techniques. I used false identification. Nobody, including Mack, is aware of it. He probably suspects my skills are beyond what one would have just by reading or observing. He and I were talking about language skills the other day and he said it's smart to never let people know how much you really know."

"What's his background?" Adele asked leaning towards Anna in fascination.

"He was a US Marine hero—a Congressional Medal of Honor recipient. It's the highest medal for heroism the US military gives. He won't talk about it."

"How old is he? He has gray in his hair," Adele asked, back on safer territory.

"I don't know. With him, age is just a number. It's not an indicator of ability. He can still run a marathon. I've seen him swim several miles in heavy waves in the Gulf of Mexico. There are credible stories of him taking on four or five guys and leaving them dead or needing a hospital. He killed my employer with amazing shooting in the middle of a gunfight with him. One of the deadliest assassins in the world and Mack took him out. MacLachlan is the best friend you could ever have and the worst enemy imaginable."

"You all seem to have a very close relationship," Adele probed.

"We are a lot alike. People like us don't really have relationships. It appeared Mack was going to give it all up for a woman, but then she got killed. There's someone else in his history. She's still around, but he doesn't talk about her. As for me, I'm not ready to retire."

The conversation took them all the way to the second hotel, where the subject of the conversation waited with Marcel.

They took the food in and placed it in the small refrigerator and gave MacLachlan his T-shirt and toothbrush.

"I explained the violent things you will do to Marcel if he doesn't talk. Adele said she'd like to watch and learn. A little blood and severed body parts won't bother her, she says." Marcel could not speak with the gag on, but his eyes bulged at hearing this.

MacLachlan looked hard at Adele and then gave her one of his killer superhero grins.

"That's my girl! Don't you worry, Marcel will tell

us his real name and everything else we ask him," he told her.

"Ladies, would you fill the ice bucket and the pitcher with slightly warm water for Marcel? I believe he's thirsty. So, we'll pour it into him and quench his thirst. And, at the same time, quench our thirst for the knowledge about Nisa he's withholding from us.

I'm sure the water feature will work fine, but, as you know, Anna, my default is slowly cutting his testicles off one at a time. You'll have to hold a pillow over his head for the surgery. Nobody alive can keep from screaming from pain during such an operation," MacLachlan said in the low, serious voice of a workman preparing to commence a job he had done many times before.

"Mack, I hope he talks before you start removing his balls. It makes even me get a bit queasy," Anna added playing along. "Remember Baghdad?" she hinted, lying.

"I don't know. It's kind of fun. Oh, fill the trashcan with the plastic liner with water, too. It won't be as clean as the bucket, but Marcel won't care by then."

MacLachlan clipped Marcel behind the neck with a knife-edged hand and picked him up and carried the hundred- and fifty-pound man into the bathroom as if he were a child. The two women followed him in and filled the containers with water.

Marcel began to come to. They wanted him aware of what they were saying to add to his terror and perhaps make the enhanced interrogation unnecessary.

"Okay, Anna. He will struggle for his life. So, I will hold him down. Let's put some water in the tub for grins. You and Adele can hold his head down and one of you pour a gallon of water through a towel and down his throat. The towel will keep his screams down and also cause the water to flow at a measured rate."

MacLachlan's matter of fact training instructions were so casual they terrified Marcel even more. He removed the bandana gag and stared at Marcel.

"The smart thing would be to avoid the terror, screaming, soiling yourself in front of these beautiful ladies. All you have to do is truthfully answer my questions, Marcel," MacLachlan said.

Marcel had a strange look on his face but did not say anything.

"Anna, please put the towel over his face. Don't fold it. One thickness of terry cloth should be perfect. Now, slowly pour a gallon of water through the towel down his throat."

At one cup of water, Marcel started trying to talk. He could not see MacLachlan smile. He motioned for Anna to stop. Adele watched this interplay of human nature, spellbound.

"Marcel, are you trying to tell me Anna is not pouring enough water?"

"No! The girl is not worth dying for. I will tell you what you want to know."

"Adele, there is a pen and small leather pad in my jacket hanging on the rack. Would you get it and take notes?" She got up, disappointed and relieved at the same time, and fetched the items.

She turned the body of the maroon Mont Blanc to ready the point for writing.

"Marcel, is Nisa still alive?"

He nodded yes.

"Where is she?"

"She is in an old farmhouse. I don't know the name of the road, but I can show you. It is within five kilometers from here."

"How many guards does she have and how are they armed?"

"Four, not counting me. They have pistols and one shotgun."

"Nationality?"

"Like me, they are Ukrainians."

"Are you working for the Russians?"

"I don't think so. They trained us. We used to be a deep cover asset for them, but not so much anymore. I was contacted by email and phone by a man. I never saw him and cannot tell his nationality from his accent. He speaks with a French accent, but so do you and I and we are both far from being Frenchmen.

"What's in it for me by cooperating with you?" Marcel asked.

"I don't kill you and you get to keep all your man parts." MacLachlan reached behind and removed the heavy wire cutters and clicked the blades again threateningly.

"Okay, okay. I got you."

"Do you have a check-in time?"

"Yes. It's nine in the morning each day."

"And, if you don't check in?"

"The guys kill the girl and burn the farmhouse down. Then, they haul ass back to our safe house in a small village in Spain. I will join them as soon as possible, if I am still able."

"Have they beaten or sexually assaulted the girl? I'm watching for you to lie. If I think you are, I will bypass the water and go straight to turning you into a very ugly woman. Do you understand me, Marcel?"

"Yes. They softened her up a little. Nothing serious. A little sex has been enjoyed, but we got some next day pills to keep her from getting pregnant."

"How very thoughtful of you. What you really mean is to prevent extraction of the rapists' DNA. I may have to kill the four on general principal," MacLachlan said.

"Has the controller talked about a ransom with you?"

"No, he said he would tell us how the exchange would be handled when he was ready. He wanted the family to sweat a little first. I got the impression we were going to turn her over to him for which he will pay us."

"When does he call you?" MacLachlan asked.

"No schedule."

"Can you tell if the call is local from the caller ID?"

"No. I am sure it is a burner phone. And he's set it so the number does not show."

"How did he get in touch with you in the beginning?"

"We have done odd jobs of a slight criminal nature ever since we got out of the military. Why not do them in paradise instead of freezing? Four of us were infantry. One guy, who gets the outside work is former Ukrainian Spetznaz. He was not Alpha or anything. Spetznaz just indicates 'special forces'."

This was not news to MacLachlan, who killed more than one true Russian FSB Alpha Spetznaz on past missions.

He had gone without sanction to recover his tactically trained intelligence analyst lover from a kidnapping. His Kate, who he was rescuing, killed another, saving MacLachlan's life.

He also flashed on the fact she had undergone twenty minutes worth of water boarding by two Spetznaz. Unlike Mr. "Marcel", who almost soiled himself over the mere thought of it.

"You say there are four handguns and one shotgun? Do you also possess a firearm?" MacLachlan asked.

"They have .38 revolvers. It's the standard for Spanish security guards. We work security when we are not on our own projects."

"Where is your .38?"

"At my flat in Palma. Drawer beside the bed. I take it you want to borrow it?"

"I might. You cooperate and you might find me paying you the price of a used car for your revolver. Again, you know the price of not cooperating, right?"

"Right."

"I'm going to cut the restraints off your wrists and ankles. You can get dressed. Then wrist restraints go back on. You and I are going to make a run to Palma and get your revolver. Is it a Taurus?"

"No, a Rossi," Marcel replied.

"Same company," MacLachlan said as he clipped

the heavy plastic wire ties with his cutters. The two women had been listening to the conversation.

"Anna and Adele. We will get back in time for the 0900 check-in, I'd like you two to go shopping afterwards. You should be able to get everything at a hardware type store."

Adele still had MacLachlan's pen and pad and prepared to copy.

"Two small aluminum baseball bats. If you need to, buy and discard gloves and balls, to avoid questions, it's okay. A couple cans of wasp and hornet spray. Get the ones with the longest range, please. More wire ties. Take one of these for length comparison. Finally, a couple cans of pest fogger bombs. The biggest and nastiest you can find. Okay?"

"Sounds good," Adele said, tearing the page out and handing the pen and pad back to him.

"MacLachlan, my underwear is wet," Marcel whined from beside the bed where he was preparing to dress.

"Could have been blood down there. So, deal with it," MacLachlan growled in a less-than friendly tone. "Let's go get your revolver."

## 2

The night passed without anyone sleeping. Marcel played the 10:00 AM call from the controller out loud. Instead of waiting as he planned, he had sent the two women to pick up the items on his list before Marcel's phone rang. They got back midway through the call from the controller and came in very quietly.

"Why are you using the speaker on your phone?" the man with the slight French accent asked with irritation.

"I am shaving. I need to get to the location and check on the guys and the girl and I'm running late," he lied.

"Well, I don't like it. Someone might overhear us."

"No chance. Every single neighbor has long since gone to work. Have you decided when and where you want to see the girl?" Marcel asked.

"I will tell you in sufficient time for you to react. However, delay your trip this morning. I am thinking about doing something which you would interrupt.

Stay put for a couple of hours. I will be back to you."
He broke the connection.

Once MacLachlan was positive the call was over,
he frowned.

"Very odd. He wants to do something without
you interrupting. I have a bad feeling about this.
Anna, what do you think?"

"Absolutely. He's going to abscond with the girl or
kill her. I don't think we have time to waste."

He nodded and said, "Let's step outside for a
moment and talk."

As soon as they were away from hearing and
sight, she preempted him by saying "I think we can
trust Adele. She said she is fascinated with what we
do and may change her major to obtain a career in
this. Whatever she thinks 'this' is."

"I've been impressed with her. She seems awfully
mature for her claimed aged. Can we leave her or
send her back to the hotel by Uber? The downside is
having a taxi or Uber see this place and associate it
with anything we do in the next half hour,"
MacLachlan said.

"I vote for taking her. I think we are stuck with
Marcel, since he knows the location and we don't,"
she said.

"We will keep him restrained. If he does anything
stupid, I will neutralize him. I trust you, Anna, but
otherwise this is the weakest team I ever took into a
recovery op. I just don't see any other option."

"Me either, Mack. Let's just roll with what we've
got and hope for the best," she said. He nodded and
brought the other two out.

The four got in and headed to the farmhouse as

fast as they could. Just like on the trip to retrieve the revolver, Marcel was cuffed in the back so was unable to unfasten the shoulder harness he now wore.

Marcel warned them of the proximity a half kilometer off. They parked the car and left Adele behind the wheel to come in hot if they needed to make a hasty exit.

MacLachlan and Anna moved through woods beside the road until the house was in sight. He dragged Marcel along restrained and muzzled by a bandana tied over his mouth. The revolver to his head may make a decent negotiating tool.

The front door was open. One door of the Audi sitting outside was open.

"What do you make of this?" MacLachlan asked Marcel, pulling the edge of the gag down sufficiently for Marcel to respond.

"Nothing good. We would never leave a car door open and definitely not the house. Something has happened."

"Okay. I'll go in the front. Anna, you next and Marcel last. Marcel, if you raise an alarm, you will get the first bullet of the game."

MacLachlan hit the door with the revolver at low ready. The first thing he saw was blood. A helluva lot of it.

There were four male bodies in the house. They apparently had been raked by a submachine gun. He saw each had a shot to the front or back of the head, depending on how they had fallen.

With trepidation, he cleared the bedrooms. All were empty. He searched the one Marcel described as the place Nisa was kept. Empty with no sign the girl had ever been there.

"Clear! Come in now. Call Adele, we have to get going!"

The two came in and Marcel cried out, kneeling at a body and sobbing.

"It is my brother, Fadey! The bastard shot him so many times!" he said through the gag.

MacLachlan was busy checking the empty brass casings on the floor.

"There are a lot of .32 ACP cases on the floor, so it was likely an old Czech Skorpion submachine gun. It's the only submachine gun I know which shoots .32 ACP. The shots to the head are accompanied by 9mm cases. This was a pro-job. Only pros do the head shot to people they have already shot. Just to make sure there are no witnesses. And there are truly none here. They must have been in a real hurry. Pros pick up their casings."

"Marcel, I am sorry for your brother. But we have to get on the trail. Anna, please keep Adele from driving up close to the house while I look at tire tracks."

He found impressions in the soft dirt. They were wider than the tires on the Audi. MacLachlan took photos of them with his phone. He used his advanced iPhone rather than the burner phone to take and keep the photos.

"The tire tracks suggest the vehicle they used as probably a luxury sedan or a middle size SUV. Nothing but old trucks and small cars have met us on the way here. So, they probably went north. Marcel, what is north of here?"

"More of the same for fifty kilometers. Just rural land. A few villages and farms. Mainly olives," the distraught man said.

"Whose car is the Audi?" MacLachlan asked.

"It is titled to my brother and me," Marcel said.

"Keys?"

"I have a set of keys."

"We may need a second vehicle. Let's take it and the van. They cannot be terribly far ahead of us, based on blood forensics. We need to get going." Anna and Adele nodded and got in the van with the feeble attack weaponry from the hardware store.

MacLachlan scooped up one of the revolvers for Anna, leaving three and the shotgun at the scene. Marcel located extra ammunition for their two .38's.

MacLachlan drove the Audi. He wanted to set a fast pace, but not one which would engender police attention.

"I'm going to continue calling you Marcel for now. We may need the undercover identity for a while. Can I assume you are in retribution mode and ready to join us instead of being the enemy?"

"I have been turned on by my client and my team killed. Nothing less than his blood will make me happy. So, yes. I have changed over to your side for the duration." MacLachlan had seen the anger and anguish as Marcel looked at this brother and his friends lying in pools of blood. He believed him.

"Excellent! Are there any ports or airports along this road?" MacLachlan asked.

"There is a small private airport near the coast we are heading towards. Rich people with waterfront vacation homes are the primary users," Marcel said.

"Know the name of it?"

"No."

MacLachlan called Anna in the van. "We are heading towards a small airport on the coast. Is your hot spot working so you can look up the name and call them? Think up some ruse to find out if a small plane is waiting to take off?"

"Yes, and okay. I will let you know what I learn. We will have to switch drivers first."

She pulled over. The road did not have any traffic except for a farm truck loaded with local vegetables ten kilometers back. Anna and Adele switched, and the younger woman accelerated hard to catch MacLachlan.

Anna found the airport's website online and, quite innovatively, winged the call.

"Hello? I am calling for my boss. He is racing towards you. He has a plane waiting to depart. There should be three passengers.

"He has not arrived yet? Tell the pilot he's on the way. Do you have the itinerary? He told me he might have to fly to an intermediate location first." She listened to the response.

"You said Inverness? Yes, it's the original destination. If he decides for me to go, is there another plane there to take me? Excellent! See you in a few hours. Bye."

She called MacLachlan and filled him in. "Damn, you're good!" was his response. "In so many ways," he said. She broke into a broad smile and perfect white teeth showed. Only Adele saw it, but MacLachlan felt it.

MacLachlan called Schutte and told him what

had happened. He accepted the mission officially and advised the billionaire's security head, they were dealing with pros. People who would turn on their own and kill with cold precision. He inquired about Schutte arranging a plane for four from Mallorca to Inverness, Scotland.

These fools had no idea they had moved the game onto MacLachlan's homefield. And the game was now officially afoot.

Before they got to the airport, Schutte called back and said a small corporate jet would pick them up there in three hours. He also said he had arranged for someone to meet MacLachlan and crew with a car and some "special items".

*Amazing what a billion dollars can do,* MacLachlan thought. He shared the information to what he was starting to think of as his team. He hardly ever worked with a team, being a sole practitioner. This was an odd one, except for Anna. Anna was a pro of apparently profound, but unknown capabilities. He was pleased with her ingenuity and glad she was along. He told her so on the phone.

"Anna, we will still push hard. If we can get to the airport in time to stop them, we will take whatever methods necessary to do it. At the very least, I'd like to get descriptions of the head guy and his hitman. We can call your and my young friend at British SIS. Remember, his fiancée is an analyst at Interpol. A few favors and maybe we have a name. I thought about having him advise Interpol now and see if they could muster enough to interdict them here. But I think the threat is too great for Nisa to be killed by them or die in the cross-fire."

They arrived at the airport in time to see a small Learjet takeoff and climb quickly.

MacLachlan mumbled an epithet under his breath.

The group walked into the two-room airport and headed for the manager's office.

"I am an agent with British MI-6, the Secret Intelligence Service. We just missed making a diplomatic kidnap apprehension. Describe to me who was on the plane we saw leave just now!"

"I'd like to see some identification and an explanation of why you have any authority on the Spanish Island of Mallorca," the manager said.

MacLachlan took out credentials matching his claim and handed them to the man, who read them and compared MacLachlan to the photo.

"Okay. You seem to be who you claim. Now, about the authority?"

"I have absolutely no authority in Spain. I do have the ability to make one phone call and put you at the root of a major diplomatic crisis between Spain and Great Britain."

Anna knew when MacLachlan and his partner, Alexis, took her into custody, they were part of a British Secret Intelligence Service team. The only odd duck was the American. Had he saved his temporary SIS identification for a rainy day? Probably so, she thought.

His bluff worked to an extent. He was given names, which he wrote down. He was pretty sure the leader's and the hitman's names were false. The descriptions were accurate and would prove helpful. The "sick" young woman was surely Nisa Faheem.

MacLachlan had enough cause to have detained them for Spanish authorities with his genuine Special Deputy US Marshal badge and creds. Or, just taken the girl and let them go.

But, alas, the arrest ship had sailed. The chase would continue into Scotland and wherever else.

MacLachlan had a small cottage in Straithlachlan on Loch Fyne. He had lectured in and toured the whole country for which his ancestors had fought the British. He still had the contacts and a solid base for operations. It beat Lebanon, where every third guy had a hit out on him. Or, the Czech Republic, where MacLachlan was supposedly buried in his Canadian identity.

Sometimes, it was tough being MacLachlan. It, however, did not worry him a bit.

"Anna, when you were coordinating operations for Guy and Solange, did you have a dossier on their competitor assassins with photos?" MacLachlan asked, being careful not to associate her with the criminal enterprise by using full names.

"I did. I was not able to get photos on all, but I got pretty good at hacking into official sites to get a lot. I believe it's buried in an encrypted file in my laptop."

"Could you locate it in time for us to prescreen a couple of similar people for the airport manager to look at?"

It took her a half hour, but she came up with an array of ten men, mostly in their forties when the photos were taken.

"Do any of these men look like one of the men who took off today?" Anna asked the manager.

He studied carefully.

"Yes, this one is definitely one of the three men. He's a few years older now, but it's him."

"Thank you, sir. Your information will be of great help to the authorities," MacLachlan said. "We are several hours away from our plane landing. Is there a nearby place for lunch?"

"We have a café walking distance to the left of the airport building. Yours is the only scheduled plane for this afternoon, so you should hear it coming in."

They walked to the café and took a corner table. By this time, he and Anna were both carrying concealed revolvers.

"Marcel, what do you want us to call you?" MacLachlan asked.

"My real name is Vanko. I have chosen Marcel because it seems kind of neutral in Europe. Let us stick with it."

"Okay, so not Ramirez either? Marcel, I am taking you at face value. You realize how serious and dangerous I can be as an enemy? You say you want to get the man who killed your brother. We can help each other get him. But there are rules. You have to take orders without question from Anna or me. You may even see some financial return when we are successful getting the girl back. I'd like to know more about her. What are her strong and weak points? What's her general health?" MacLachlan asked.

"She is a spoiled rotten little bitch. She has a superior attitude. She could be a bit attractive if she wasn't always sneering at people. She is healthy. She will probably lose some of her baby fat during this. I doubt she will lose any of her attitude."

MacLachlan turned to Adele.

"Your opinion on Marcel's assessment, Adele?"

"I think he's correct. In her quiet moments, she's not bad. She has some real hang-ups about her looks. They, and being spoiled, make her act worse than she really is. She is my friend, but a very trying friend."

"Mack, you and Anna are professionals. Yet, you came in unarmed."

"True. Both of us usually have access to whatever we need. Anna is particularly adept at securing things. In my case, I have always found if you need a weapon, find someone who has one and take it," he said.

"Like you now have some pistols?"

"Yes. And perhaps more will be waiting for us on the plane when it arrives."

MacLachlan knew his new team had questionable experience for this type of operation, with the possible exception of Anna.

Anna, her brilliance and usefulness notwithstanding, was still somewhat of an unknown quantity.

He watched her kill her former employer in cold blood. Admittedly, after the woman killed their Lexi, he was already beginning to press the trigger to do the same thing. She just did not give him time to decide. Spontaneity, MacLachlan knew, was a double-edged sword. A very sharp one.

He was not sure what her future plans were. If she was going to resume her previous career as a travel and weapons logistics provider, he was going to counsel her. There was a semi-legal way to pursue such an endeavor. The way she did it before was illegal. He would press for the former. It was none of his business, but he truly cared for her and had successfully kept her out of prison for her years with the team of Guy and Solange by negotiating her to be a protected witness for the Crown instead of a defendant.

He did not question Anna's devotion to him. She had proven it.

Adele was an interesting one. For a college student, she adapted to this life of violence quickly and seemed to relish it. She would be an interesting catch for Anna's service. MacLachlan did not think it was an original thought. He observed their interaction and knew Anna was quietly interviewing her.

"Earth to MacLachlan," Anna said. "I'd give a Euro for your thoughts."

"For you, they are free. I was thinking about each of you. This is an unlikely team, but you and I are going to make it a cohesive, effective one, Anna."

"We aren't already?" Marcel asked. MacLachlan knew he was a smartass. He cut him some slack. His attitude allowed him to move in circles where MacLachlan could not.

"I don't know, Marcel. You have seen violence. I have not seen you deal it out under fire yet. I think the time is coming soon, though.

"Adele is adapting to all of this admirably in view of being so new to this sort of thing.

"On the plane, we will review some basic combat techniques. Real basic. Both firearm and hand-to-hand. Just verbal stuff. We don't have a place to really practice yet. My place in Scotland is too far from our destination to use."

MacLachlan having a place in Scotland came as a

surprise to the two younger members. Not to Anna, who had been there surveilling MacLachlan after Alex's funeral. She was really good at covert surveillance. MacLachlan had felt her presence. Yet, he had never seen her. Not once. And, he had been doing constant surveillance detection routes and routines for over thirty years.

"What do you think of Adele working with me after this is all over?" Anna asked as the two were stretching their legs around the small airport.

"You've been pretty subtle, but still feeling her out all day. If you will let me, I want to help you get started again on your business. I will only do it if you agree to some changes. It has to be a legal operation. I believe you can do the same work and keep it legal. Some niceties like a firearms importer's license to move guns around legally, vetting customers, too many ideas to talk about here and now," MacLachlan said.

"I might even invest a small amount with no expectation of it being paid back. You know, just to get you rolling," he added.

"I guess it would be unprofessional to kiss you right now?" she asked.

"Could you save it for after? I can run a tab on kisses like other people do on drinks."

"Consider it done! And of course I would value your input. You and Lexi kept me out of prison once. I don't want to worry about going now." MacLachlan did not believe it for a minute.

"On another subject, I wonder what Schutte is sending us. He hinted at weapons. Even in Inverness, I believe we can get them in at the private airport without paperwork. Using them may be a different matter," he said.

"Why did we leave several revolvers and a shotgun at the massacre scene?" Anna asked.

"It was a feeble attempt to leave evidence of a professional hit on an armed criminal gang. Which it actually was in the broadest sense. A shotgun is no big deal. A couple of handguns are. We just needed a couple handguns until we are supplied arms on the plane or in the car waiting at the airport in Inverness."

They heard the high-pitched whine of a small jet changing throttle overhead. It had to be theirs.

They went in and the airport manager verified it to be their jet. It landed and taxied in. A fuel truck met it immediately. The pilot walked towards them. The copilot observed the refueling.

"Mr. MacLachlan? I'm Glen McKinney from Inverness," he said with a brogue and the correct pronunciation of the city, with the accent on "ness".

"I'm Mack, this is Anna. Thanks for coming so quickly, Glen."

"My pleasure and my job. I also have some items waiting back in Scotland for you. No need to risk bringing them to Spain. They are labeled 'scientific equipment'. Odd-shaped cases, but I dinna know a thing about scientific equipment."

MacLachlan gave him a conspiratorial grin.

"Aye, we scientists like to keep our tools rùn," MacLachlan surprised the man with Gaelic for "secret".

The pilot winked and made a pre-boarding announcement on the tarmac.

"We offer coffee, tea, sodas and some wee snacks

on the flight. Just be advised, the only toilet is under one of your seats. It's a three-hour flight. If you need to have a wee or worse, I'd advise doing it now."

Adele and Marcel all but sprinted to the lobby where the restrooms were located. MacLachlan and Anna headed there, just not at a run.

The flight from Mallorca to Inverness, Scotland took three and a half hours.

The pilot presented a manifest to MacLachlan to sign, which he intentionally signed with an undecipherable signature.

"If you go into the executive terminal over there, they will give you keys to a car. I loaded your scientific gear into the boot before coming to get you. Clear Immigration and then pick up the car and drive off with no further ado."

"Thanks for a prompt and good flight. We may be seeing you again," MacLachlan said. After clearing Immigration, they gathered around the boot of the gray Volvo sedan and loaded their carry-ons into it. With the team blocking his action from unwanted view, MacLachlan looked into the "scientific equipment" cases. There were four Pelican cases. Two were short rifle cases and one which carried four ubiquitous Glock 17s. Each rifle case had a very "scientific" Heckler & Koch MP5 semiautomatic carbine. MacLachlan smiled broadly and lifted something out of one of the cases to show the others.

"You have probably seen these in action movies. They are silencers, more correctly called suppressors. In the US, they have to be specially licensed. Not so in much of Europe, where they are encouraged for hunting and target shooting because of noise reduction regulations and hearing protection. These are a Godsend for the type of work we are going to do." The fourth box had enough 9mm rounds to hold off a siege.

"We'll find a place to familiarize everyone with these. But first, we need to do some sleuthing here at the terminal. Let Anna and me handle this one. You two are a bit young to be what I'm claiming. And she's close."

MacLachlan and Anna walked into the terminal. It was small enough to have a manager who also served as dispatcher and all-around factotum.

There were a couple other people in the lobby.

"May we speak with you privately?" MacLachlan asked.

The manager, a man named Childress, led them into a small but nice office and bid them sit down.

MacLachlan held up the British SIS or, as it is more commonly known, MI-6, credential. It was a genuinely-issued one he had neglected to return from his last visit to Scotland.

"What we need to speak about falls under the Official Secrets Act, so you cannot share any of this with your wife, coworkers. Not even in your prayers, okay?"

The man nodded, but with a quizzical look on his ruddy face.

"You sound like an American, not some James Bond bloke."

"Raised in Canada and moved home," MacLachlan lied and continued before further questions.

"A plane came in here a few hours ago. At least

two males and a female. She may have been drugged and needed help walking. My associate and I have been chasing them around the world," MacLachlan said.

"Aye. I remember them well. One was an obvious posh. He was in charge. Then, a dangerous looking guy. Looked like a soldier. The third man looked like a secretary or personal assistant type. The girl was a bit haggled. The soldier walked beside her and steadied her some."

"It's them, alright," MacLachlan said to Anna, nodding his head more for theatrical purposes than anything else. She made the appropriate face, playing along.

"Mr. Childress, will you give us as detailed descriptions as you can? Even accents," Anna asked.

"The posh was small, a bit overweight. Not fat, just soft looking. Except for his eyes. They were real dark and real cold. He had wiry black hair. Wore slacks and a golf shirt. Carried a blue blazer. We get almost nothing but posh clientele. This chap's outfit cost as much as my car."

Both took copious notes.

"How about the 'soldier' looking man?"

"Just like you. Age, build and look. His accent was probably German or Swiss. Not a man I'd want to get in a tussle with at my local," Childress said, referring to a bar fight.

"He was dressed in dark clothes. Kind of marched instead of walking. Looked like a damn Nazi to me."

"The girl?" Anna asked.

"Upper teens, low twenties. Average build. Haggard looking for a young person. Looked tired, beaten down, and hungry. She was wearing a cotton dress like cleaning ladies wear. Light gray with white on it. It was pretty wrinkled. And I almost forgot! She wore slippers, not shoes. Her hair was black and thick. Also, as tangled as a haggis' nest." MacLachlan grinned at the use of the fictitious animal's nest.

"She looked like a homeless person or a druggie. Usually, the 'wives' we see look like showgirls."

"How about the PA?" MacLachlan asked.

"He was a skinny little guy. Glasses on top of his head. Dark wool jumper and tan slacks. Mousy wee man. Followed close behind the posh. Canna speak to his accent, because he said nothing."

"Did they have a car here? Or, have someone pick them up?" MacLachlan asked.

"Apparently, this was an unplanned trip. He had me call a car service instead of a taxi. Demanded a big car or estate wagon. I called a friend, and he sent an extended length Defender. The posh complained it would ride like a truck. I told him the Queen drove one herself on hunts, or at least did before she got up in years. He just shrugged, unimpressed."

"Can you call your friend and find out where the service took them? Use finding something on the plane as an excuse. Like an envelope stuck in a seat cushion. Say you haven't opened it, but it feels like cash. I'll provide a cash envelope if required."

Childress dialed a number he clearly knew by heart.

"Denny. It's me. Where did you take the three blokes and girl from the Mallorca plane today? They wanted it kept mum? Strange. One of them lost an envelope with what looks like cash wadded up in it. I thought they might want it. Oh? You'll drop by and pick it up and take it to them? Alright. Send someone over. Damn weird posh, if you ask me. Yes, I know. All of them are. See you or one of your boys soon." Childress hung up; mission accomplished.

"Thank you. Remember, this is government business you are doing. You can't mention it to a soul," MacLachlan said.

"When the man gets here, walk out and wave as he leaves. We will use your wave as a sign he's the one to follow," Anna said.

She and MacLachlan went back to the Volvo, popped the boot and loaded the two H&K rifles and two Glocks. They screwed a suppressor onto the barrel of each H&K. They took four boxes of fifty rounds each and put everything in the front of the car.

They removed all the luggage and the remaining boxes with Glocks and ammunition and left them with Marcel and Adele.

"Once we get a location, we'll be back and the four of us will formulate a plan for tonight or early in the morning," MacLachlan said.

The two professionals got in the Volvo. MacLachlan backed it in beside a hangar, but where they could see a vehicle arrive and leave the office.

Soon, a black full-size saloon arrived. MacLachlan was not sure what it was. A Vauxhall?

They saw Childress hand the rumpled envelope MacLachlan provided with fifty Euros in it. They spoke for a while, then the black car backed up and left. The two in the Volvo watched Childress give the wave signal and pulled out onto the road.

MacLachlan hung back until they reached a main road. Then, he slipped in two cars back.

"Tailing someone in only one car is a pain. You should have three and radios," Anna observed.

"We seldom have such a luxury. Not like we are a federal agency," he said.

"I don't know. You seem to be able to come up with all sorts of IDs!" Anna said.

"I have to be careful. The Marshal's badge and creds are real. The others were real but are out of date. Sir Walter at SIS would have a kitten if he knew I was using his agency's credentials. I often wondered, though, about what goes on in his devious spymaster mind. He knew I had them and did not ask for them back. He has a memory like an elephant—okay, not anything approaching your eidetic one—but still remarkable. I may be unpaid SIS reserves and he forgot to tell me."

"Surprising, since I know he got a report on the way you looked at the damn ambassador who wanted me in prison instead of signing my "deal". I remember those out of order remarks the creepy diplomat made about you as an American! I thought you were going to climb over the desk and rip his throat out," Anna said.

"The pompous ass was too stupid to know how close I was to killing him right there, Anna. His regional security officer knew for sure."

"It was a close call, but you did everything right to get me a deal. Something I will always credit you for and one of the reasons I would do anything for you."

"One reason?" MacLachlan asked rhetorically with a smile.

"Yes. I will leave you to figure out the others," she said as she reached over and caressed the side of his face.

They hit the A82 and the black car sped up.

"Damn! The lorry in front of us is not speeding up. If we pull around it, the black car will make us," MacLachlan grumbled.

"Honey, we are in a gray Volvo. How noticeable will we be anyway?" Anna asked.

"You have a point," MacLachlan said as he powered around the lorry and punched throttle on the Volvo. The turbo-powered sedan leapt forward.

After fifteen minutes, they saw the black car slow and take an exit, without using turn signals. The Volvo followed.

They came to a roundabout. The black car took the third turn. So did the Volvo.

"I don't mind driving on the wrong side of the road, Anna. But those roundabouts drive me crazy. Especially in traffic when I am in an unfamiliar place."

Having learned to drive with roundabouts everywhere, she did not follow, but did not press the matter.

In ten minutes, the black car slowed and turned into an estate. MacLachlan passed the entrance, and both looked back.

"It's a small castle!" Anna exclaimed.

MacLachlan pulled into a small side road and did a Y-turn. He drove to the entrance and parked opposite. They could see traffic if it left the castle, but the other vehicles were unlikely to notice them.

They were rewarded by seeing the black car turn

onto the main road in the direction from which it came.

"We are left with a decision. We know the girl is alive. Do we go in, guns blazing, in daylight without an ops plan? Or do we wait until we do some surveillance. Then, we could assess their strengths, and formulate a plan. Most likely it would be to go in like Apaches an hour before dawn." MacLachlan knew what he wanted to do but wanted to see Anna's operational sense in action.

She thought a minute.

"We put a plan together and hit them when most are asleep."

"My inclination, also, Anna. I don't believe they would bring the girl here by corporate jet and kill her right away. They have not even proffered a demand to Faheem yet.

"How about we park the car out of sight and go in through the woods and take a look during daylight?" he asked. Anna nodded enthusiastically. She may be an intellectually brilliant and highly complex individual, but first and foremost, Anna Visser was a person bred for action.

MacLachlan found an out of the way place to hide the Volvo. They entered the woods half a mile north of the castle grounds.

They moved carefully through the trees to what they estimated to be several hundred yards from the grounds.

"Scan for game cameras in trees. Often, they are less than six feet up so they can be readily serviced. Also, look for small sending devices which are a small bit lower-to-the ground. They shoot beams small animals like squirrels and rabbits can go under without breaking the beam, but something as tall as a person would break it. This does not look like red stag country, so I think they would be no more than waist high. But as Will Grafton says 'Ya just never know!'"

They spotted a game camera in the distance. Whoever put it up was more interested in his convenience finding it than camouflaging it. The camera, affixed five feet up a tree, was fluorescent lime green.

MacLachlan just shook his head. He focused on the way it was pointed, or "watching". Making allowances for the probable cone of vision of its lens, they skirted the area. They did not find any laser or microwave motion detectors.

The woods abruptly stopped a hundred yards from the castle and several small outbuildings.

"Nice place," MacLachlan said in a low voice. He knew it was more difficult to hear someone speak softly than to hear a whisper.

"Yes. Why don't you buy it? It's bigger than your cottage on Loch Fyne."

"It is. But, since I have the place in Florida and my cabin in the woods in Virginia, I like holding the upkeep down."

He touched her shoulder and pointed to a man with a gun patrolling the grounds. He was dressed like a Scottish gamekeeper in a Barbour jacket. He was appropriately armed with a shotgun.

However, he did not saunter like a gamekeeper would. He walked, stopped and checked each direction and moved on furtively though in plain sight. He appeared to MacLachlan to be a trained security or military man.

A matching man approached him from the opposite side of the castle. They spoke briefly and continued on their rounds.

After a half hour of watching, they saw the two men three times. It took ten minutes to make a given round. Their regularity was a flaw in security, MacLachlan noted to Anna.

"It will be interesting to see if the patrol and its regularity are run for a full twenty-four hours," she observed.

"I see a camera on the corner of each house. They are set to watch around both sides. I have no way of telling what the cone of vision would be. Let's circle the castle in the woods and see all sides," he said.

After a full circle, they found no cameras on the middle of the four walls. It appeared a direct approach to the front entrance or middle of the rear façade may be the only one blind to surveillance cameras. They did not know if any or all of the cameras had night vision capability, so had to assume they did.

"The front door is befitting a castle. It would take ten serfs with a ram to breach it. The rear and side doors, not so much," he told Anna.

"The good news is, since the castle is probably several hundred years old, electricity was added in last seventy-five years or so. I spotted where it comes in. We can kill the power. I doubt they have the cameras on backup. I could be wrong, of course. At three-thirty or four in the morning, only the guards would realize the power was cut."

"I just thought of something, Mack. We will need

some high lumen torches for the op!" Anna said. He agreed.

They disappeared into the woods as wraithlike as possible.

They planned in the Volvo on the way back to the airport.

"I don't totally trust Marcel yet, Anna."

"Nor do I. Maybe after the op, I will. We need to get another big hotel room and stay where we can watch both and control the guns," she said.

MacLachlan saw a "For Sale" sign. It was at the beginning of a twisting lane. He braked the car and drove down the lane. There was a small cottage at the end. Peering through the windows, they saw it even had minimal furniture still in it.

"Anna, call the estate agent's number listed. Pour on your French or German accent. Your choice. Just pick a name to go with it. Say you saw the sign and drove down the lane. You might want to see it. Just what you've been searching for. But you are not available until the end of the week. Probe about it. Is the electric still working? Water? You know."

As they pulled into the executive portion of the airport, Anna finished speaking with the realtor.

"We should be good. She pushed for an offer. It's been on the market a while. Water and electricity are on. It does not appear anyone will be coming to look at it for the next few days. By the time I am supposed to call her back, we should be wheels up going... well, somewhere!"

"We'll pick up some powerful flashlights, sleeping bags, radios, and just use take-out to avoid food preparation," MacLachlan said, thinking aloud. "Maybe some folding chairs and whatever we see which looks like something we can use. We can do some dry fire orientation on the weapons once we get there for the other two. Even with suppressors, I would hesitate to fire real rounds so close to the castle."

They picked up the minimally needed supplies and returned to the old farm to set up temporary camp.

MacLachlan watched with interest as Anna removed a lock pick from a hidden compartment in her purse. She had the front door open in seconds.

*I really need to find out where she got her training and in what areas,* MacLachlan thought.

The two women drove to buy takeout dinner. After they ate, MacLachlan went through the manual of arms for the Glocks and MP5s. Anna seemed handy with the Glock 17s, but was experiencing one of MacLachlan's favorite firearms, the Heckler & Koch MP5, for the first time.

"We have not had time to conduct much surveillance. Anna and I determined they have corner cameras. Unknown if they are infrared. They are fixed but probably have 180-degree lens watching around all four corners. There is likely another security officer inside monitoring them and the two patrolmen's radios. We know there's a pro inside, the owner, Nisa, and an accountant.

"While the accountant appears mousy, don't take him for granted. Folks are not always what they seem. It was not unheard of for a Russian ambassador's driver to be the embassy's KGB head. I assume it's probably still the case with the new FSB.

"Anna and I will take out the sentries as quietly

and humanely as possible. They may not be bad guys, just hired help.

"Our two weapon types are semiautos. They spew brass casings to the ground. Brass casings are evidence. Pick them up! As a matter of fact, we should take our .38 revolvers. Use them first. Revolvers don't eject brass until you choose to remove your empties. With a Glock and a revolver, there are twenty-three shots without reloading. Two extra mags apiece will give another thirty-four rounds. I am not including the ones in the chambers. I tend to not fully load a semiauto with a full mag and one in the chamber. Not having the magazine full to the top gives me even more comfort about an already reliable handgun.

"I want you to always keep your trigger fingers locked straight and along the slide until you are ready to fire. Like this," he said, demonstrating the safer hold.

"Practice loading and racking the slides. If you find it difficult to rack, pull back the slide with your weak hand and push the lower frame forward at the same time with your strong hand. You will be surprised how much easier it makes working the slide."

Everyone rested until two-thirty in the morning, when MacLachlan awakened them.

"Time to go."

Once everyone was gunned up and by the Volvo, MacLachlan explained the simple ops plan.

"Each of you has a small walkie-talkie. We will observe radio silence, except for emergencies.

"Marcel will be on the road at the beginning of

the lane to the castle. Lights out and out of sight of the main road and any police patrols.

"Adele: walk in with Anna and me. We will position you away from the castle where you can see what's going on. You will be the immediate backup to either of us who needs assistance. Click your radio twice if you see someone behind us.

"Anna will take out the first guard to circle the front. I will take out the one who's still in the rear. We will try to use non-lethal take downs, if possible. Once we take down our person, communicate it by group text.

"Anna, take the rear door. I will come in the front. We will look for Nisa. Anyone we encounter is deemed a threat and we will do whatever is necessary to neutralize them. If we have to kill, do it. All are direct accomplices in a felony kidnapping. To hell with them and police procedures.

"Once Nisa is in hand, whichever of us has her will move her outside and remain in a dark spot. Use the radio to tell Marcel to come in hot. Pick us up and Adele on way out. The first thing we want to do is get Nisa in the car.

"Remember: the mantra of executive protection is "cover and evacuate"!

"Everybody on board? Questions?"

There were none. The plan was simple. It would likely go awry. They all did. Then, they would "improvise, adapt and overcome", as Marine Gunny Highway said in the movie Heartbreak Ridge. And, Marines have claimed it as their own ever since.

They got in the Volvo and drove in, lights off.

Adele was dropped at the edge of the woods, where she could see, but not be seen.

MacLachlan went right and Anna left, furtively towards the castle.

They paused in the darkness as one patrol appeared. Before the other met him, Anna dropped in behind him and began to trail him. MacLachlan crouched in the doorway shadows awaiting the next one to appear from the opposite direction.

When he did, MacLachlan stepped out and sprinted fifteen feet, hitting him hard from behind. The man went down with an "Oof!"

MacLachlan gave him a hard punch to the back of the neck, putting him down. His shotgun flew to the side and hit the ground. The guard sprang back up and reached for his handgun. MacLachlan open handed him on the chest and drew the .38. He fired once and the man went down for keeps.

MacLachlan checked for a pulse for verification. There was none.

Dragging him into the shadows by the house, he unloaded the double barrel shotgun, obviously chosen for a gamekeeper illusion, and tossed it away.

MacLachlan quietly tried the front door. It was locked. Not for long.

He went in, MP5 now unslung, and checked the lower floor. He saw a light on in a room and approached it. It was the security room, and he could see the video screen. A man was sitting dozing at the desk. The sound of the shot must not have carried into the castle. A base station radio was in front of him.

A knife edge hand to the rear of his neck knocked him out.

He looked at the camera screens. As he thought and hoped, there was no coverage in the direct front and rear. Bad security. There was no sign of Anna and no radio call, so he had to assume she had neutralized her target.

As MacLachlan was erasing the surveillance film CD, the radioman recovered and clawed at him. He pushed MacLachlan backwards and began to draw an unseen handgun from his pocket. MacLachlan throat punched him and he died in his chair.

MacLachlan finished erasing and turned off the screens and radio. He left the room. He started up the steps as a large man appeared at the top, now five steps up.

The man hurled himself on top of MacLachlan and the two tumbled head over heels down to the landing at the bottom. The steps were original stone, worn by several hundred years of use. But they were not softened by the use. Each bump along the way was painful for the two men. They were seeking an advantage even while falling.

The luck of the draw, and nothing else, put a battered MacLachlan on the bottom. His MP5 was halfway up the steps and unreachable.

The man, bleeding from the nose, aimed a punch which would take MacLachlan out of the fight.

Before he could throw the punch, MacLachlan used the fact the man had straddled him too high on his chest. The former Marine was able to place both heels flat and arch backwards. He threw the man over him, and his head slammed into the stone wall hard.

MacLachlan was up instantly and kidney-punched him as he tried to stand.

He then raked the inside heel of his shoe down the back of the still squatting man's ankle, causing a scream. He kicked between the man's legs from behind, hitting his target the most effective way. He used his shin instead of his foot. His adversary went down doubled-up. Grabbing his belt from behind, he slammed the man's head into the stone wall several times as hard as he could.

This was not martial arts with its rules, or boxing with Marquis of Queensberry rules. This was one man walks away and one man dies rules. Street rules.

MacLachlan, every spot in his body aching, touched the man's carotid with two fingers. Nothing. He stood up. The man had a tattoo on his exposed forearm.

MacLachlan recognized it. Russian Spetznaz Alpha. From the KGB days even before the FSB. Their Tier-1, along with Spetsnaz Vega.

There was no time to contemplate on beating one of the best of the best. He had to find the girl and exfiltrate.

Unsuppressed shots came from the downstairs back. As for so many years, MacLachlan ran towards the sound of gunfire.

He heard the mechanical sound of the suppressed action of Anna's H&K firing intermixed with louder pistol shots. Two different sounds of pistol shots. Maybe a 9mm and something smaller. But, not by much.

He slung the H&K and drew the .38 revolver. The new breed would not pull anything without a slide. MacLachlan wanted every trigger pull to go "bang", and no brass to police up later.

He cut the corner like a pie and peered into the eyes of the personal assistant. Or whatever he was. The man aimed a Walther PPK at him. Either a .32 or a .380. It did not matter much to MacLachlan as he fired the revolver.

The man went down. He was dying. There was nobody else there. Apparently, Anna had followed the other shooter as he exited. With the girl? MacLachlan scooped up the little Walther. He liked them. As a backup maybe.

He heard Anna yell "Stop!" and a car started.

MacLachlan was still closer to the front of the castle than the rear, so he turned and went out the front door.

He rounded the corner of the stone building and looked towards where Anna was aiming her H&K at another building.

It became apparent it was a garage when the wide door disintegrated. A supercharged Range Rover powered through the debris.

The windows were black. Anna could not see whether Nisa was in it. She could not risk firing at anything other than tires, which she did.

MacLachlan saw the driver's face clearly. His expression was fear, anger and a myriad of emotions.

MacLachlan rammed another magazine into the MP5 and almost emptied it in the approaching Range Rover's grill. Despite Anna's accurate shots, the tires were still inflated. They had to be run flats.

He hoped the small 9mm bullets could penetrate the grill and punch holes in the radiator. He aimed at the man's face but knew he could not fire with the girl in the back seat.

Bullets fired into or out of a car windshield did weird things. The one thing they seldom did was go straight. He wanted to bring the girl back. Not her body.

The driver aimed the SUV at MacLachlan who jumped aside in just the nick of time.

"Marcel, come in hot and try to ram the Range Rover coming at you. The girl is in the back seat," he yelled into the radio. Anna was running towards him, reloading her MP5.

"Don't hit him head-on. As you meet him swerve into his front tire from the side."

Marcel almost executed the maneuver. However, the much larger SUV avoided the hit, swerved to the side of the road and the driver recovered.

Marcel and the Volvo spun to the other side and went down an embankment.

Marcel steered clear of trees and came to rest with the front wheels in a stream. He tried to reverse out but was stuck. Adele, near the trees where he entered the woods, had dived for her life as the Volvo careened by.

"There goes our chance of pursuing them!" MacLachlan said aloud. "What a cluster!" he said under his breath grading the op badly. He knew they had to develop a new plan, not evaluate the disappointments of the old one.

"Anna, will you call Mr. Childress at the executive airport and see if there is a jet just reserved for the parties who came in yesterday?" She nodded as

MacLachlan handed her his phone with the number queued up.

"Adele, get the guard Anna subdued around back and march him around here at gunpoint. Remember, finger off the trigger?"

"Ah, Mack. The guard has to be permanently subdued," Anna said as she sought the number.

Adele responded, "I copy, Anna."

"I'm going to check for a tractor or something to see if we can recover the Volvo."

There was a small Kubota tractor with a front-end loader shovel on it in the barn. MacLachlan started the diesel and drove it out. The next trip in located a logging chain, which he tossed in the shovel. He and Marcel rode out the lane to where the Volvo entered the woods. The chain was not long enough to reach from the lane to the car, so they entered the woods with the tractor, hooked it to the Volvo and pulled it out of the stream. Marcel guided it backwards as MacLachlan pulled it up the incline with the Kubota.

The Volvo had some superficial scratches, but nothing to prevent it from operating.

They drove both vehicles back and MacLachlan took Anna aside.

"Mr. Childress has not heard from his mysterious kidnapper yet. He promised he'd call if he does," she said.

"Very good! Let's talk with the PA before he dies."

"Do you think we can negotiate with him?" she asked as they approached the man lying on the hallway floor.

"What is, or rather was the name of the Russian?"

"Liev Jovanovich," he said, pink froth on his lips.

"Was he your boss?"

"No, I worked for Mr. Faheem. Zaid Faheem."
MacLachlan kept a stone face. Anna did not have to,
sitting in the rear, and her mouth dropped open.

"What was Mr. Faheem's relationship to the
victim?"

"She's his niece." Again, MacLachlan showed no
discernable facial expression.

"What was Mr. Jovanovich's job?"

"He was Mr. Faheem's full-time enforcer."

"Tell me your name. I am afraid your time is
running out."

"My name is Stuart Smythe-Henry. I'm an
accountant and business manager."

Blood was starting to trickle down one side of his
mouth.

"Do either you or the enforcer have wives or
families?"

"The Russian does not. I have a boyfriend in
London."

"Where do you think Faheem would run to now?
Anywhere local?" MacLachlan asked.

"No. He'd stand out like a sore thumb. He'd want
to get himself out of Scotland. Maybe London, maybe
Jordan where he came from, though I doubt he wants
to go to a place his brother could reach him." Those
were his last words. He died unceremoniously in
front of them.

"Anna, let's just take a revolver and a Glock
apiece and ride down the road. We did a lot of
damage to the Range Rover. Maybe we will find it."

"Marcel, we'll be back after a run down the road to see if we can spot the Range Rover."

Anna reloaded the handguns and MacLachlan drove the scratched but completely usable Volvo.

Five miles up the road, they saw the Range Rover on the side. MacLachlan expected this from the fresh coolant stains they saw dribbled on the tarmac.

They got out, guns available but unseen. The car was empty. The tires had just been marked by Anna's bullets. They did not look like bullet marks to a casual observer.

The grille was broken but, again, did not scream out what had happened without a forensic investigation.

"There are a man's and smaller footprints on the shoulder of the road," Anna advised. He looked at them.

"They are walking north. Away from the airport. Maybe there's a town where they can rent a replacement vehicle."

However, rural Scotland is not known for auto rentals outside of cities. They drove on and came to a small store with two Esso pumps in the front. One was gasoline, the other diesel. They walked in very carefully.

There was one teenage attendant.

"Hi. We are trying to catch up with some acquaintances. A guy from Jordan and his niece. We found their car broken down a few miles back, so they were probably on foot."

"They were here. Half hour ago. Bloke bought my old Austin for a thousand quid cash."

"What does it look like?" Anna asked.

"Rusted out maroon. Fifteen years old saloon. You can follow the smoke trail. My lucky day, though! The rust bucket's insured. I'm going to report it stolen."

"How long since they drove off?" MacLachlan asked.

"Twenty minutes."

"Did he ask directions anywhere?"

"Yeah. To the next city with an airport or ferry. I told him Ullapool had a CalMac ferry over to Harris in the Outer Hebrides. I'm pretty sure he's heading there."

MacLachlan pressed twenty pounds into his hand for "petrol for your new car".

He pushed the turbo Volvo hard but did not catch them before reaching Ullapool. It did not take long to find the ferry terminal. A CalMac ferry was docking, and they saw a man and young woman getting out of an Austin meeting the description the service station attendant had given them.

MacLachlan pulled the car up, blocking the Austin.

Both got out and quickly approached Zaid and Nisa Faheem as they got out of the car.

"Zaid! So glad we caught up with you. Kadar sent us to pick up Nisa," MacLachlan said.

In a lower voice, he continued "You pull a gun, and you will be as dead as the Russian and your PA. Do you understand me?"

Anna had already moved around the car and taken Nisa by the elbow.

"Get on the ferry. I have no authority to take you into custody. What happens later between you and your brother is up to him. Take too long to think about it, and I will yell "He's got a gun!" and drop you with my bare hands like I did the Spetznaz. Then, I will put a revolver in your hands. The very one used to kill your PA. And we will disappear, leaving you facing a murder charge."

Zaid Faheem was a smart man. He knew he was way out of his league here. He turned and almost ran to the ferry ticket counter. He never looked back at his niece.

Anna put her in the rear of the Volvo and got in beside her.

MacLachlan quickly left the ferry terminal. As he drove, he saw a medical practice on North Road.

"Nisa, do you need to have a doctor look at you for any reason?" he asked.

She did not respond. She may have been traumatized. More likely, she had a sour disposition. Her unpleasant disposition did not take long to manifest itself during the drive back to the castle.

MacLachlan called Schutte on the burner phone.

"We have her. She is uncommunicative, but her health seems alright."

"How about the kidnappers?"

"She was kidnapped by her uncle, Zaid Faheem. He just boarded a ferry to Harris, an island in the Outer Hebrides of Scotland. We got her in a crowd, so there was no way to take him into custody. I figure the father will want to handle him. If he wants the police to arrest him, he'll be in Harris in two and a half or three hours. He will land at the CalMac ferry terminal."

"I'll talk to the boss. I have no idea how he will react to this turn of events. Any casualties?"

"Yes. Zaid had a Russian Spetznaz Alpha enforcer. He also had a little PA fellow with a Walther. Both are deceased. The area should be cleaned up by the time I get back to Zaid's castle near Inverness. It's going to look to the Scottish police kind of like what it was. A fight between a suspicious and well-armed crew at a castle and a gang of thugs from the Ukraine. It will smell to high heaven of illegality."

"Good job. I will send a plane for you to escort Nisa and Adele back to Paris. Kadar may want to meet there. I just do not know, Mack. Include Miss Visser on the flight as part of your team." Team. The word reminded MacLachlan of something as the call terminated.

He pulled into the lot of a small café on the edge of Ullapool and stopped.

"How about some coffee and a sandwich or pastry? Are you hungry, Nisa?"

The girl glowered at him. He turned in the seat and stared into her eyes for a long minute before saying, "You listen to me, you ungrateful little brat. Four people on my team risked their lives to get your worthless ass back to daddy. You will answer any question Anna or I ask you, or we will drop you off barefooted in the middle of nowhere. Neither of us need the money. And you are beginning to not be worth the trouble."

"A sandwich and a Diet Coke," she spat out. Anna nodded indicating the same.

The real reason MacLachlan wanted to stop was to call Marcel and tell him to get out of the castle and lay low while Nisa was there. MacLachlan was sure the young woman with the unusual personality would go bananas upon seeing him.

He called and told him to tell Adele to keep quiet about him and for him to go to the hide and wait. Marcel understood and agreed.

Anna called Adele a few minutes later as they were driving and eating. They saw a first hint of a smile from the billionaire's daughter as Anna handed her the phone and she spoke to her friend.

Marcel and Adele had been busy. And, effective. The Skorpion the Russian used on the Ukrainians was lying on the floor. Marcel said he carried it by the tip of the barrel, using a washcloth to prevent finger-prints. All bodies were left as they lay.

Kidnap victim and friend greeted each other with screams and a hug. Nisa became animated. Adele took her aside and told her some of the things, dangerous things, she, Anna, and MacLachlan had done to secure her freedom. Even Adele was unsure of any sense of appreciation.

"What a bitch!" Anna commented privately to MacLachlan.

"The important thing is we were paid to bring her back, not to like her. She is completely unlikeable. Wonder what she'll do with over a billion Euros when daddy cashes in?" he posed rhetorically. Rhetorically, because neither he nor Anna cared in the least.

Schutte called with the arrival time for the char-tered plane to Paris. He said it would be the same plane and pilots. They only had several hours to wipe the place and pick up anything left at the old farmhouse.

After the call, MacLachlan told Anna the times. He also said he had to go see someone. He did not have to tell her whom. He drove to the old farmhouse they referred to as their "hide" and paid Marcel. They wiped the place down and removed any remaining belongings.

"Marcel, here is two thousand Euros for the revolvers and one thousand for your transportation to Spain or wherever you want to go. I don't need the guns, but there's no way you are going to be able to transport them. I can.

"I doubt there will be any reason for the police to be interested in you. Everyone other than Nisa is dead. She will think you were killed at the farmhouse.

"We will be leaving in a couple hours. If I were you, I'd get out of the UK right away. Good luck to you," MacLachlan said, and they shook hands.

MacLachlan gave him a ride to a bus stop and left him standing there, his clothes in a bag and three thousand Euros richer.

"I'm on the way back, Anna. We need to leave early and get her something to wear on the flight and to see her father. Also, whatever she needs to make herself presentable in the way of makeup. She should be able to use soap and shampoo there and take a quick shower now. She should steal whatever she needs from her uncle's castle. He owes her. Let's wipe everything at the castle one of us may have touched. Don't worry about Nisa's prints. See you in twenty minutes."

By the time MacLachlan returned, Nisa was freshened and only needed new clothes and shoes. Those were obtained at a store in downtown Inverness. MacLachlan stood by the River Ness and thought. There was no way in hell he was going shopping for anything with the brat. Anna and Adele kept her more or less in line.

They arrived at the airport in time to meet the arriving jet. Neither Schutte nor Faheem were on it.

"We have the "scientific" gear," MacLachlan told the pilot from the original flight. "Will it be a problem flying into France?"

"We can handle it," the pilot grinned. "One of the benefits of flying charter jets."

They boarded. Adele already gave Nisa the admonition about the toilet under a passenger seat.

It was dark when they set down at an executive airport distant from Charles de Gaulle.

There were two Mercedes SUVs awaiting them. Schutte, a couple of his security men and the drivers were there. No one from the Faheem family came.

"Congratulations, Mr. MacLachlan. We will put Nisa and Adele and their luggage in the second car. You and Miss Visser ride behind in the lead vehicle. I see the transport cases I provided are with you. We don't want any connection to them, so please dispose of them in the way you deem most appropriate," Schutte said.

"I will debrief the girls on the ride to the boss' hotel. It is impossible to tell if he will wish to thank you in person. My boss is virtually impossible to predict. You will be provided a waiting room. Leave your luggage and equipment in the SUV. It will be safe and the driver will give you a ride to the hotel of your choice after you and I consummate our arrangements."

Kadar Faheem met his daughter in the lobby. He did not even look at MacLachlan or Anna. The daughter ran towards him and stopped short of hugging distance. With great deference, she stuck out her hand and they shook like strangers.

"No wonder she's such a cold fish," MacLachlan said to Anna between clinched teeth.

Both of them scrutinized Faheem. He was a medium height, bearded man in a thousand dollar plus suit. He showed no facial expression, nor any particular joy in having his kidnapped daughter back.

One of Schutte's men ushered MacLachlan and Anna to a waiting room on the penthouse floor of the hotel.

Anna looked around the period antiques.

"Shame we don't know how long we have here before being summoned. We could put this nice room to good use," she said.

"Don't worry. I will find us a nice room for tonight. It will have less fragile furniture."

"One of the many things I love about you, Mack. Your furniture planning," she smiled.

They sipped cold Perrier water and only had to wait fifteen minutes for Schutte to appear.

"Mr. Faheem decided to remain at arm's length. He sends you his appreciation for the amazingly fast, safe return of his daughter.

I would like to debrief you and assure there are no loose ends to which either of us must attend," Schutte said.

"Please give an executive summary of your actions over the past few days."

MacLachlan recounted each step of the investigation, the ops plans, recruiting one of the kidnappers, and steps taken to hide their actions.

Schutte handed MacLachlan a thick envelope.

"Here is the agreed upon fee for retrieving Nisa. There is one more thing," Schutte said.

"Yes?"

"My boss is convinced his estranged younger brother was working against him. He thinks he was working with one of the two Russian pharmaceutical companies. His beliefs are not based on any intelligence I obtained for him. It is pure speculation but makes sense. Russians are seldom gracious losers. A billion plus Euros breeds a lot of angst.

"Zaid is actually a half-brother. He has always been jealous of my boss' success and him inheriting virtually everything. My boss is very mad over him kidnapping Nisa. I have two men with eyes on Zaid right now in Harris. He is trying to lay low.

"Mr. Faheem would like you to make sure he never hurts the family again. He has authorized me to pay you a hundred thousand Euros to make sure Zaid disappears permanently."

MacLachlan let it sink in for a moment. He was halfway expecting it and already had an answer.

"Thank Mr. Faheem for his confidence, but I have to turn him down. It may be possible I have had similar assignments in the past, but they were direct actions for US national security. Private assignments are something I decided to avoid a long time ago."

Schutte was clearly disappointed. Until Anna spoke up.

"I may have some proven connections who could help you. Would the stipend be the same?"

"Yes."

"Keep your men in place and give me two days. I will contact you either way."

Schutte looked at MacLachlan for some sort of reaction.

"Ms. Visser and I are independent operators. She is quite expert in certain fields. This is one of them. But one where she will be on her own."

Schutte's number was on MacLachlan's phone. Not knowing if MacLachlan had given it to Anna, Schutte passed a business card to her.

"My phone is encrypted. Any conversations we have other than face-to-face must be encrypted. Despite the encryption built into modern cell phones, they are not impenetrable. Let's settle on an encryption app and use it for texts," Schutte said.

They decided on a well-respected app. MacLachlan's "special" phone's encryption was at AES or Advanced Encryption Standards. It had no Wi-Fi, open source data collection, or Bluetooth as entry portals. For everything else, he used his iPhone or SAT phone with encryption apps. He was pretty sure neither Schutte nor Anna would have a model like his special one.

MacLachlan stood and said, "I am glad we were able to deliver on the Nisa matter with her safe and speedy return. If we are to hitch a ride with one of your security cars, I will let you two speak privately." He stood, shook hands with Schutte and left.

Anna met him in the lobby not long after.

"Let's go to your place and organize our plans," he suggested. "I checked on my smartphone while you were finishing up with Schutte. It's only a three-hour drive to Leuven from Paris. It's only 208 miles on the E16 and E19.

We can have Schutte's driver drop us at Europa Car or some rental agency. We'll just have to transport the weapons in their Pelican cases and hope the EU's stupid idea about open borders won't blow up in our faces."

"Sounds like a good idea. Are you mad with me for taking on the assignment regarding Zaid?" she asked tentatively.

"No. A little disappointed. I'd hoped you would start and run your business legally. But it's your call. You know the risks as well as anyone, Anna."

She did not respond.

Schutte's driver took them to a rental company. MacLachlan did a one-way hire on an E Class Mercedes. He got Schutte's driver to bring his vehicle close to the trunk of the Benz and help block the transfer of the "scientific" gear into the trunk, or boot as MacLachlan usually forgot to call it in the UK or Europe.

Once they got out of Paris, MacLachlan pulled into the first rest area. After going into the restrooms and getting coffee au lait at a nicely equipped restaurant, they got back into the car.

MacLachlan handed the envelope to Anna. She had a funny look on her face before he could speak, and a tear rolled down her left cheek.

"Is this goodbye, Mack?"

"No, silly. I want you to take half for our job just now. You don't have to count, just guess half and take it."

"Are you sure this is not goodbye?"

"I am sure."

"How much is here?"

"Supposedly a hundred thousand Euros. Not bad for less than a week's work."

She eyed the bundle, walked her fingers across half its thickness and separated it.

"It was your op. I was just along for the ride. You should take the lion's share, Mack."

"Consider the money my contribution to the rebirth of your business," he said.

"I'll pay you back."

"I don't want it back. You earned it."

"Even though I have already made the call to set up the hit on Zaid Faheem? I know you weren't in favor of it. You'll still help me?"

"I will spend a couple days with recommendations, then I will return to Florida. Or maybe my cabin in Virginia. I think it would be prudent for me to stay away from Scotland for a while. Let things settle down. The regional detective chief inspector will have six murders to deal with. Then, he or she will have to coordinate with the detectives on Harris for another one which will be easy to see is connected."

"Do you think you will see your friend when you are in Virginia?" she asked.

"My friend, Will? I don't know. I have not thought about it."

"I was thinking more of the woman who works for him," she said.

"Kate. If I go to see Will, I will probably see her. She's on the same floor of the same building. Otherwise, I don't know. Why?"

"Just wondering," she said and let the subject drop for now.

They arrived in Leuven, and she opened her apartment for the first time in a while. It required some airing out. They went for groceries and soon it was home again.

Anna called an assassin whose work her former employers had admired. He accepted the offer on the hit on Zaid Faheem in Harris, Outer Hebrides. Anna took the normal twenty-five percent fee. She wired half the money, net of her fee to him from an existing Isle of Man account. It was the one to which she had specified Schutte to wire the full amount. Her as yet unnamed company was off and running. And, she had twenty-five thousand Euros, plus the fifty thousand from MacLachlan. She did not discuss the transaction with him, though he suspected what was happening.

She sat down, her long legs curled under her.

"Where would you start?" she asked.

"I would divorce my home from my office. I would set up a shell company to own the business. Then, let a friend like me lease the office space. Apply for the business license in the name of the business instead of your name.

"Do you still have access to a forger who can create identification and a fake legend for you? And an older male," he asked.

"I do, in fact. It will cost at least five thousand Euros each," she said.

"Do it. Have the legend reflect a long history in legal arms trading, then apply for a weapons importing and sales license. Show yourself as a clerk and the false identify as the proprietor."

"Would you be the older male?"

"For purposes of obtaining the license only, yes. Next, find a small office. I will lease it. As the secretary, you can furnish it. I would stay modest and spend whatever it takes on a top computer system. I have a young hacker friend who would travel here to set up the safeguards you should have. Dark web, virtual private network, automatic saving to a secret cloud, and so forth."

"Should I warehouse weapons?"

"I have not given it a lot of thought yet. At first blush, probably. You will have a legitimate license including automatic weapons. Then, you could ship from an unknown address instead of drop shipping from whoever your supplier is. No need giving them away, too.

"How important is it to stay here in Leuven? It could make sense to move four hundred miles to Switzerland."

"Unless it has massive benefits, I'd rather stay here.

"On a related subject, the Katholieke Universität Leuven is one of the hundred largest universities in the world. I was thinking if her parents would pay her tuition if she transferred to KU Leuven, I would hire Adele as a college intern. If she's as good as I think she would be and the business grows, she would have a career here," Anna said.

"I realize you have been planning along those lines and agree. I have one last question before you put all of this into action. You have had more than a taste of field work. You like it and are good at it. Do you think you can sit in an office and make money instead of dashing about on operations yourself?"

"Oh, absolutely!" she lied. MacLachlan did not buy it for a minute. But people are who they are and this was none of his business.

"Now, I have a question for you, Colonel MacLachlan. My treat for dinner, then bed? Or bed, dinner, and bed?"

"The latter please."

After, they kept it light with sushi at Kintsugi and returned for a bottle of wine and turned in early.

## 3

They made the background contacts the next morning. They prepped for the false identification with a visit to a theater props store. MacLachlan bought a high-grade grey mustache and some gray powder to add to his already graying dark hair. Anna bought a red wig. Both got glasses with plain lenses. MacLachlan picked round tortoiseshell frames. Anna picked dark green designers.

MacLachlan wondered at her choice of a red wig. Did she know about Kate? He decided not to say anything.

Their purpose with the disguises was to change focal points for the photos, not try to trick photo identity programs at airport and border surveillance cameras.

They obtained several sets of passport-sized photographs of each and posted them to Anna's forger in Brussels. He promised a one-week turnaround in an encrypted text.

MacLachlan contacted his late teens hacker in

Finland and offered him ten thousand Euros of Anna's money to make the two-hour flight for the day to set up the computer system. He told the two on a conference call what computer equipment to buy. He said he would put it all together and provide additional security software.

They could do little except fill out applications for the various licenses until they had the identification in hand.

Anna called Adele and told her about her college intern idea. Adele was thrilled and spoke with her parents. She was on summer leave and the timing was perfect.

Her parents approved and Adele applied to KU Leuven. Her grades at the Sorbonne virtually guaranteed her acceptance.

Later in the day, Anna received an agreed upon message indicating the assassin had killed Zaid Faheem. He sent an email with a newspaper headline attached. It verified the hit. She had her banker wire him his final thirty-five thousand Euros. Using an email from an Internet café, she sent the news article to Schutte. The deal was done.

Commander Zero, as hacker Elias was known on the Web, promised to fly in at the end of the following week. MacLachlan and Anna had ten days to find an immediately available office and buy the computers.

The time waiting for the false identification packages to arrive was spent on runs around the city, quiet lunches and dinners. Anna spent every free moment reconnecting with former contacts.

The driving licenses, working credit cards, passports and historical legends arrived on time. Now, they could move forward at full speed.

Anna found a realtor who specialized in office leases. She and MacLachlan, who portrayed her boss, donned their disguises and checked one another closely with a three hundred sixty degree walk-around.

They found a small office suite within a six-block walk of Anna's apartment. It had a reception area, an office, and a work or supply room. The toilets were down the hall.

MacLachlan made a cash deposit. "I did not expect to find the perfect office on a first look, so I did not bring a check," he told the realtor. Glad to get Euros in hand, she smiled, and they signed the lease for occupancy after a cleaning MacLachlan required.

After the cleaners had completed their job, MacLachlan and Anna had a security company install cameras, alarms and a heavy-duty lock on the door without advising the rental company

The next few days were spent obtaining a business license and applying for a weapons dealer license. Once they had the business license, they went to a nearby bank and opened a business checking account. Checks would be delivered in a week, but all they would be used for was subsequent rent, office equipment and supplies. Utilities were included in the rent. Most things would be paid for by automated bill-pay or private Swiss account electronic transfers.

They bought the computers and associated equipment per Elias' list. It went straight into the boot of the rental Mercedes and to the new space.

Elias arrived with software and detailed instructions already in writing. He hooked up the equipment and spent the rest of the day instructing Anna and talking about her forays into hacking. The nineteen-year-old hacker fell head over heels in love with her. MacLachlan sat back and tried to keep a straight face. He wondered if he was so goofy at nineteen. He knew he was not as smart as Elias at any age. The kid was past brilliant and already a millionaire. A person who had never seen the inside of a college.

The firearms dealer and importer license would take the longest. She needed it to buy and stockpile some basic guns and ammunition at dealer discounts to be able to sell them at a large markup. She began to make marketing calls to all her past associates.

There was no worry about court trials with both of her former employers dead.

Adele arrived and immediately went to KU Leuven with Anna and was interviewed for her almost guaranteed acceptance.

MacLachlan took the two beauties out to dinner. Everyone had a great time. He kissed both goodbye and moved to a room closer to the airport for the evening.

He left for Dulles Airport in Northern Virginia the next morning.

MACLACHLAN ARRIVED in Dulles and took an Uber on his false identity credit card to a Dunkin Donut shop near the airport.

He had a cherry filled donut and cup of black

coffee. As he sat at the window, he watched for a tail, part of his surveillance detection protocols. None were obvious.

He finished and walked right from the entrance carrying a scarred leather carryon.

Continuing to scan the front and both sides, he cast the occasional furtive glance to the rear. Still clear.

He used a key to enter a storage facility. Going to a garage-like unit, he opened the heavy, saw and wire cutter resistant, high security padlock.

The unit, like the one he had near the airport in Sarasota, Florida, was air conditioned. It smelled fresh inside.

He grinned at the matt black older Jeep Wrangler hardtop. It had thirty-five-inch tires on black mag rims, a snorkel, and a winch. None of this was for street creds. He used all of it off road.

He hung his blue blazer on a coat rack. It was hot enough out he did not don a windbreaker.

The gun safe had a couple of Glock 19s, his past everyday carry piece. Since he did not have a coverup and would be seated for several hours, he put it in an ankle holster inside his left calf. The khakis had a wide enough cuffed bottom hem and covered it acceptably.

He clipped a Gerber 06 automatic knife to his left front pocket.

MacLachlan unhooked the trickle battery charger on the Jeep. The vehicle, cursed by Will Grafton as "your bumpety-ass Jeep" and christened the Bat Jeep by Kate Mahris, fired up immediately. The exhaust was relieved. It was moderately loud, until the

Australian supercharger cut in. Then it sounded like an uncapped racecar.

MacLachlan had installed a peephole in the garage door. He looked out. The way appeared to be clear. He pressed the automatic door opener and drove out. Leaving the Jeep idling at a low burble, he closed the door and put the padlock back on until next time.

He drove out of the facility and did a couple of right turns to see if anyone was following him. Then, it was I-66 South towards Front Royal. He stopped along the way to pick up groceries for a week.

MacLachlan exited and drove to Cedar Creek. A ford across the stream and mile along a two-track path later, he saw his cabin on a rise across from a swimming hole in the creek.

MacLachlan was home. Or at least one of his three homes. The Florida one was inherited from his grandfather and destroyed by a Hezbollah attack over a decade ago. He had rebuilt the house from the original blueprints. The new house did not have the presence of his beloved grandparents to him. It was just a house, albeit one in paradise. What was cheap land when it was built now represented over several million dollars in real estate. The cabin in Virginia was hardly worth more than he spent to buy the land and build it. He had not spent enough time in the one in Scotland to know what it meant to him. So many homes. So few really mattered.

There was something missing. As smart a man as he was, he did not know what it was.

Will Grafton knew what it was. Apparently, Anna Visser did as well.

And one other person in the world did. She was conflicted as to what she wanted do about it.

———————

HE AIRED OUT THE CABIN. His recently installed solar system on the roof of an outbuilding behind the cabin kept the temperature in both between sixty in the winter and seventy-five degrees Fahrenheit in the summer. Ceiling fans were kept running on low in both.

This technology was in the Florida home, but not yet in Scotland. Maybe one day.

He checked the outbuilding. It and the sixteen-foot Kevlar fiber canoe and mountain bike within were untouched. He checked the .357 magnum revolver which was still clipped, loaded and hidden, under the workbench.

It was hot as hell out, so he grabbed a towel and walked to the bend in the creek which formed a perfect swimming spot.

Unlike the summer tepid Gulf of Mexico, the water was cold when he plunged in. Only two people had ever swam with him here. One was dead and one was pursuing a very successful career. Perhaps it was meant for him to swim alone, he pondered.

After the swim, he brewed a pot of coffee and fixed a sandwich for dinner. He sat on the porch and ate, thinking about smoking a Cohiba Churchill cigar afterwards.

He had trimmed and lit the cigar, blowing out its first aromatic cloud when his iPhone rang.

He did not figure it to be one of the nuisance auto warranty calls and answered it.

"Slickmeister."

"How ya doing?" MacLachlan asked.

"Finer than frog's hair. This is not business, so we are good on an open line."

"That's good, I performed the job to which you referred me and owe you lunch or dinner or something."

"Yeah. You got back to Dulles at eleven-thirty. Nice flight?" Will Grafton asked.

"You and your damn electronic leashes!"

"Gotta watch my boy. There are those—not me, of course—who think you are a national treasure."

"Yeah, right."

"I'll take you up on lunch or an early dinner. Soon. Like maybe tomorrow. There are some matters Kate and I would like your opinion on."

MacLachlan was not up for an assignment, if the conversation was leading towards one. "Kate", however, perked up his ears.

"Name it."

"Meet us at the Italian joint we've gone to before near Langley. I'll ride with her in her new Japanese luxury hot hatch. You drive yourself in your bumpety-ass old Jeep. With all your money, one would think you could get a new one. I understand the new Jeeps ride real well."

"I understand the same thing. But then, what would you have to complain about?"

"I'd find something, Slickmeister. See you at eleven-thirty. I'll perform my usual rituals." Grafton broke the connection.

"No business?" MacLachlan said aloud. "Then, why is he performing his usual rituals? Having his tech team do a technical surveillance counter measure sweep for bugs?"

MacLachlan was pleased about the invitation. He grinned around the stogie clamped between his teeth.

The next morning, he showered and shampooed outside. Inside, he looked in the mirror and decided he would not shave, just touch up. He had been wearing the three-day beard look for some months. If he had known it was considered chic casual, he would probably have shaved right away.

He put on his Washington uniform, though he would be some miles from the capitol. Seeing how far downhill the former Camelot had slid both saddened and infuriated him.

The uniform was a dark blue Brooks Brothers suit, white LL Bean Oxford cloth button down, maroon silk tie and black cap toe Oxfords. The shoes were the most special part of the outfit. They had thin titanium toe caps which could deliver a fatal kick, yet not add to the weight of the shoe. He had used them quite effectively in London last year against a group of illegal thugs from Eastern Europe. They had made the mistake of assaulting a young couple on the street in MacLachlan's view. All went to the hospital. One remained in a coma for some months but awakened in time for his trial.

Looking as good as he could look, MacLachlan mounted the Jeep for the drive up I-81 North to I-66 East, then into the heart of non-DC government country.

He arrived, as planned, thirty minutes early. He

circled the area where the restaurant was situated to check for surveillance. He did not see any. Restaurants like this were frequented by intelligence and law enforcement agents and people they were meeting. Their proximity to spy central, Dulles Airport, made them a convenient choice for both good and bad trench coat wearers.

MacLachlan hated places like this. He knew Grafton, with his in-your-face attitude, loved them. It may have been the only chink in his OPSEC. Well, there was always forgetting his damn gun now he was a muckety-muck.

He parked the Jeep in the shade at a strip mall next door and walked over to the eatery.

There was an outdoor dining area which was not open. It gave him cover and a place to wait out of sight.

He saw three men leave with large cases. Their coveralls said ACME Electrical. *Yeah, right,* MacLachlan thought. *They are Will's boys doing a technical security countermeasure check.* He was glad his friend was staying sharp. He doubted, great target he was, he still went armed. Kate had told him when they were closer, she carried when the two of them went out, knowing he probably did not.

Kate had been taught by the best. Then, received a post graduate course from him. Her prowess had allowed her to put one in the groin and two in the chest of a Spetsnaz who shot MacLachlan and was planning a kill shot. Kate's after-action psych had had a time with her interview and the crotch shot.

He saw a racy four door hatchback arrive. The driver was going too fast, but obviously had driver training. It stopped quickly and MacLachlan could tell from the shudder the ABS system had kicked in because of the fast stop. The lanky Grafton climbed out. His normal grin was replaced by a look of mild irritation.

This made MacLachlan smile. Smiling was something he had not been doing regularly for a year or so.

Grafton had graduated from Tony Scotti's famous driving school. He had urged MacLachlan to go. And, he had.

Now, the curmudgeon could not tolerate a ride with a beautiful redhead who drove too fast, although extremely well? This was fodder to tease his friend and mentor about.

As Will Grafton walked towards the restaurant's door, he saw MacLachlan in the shadows. They went back to the eighties together and he had started as MacLachlan's boss but stayed his mentor and best friend over the years.

Grafton's scowl turned to a wide grin as he approached his younger friend. They shook hands and hugged like the brothers they considered themselves.

Kate, who generally operated at warp speed, clicked around the corner in her iconic, red-soled, high heels and saw them. She gave MacLachlan a long hug.

"You didn't hug me for like ten minutes," Grafton said.

"Will, if you felt half as good as Kate, I would have," MacLachlan countered, earning a quick kiss on the lips. She whispered in his ear, "I've been worried about you," and released her full body hold.

"We better get inside and eat. Since you are buying, I've been saving up for this and am starving," Grafton said.

The hostess who knew Will Grafton and Kate well, escorted them to a private corner.

"Everything was checked out about fifteen minutes ago," she whispered in Grafton's ear.

They were twenty-five feet from the nearest diners. Not enough for Top Secret. But, workable for lesser topics.

Grafton ordered surf and turf. At this restaurant, it was the pretty standard filet mignon with a lobster tail. To celebrate, so did MacLachlan. Kate stuck with an antipasto salad. She was always watching her figure. Just like everyone in her proximity was.

"Is this too business-oriented for a glass of wine?" MacLachlan asked.

Grafton looked at his watch as if it would give him permission.

"Meetings are done. End of the week. Not a world-shaking sensitive subject. Why not?" he said.

MacLachlan ordered a bottle of California Pinot Noir. He gave his friend the honor of sampling it when it came, and glasses were poured.

MacLachlan raised his glass.

"To the two people in the whole world I care the most about."

Grafton knew it to be true and smiled. Kate did, too. But Will Grafton was sitting in a position where he could see a tear run down her cheek.

"To friends and associates," she toasted without the emotion the tear had given away.

The lunch was as convivial as three friends, two

of which were former lovers, could be.

*"Former lovers forever, or lovers on sabbatical,"* MacLachlan wondered.

After lunch, Grafton broached the subject he and Kate wanted to speak about.

"Remember when you did a capstone week of lectures at the end of the Tactical Analyst School? When you met Kate, I believe," he began.

"Actually, we met at the airport as I was coming in. She just didn't know who she was flirting with," MacLachlan corrected, getting a dirty look from Kate Mahris.

"I don't flirt, thank you!"

"Hmm...it's so rare beautiful women flirt with me, I hardly think I'd be mistaken."

Though she did not buy it for a moment, Kate decided discretion would be the better part of valor, as Falstaff said in Henry IV.

"Anyway, word of how effective it was, has spread around the intelligence community. Several members have training academies. The rest have training courses before or after sending agents to the Federal Law Enforcement Training Center. Have you instructed at FLETC?" Grafton asked.

"Yes, once years ago. It's only about a five-hour drive from the place in Florida."

"Because you have two real vehicles in Florida. Not bumpety-ass ones," Grafton reminded him.

"I do, though I got rid of the Jag and got a very special Mustang."

Grafton did not want to discuss the subject he started and continued on the training topic.

"Anyway, several have approached the ODNI,

since we retained you for the capstone, to see if you would deliver the same week to their academies or their folks at FLETC. This will be for 1811's and 0132's exclusively. Agents and Intelligence officers. Don't expect any uniformed officers as students.

"You have mentioned wanting to wind down and avoid being shot at for a living. Here is a way," Grafton proposed.

"A good way. How set would these schedules be, Will?"

"Pretty far out. You could still take some missions and work around them. The pay would be what we paid you. Most will be in Northern Virginia and the rest would be at FLETC. So, there's a degree of travel comfort in sight of you being a reasonable drive from home. One home or another."

"Expenses for the week, wherever it is?"

"Yep."

"This sounds appealing, Will. Who will parcel out the assignments?"

"Your friend across the table. She will likely do the intros also. She is prepared to tell you why now."

He turned to Kate.

"Mack, as you know better than anyone, my kidnapping and your rescue greatly affected every aspect of my persona. I'm still getting counseling and it's over a year later.

"I love travel and adventure. I don't mind shooting people who need to be shot. Like the Russian guy when you broke me out. But, the captivity, twenty minutes of waterboarding and the torture. I just cannot endure another session of it," she said.

"I understand perfectly. And, I will say this in

front of your boss and my best friend in life. You can retire any moment you wish and have several places to live, any car you want to drive, go anywhere you wish to travel and never worry a second about money."

"I have some goals to achieve first, Mack. One day, perhaps."

"Just remember sand pours through the hourglass pretty consistently. We cannot control time," he said softly.

This was her old Mack speaking now. She welcomed him back in her heart. She also wished she could give him a different, more immediate answer. But not yet.

"So, you are good with this proposal to run seminars?" Grafton asked.

"I am," he said. He liked instructing. He certainly did not need the money. Most of what he made went to charity. One in particular. What this guaranteed him is much more contact with the redhead across the table and something interesting to spice up sitting around, fishing and having too much fun.

MacLachlan paid the bill, not worrying about the three hundred fifty-dollar tab.

"Let me go out first and scan the area before you come out. Arriving and leaving are the two most dangerous times for targets."

"You think I'm a target?"

"You've been a target for forty years, my friend. You're just a bigger one now. An unarmed one."

"How in hell do you know I'm unarmed?" Grafton asked.

"It's my job to know these things. Kate is making

up for it. She has a larger purse. When I moved it, it was about a Glock 19 too heavy for just makeup and money."

"Exactly why you are the Slickmeister who I want to teach this course to young men and women preparing to go into harm's way," Grafton said, and Kate nodded.

MacLachlan did his scan. Kate brushed his arm with her hand as she went by to get her luxury hot hatch car. If it was possible to give a look at once sad and happy, she did.

The two friends stood in silence. They had known each other so long, both swore they could communicate without talking.

Kate roared around the restaurant and stopped for Grafton to climb in. Will nodded and then they were gone.

Though still aware of his surroundings, MacLachlan walked back to where he had parked the Jeep, his mind flashing on a myriad of thoughts.

He headed home to his cabin forty miles southwest.

———————

MACLACHLAN HAD JUST SAT down on his front porch when the SAT phone rang.

It was Schutte, someone he did not ever expect to hear from again.

"I'm calling from the hospital. I was shot this morning and several of my men killed. A professional team hit the boss's home. They took him, his wife and the daughter you retrieved.

"The chief operating officer of the conglomerate is number two. He was in on the whole original kidnap of Nisa. He has authorized me to offer you a seven-figure stipend to take a team in and bring the boss and his family back to safety. Again, no government. No police. The Faheems have been moved to the Czech Republic. I will verify the exact amount we will offer you when we speak tomorrow. The one he has in mind will take a vote of the board of directors. Do you have contacts there?" Schutte asked.

"Yes. Very good ones. How are you so sure they are in the Czech Republic?"

Schutte chuckled.

"After Nisa's latest episode from which you brought her back, Mr. Faheem had a GPS tracker inserted under her skin. The indignity of putting it in one of her round ass cheeks did double duty as punishment for what her last escapade cost him as much as for security. I have the exact coordinates of her location, about forty kilometers east of Prague. To further validate, the Faheems all have the latest generation iPhones. My number two, who was on holiday during the attack, has performed the "find my phone" on all three. They coincide with the tracker in Nisa's right butt cheek."

Now, it was MacLachlan's turn to chuckle.

"Please tell me how many men were involved, how did they operate and what were their arms? Anything on vehicle descriptions?" MacLachlan asked.

Schutte answered all with confidence, as he was an eyewitness himself.

"Eight men, no face coverings, dark jumpsuits,

pistols and automatic weapons. Flashbang grenades. Bags over victims' heads."

The several things struck MacLachlan odd, and he shared his thoughts with Schutte. One was leaving anyone alive. Pros kill witnesses. Especially when they could give good descriptions as Schutte just did. Two, not immediately getting rid of the phones. Last, why outside of Prague? Yet in every other aspect, this appeared to be a smooth, well-planned professional snatch. Schutte had the same thoughts. He suggested not throwing away the expensive phones may suggest they came from some-where they would be a source of great pride or a hot commodity on the black market. Either way it was a sophomoric mistake.

"I take it no ransom request yet?" There had been none.

"I will accept the assignment and head for Prague right away. I will make a stop en route and mix up the route I'm taking. It may take several days to get a team there and coordinated. Let's keep one another apprised of any new developments. As we thought before, we should learn about the captors from the nature of the ransom. Have your chief operating officer demand proof of life and stress how much time and red tape he will have to expend meeting what-ever the request is.

"I hope you recover soon and fully. I will talk with you from Prague unless something new comes up," MacLachlan said.

Schutte gave him the coordinates now as a precaution. MacLachlan wrote them on his notepad.

"Thank you. We'll talk tomorrow at the latest

unless you are flying over the ocean then," Schutte said and hung up.

MacLachlan obtained business class tickets from Dulles to London. He booked on Air Canada, leaving at 6:00 PM the following day. There was no way he could make the flight today from his cabin far south. Besides, he had to make a number of phone calls. This was not going to be a solo op.

One call would be to Tomás Studrich, a former Czech agent under both communist and democratic regimes. He was in his mid-seventies, but MacLachlan had seem him and his former associates in action. MacLachlan recruited them to help him save Tomás's beloved niece, Kate Mahris, last year.

He would also call a scientific idea man for the government. His section was so sensitive it did not have a name. And he was scary smart. But, if you wanted to find out about designer drugs for intel use, drones, or special weapons, he was your man.

Then, he would call Gunny. The grizzled former Marine Master Gunnery Sergeant had helped him before. Studrich's age, he could still take several thirty-year olds in a bar fight. More importantly, his knowledge of explosives was encyclopedic.

Lastly, he thought he would try Paul, the helpful giant at the nightclub in Palma, Mallorca. Paul's French Foreign Legion service would fit right in.

This, MacLachlan thought would be his dream team. The only one he wanted but could not have was Rory Murphy. Rory was British Secret Intelligence Service, more commonly known as MI6.

It was his background in hostage rescue in which MacLachlan was interested, not his intel experience.

Rory was formerly a member of the British SAS. MacLachlan was confident Rory knew someone he could recommend from his old regiment.

While it was usually mandatory to have a team train together, he did not have the luxury of time on his side. By choosing absolute professionals on his dream team, MacLachlan thought he could somewhat compensate for the training requirement. Anna would handle weapons and equipment.

Rory was unavailable and would call him back.

His first call was to Kate.

"Kate, it's me. I want you to be aware I will be gone for a while. There is a project in Eastern Europe. Tomás will be involved. I'll be in contact with you in a month or less. This is your ears only." He never wanted to create a situation where Grafton, her boss and his friend, could appear complicit if an op went south. His official position had to remain above board.

She was not in, so he left the message on her voicemail. Not what he wanted, but he needed to scramble.

He called Anna. She was still in the office despite the late hour in Leuven.

"Hi, how's it going?"

"Oh! Mack! I am really busy. Shocked at it, as a matter of fact. Thank goodness I have Adele here helping. She's really getting into this darkside stuff," she said. "Do you miss me?"

"Of course," he said.

"Have you seen Kate yet?"

"Briefly at a business lunch with my old friend."

"How did she look?"

"Like you, she always looks good."

"Despite your Texas charm, you sound serious," she said.

"I have a big op and would like it if you would handle some weapons and equipment logistics. I'll need the items in the Czech Republic. Are you up for it?"

"Give me an approximation of what and I'll let you know."

"Ten carbines with suppressors. One sniper rifle. Pistol caliber like 9mm or rifle caliber like 5.56 NATO. Ten Glocks, 17s or 19s. Belt holsters. Two short-barreled shotguns. Ammo for all. Two hundred rounds for the long guns, one hundred for the pistols. A box of flash bang grenades. A box of smoke grenades. Ten Kevlar vests with added steel plates." He thought for a minute.

"Probably three 2XL vest carriers for the plates, seven XLs. Magazine pockets in the plate carriers, please. They won't be under a shirt—they will be the outer layer. A long-range hearing amplifier. Several pairs of good binoculars. A silent drone and computer paired to it. That should be a good start," he finished.

"So, you are planning to make my whole first year in one order, huh? What can I know?"

"Hostage rescue. Whole family. You just met the bitchy daughter."

"No! They got Mr. Big?"

"They did."

"I hope they are paying you in seven figures," she said.

She was a friend. Sometimes a lover. But this was business.

"With what you are going to have to charge for my order, I hope so, too," MacLachlan said.

"I'm comfortable with most of it. Basic stuff. I don't know anything about drones. I will put Adele on drone research duty."

"I wish you were here on this one. But I would never pull you away from your new business at this juncture," he said.

"Thanks. I really couldn't leave right now. Anything else you can think of, Mack?" she asked.

"Maybe a sniper rifle. Just a hunting model in a long-range caliber. Bolt action, scope and suppressor. Should be the easiest thing on the order, since it's what most European hunters use, including with a suppressor."

"Do you want 6.5 Creedmoor, 7.62, .300 Win Mag, or .338 Lapua?"

"I love it when you talk calibers!"

"A turn-on, huh? I'll remember."

"I will know better when I get there and see what I'm dealing with. The rifle won't be a problem at the last minute like the more military hardware will."

"Actually, I can move military hardware easier. It's the police and civilian items which are difficult sometimes. As ubiquitous as Glocks are, they can be tough for anything other than a government contract for soldiers or police," she said.

"Since we are in their homeland, how about CZ-75s? I prefer the B model with the hammer drop," MacLachlan suggested.

"May be easier. Would you be just as happy with them?" Anna asked.

"Probably. There are likely more of those in military holsters around the world than Glocks, Berettas, or SIGs. Just a feeling. I've never seen the stats."

"On the ammunition, do you want Geneva Convention compliant hardball?"

"You are kidding, right?" MacLachlan asked.

"Damn! Thought I had you! However, if we go with pistol caliber for the carbines, we might want to use NATO spec full metal jacket instead of hollow points. They would feed more dependably," she said.

"You are right. Pistols should be hollow points. I like one hundred twenty-four grain if available. If the carbines are pistol caliber, go with the NATO spec," he said. "Plus, they are hotter loads than most commercial 9mm's. Oh! We will need ten gas masks. Israeli if possible," MacLachlan said.

"We'll need a full-size SUV. US definition, not sporty pickup trucks like the Europeans call SUVs. Land Rovers, Land Cruisers or the like. And a big van, like a Mercedes Sprinter with closed sides.

"Two history tidbits: the Germans sued the US for copyright infringement in WWI. They said we were shooting them with 1903 Springfields which infringed upon the Mauser 1898 copyright. They were right and we paid them for each 1903 we fielded against them. Secondly, they sued us for the 1897 Winchester pump shotguns we used against them in the trenches. Said they were inhuman, unfair or something. Whatever the official court decree, we continued to blast away at them with our twelve gauges.

"The hidden lesson is, I could give a damn about the Geneva Accords. They are a bunch of BS to me!"

"You are so full of little ditties! I may be able to

use those in my business, though. Be safe, Mack. And be happier, okay?"

"I promise the trying to be safe part." He broke the connection with the striking blonde. She seemed devoted to him, but not in a long-term relationship way. Brilliant, beautiful, and possibly a psycho. He watched her kill the assassin who killed Lexi, with a smile on her face. She was like playing with a beautiful venomous snake.

He checked the weather for Prague. It was in the range of 6oF throughout the month.

He packed his toiletries kit, with the fiberglass dagger hidden in the seams, socks and underwear, several black compression pullovers, black windbreaker and ballcap, and black cargo pants. His usual flight uniform was blue blazer sans tie, dark gray slacks, Oxford cloth button down, and his lightweight cap toe lace-up shoes.

The only line of work he had ever had was tactical in nature. However, MacLachlan always thought dressing in tactical clothes, boots, watchbands and belts was a sure give away outside of operations. He always assiduously sought to avoid attention.

Similarly, he never openly displayed his sidearm, even in open-carry states. He preferred his gun to be a surprise to someone bent on assaulting him. Even with the general populace, it drew attention to him. *Bad damn OPSEC!* he thought to himself.

He placed a call to the retired member of Czechoslovakia's Security Information Service, BIS, and the Communist agency which preceded it. He had been a tough operator and proved to Mack he still is.

"Tomás, it's Kate's friend," MacLachlan began on an open line.

"Why have you not married my niece yet? She's crazy about you," came the answer in slightly accented English.

"It's not for lack of trying. Her career seems to be her focus currently."

"Ah, the vicissitudes of youth..."

"I will be in your neighborhood in a couple days. I owe you dinner. And may have a business deal you'd enjoy."

"Call me when you arrive. I will make myself available for a friend." He hung up. Literally. MacLachlan had used the rotary phone in his home in Prague.

The old spy followed as much tradecraft as MacLachlan. They met when Kate had been kidnapped. MacLachlan thought he was looking at himself in twenty-five years. Studrich thought the same in reciprocal.

The next call was to one of the two brilliant nerds MacLachlan knew. The first was the nineteen-year-old Finn who helped Anna set up her computer system and bulletproof security. This one was an idea man for the government. If the army was ever going to carry ray guns, this would be the person who developed and refined them.

"Hey, Drew. It's MacLachlan."

"What's up, Mack?"

"I need your advice on a couple things. One is so basic, I am afraid I will insult your intelligence."

"Insult away!"

"Okay. In a hypothetical situation for hostage

rescue, what drone would you recommend? I want one which could deliver and dispense a gas and/or an IED. So, it would have to be bigger than the ones kids goof around with and smaller than the ones the military uses. Plus, I would have to figure out how to drive the darn thing," MacLachlan explained.

"Oh, so easy!" Drew told him two makes and models of drones which met his criteria. They were about three thousand dollars each, but either would do.

"Along the same lines, what gas could be dispensed to make people drowsy, but have no danger of poisoning them? I know the Russians used a fentanyl derivative at the Dubrovka Theater, but some people never woke up."

"Yeah, Spetsnaz FSB Alpha did it. Screwed the pooch for sure. Forty special operators and a hundred seventy theater goers died. A gentler approach might be one of the human pheromones. Or maybe something like diazepam. May not knock 'em totally out, but neither will kill anyone. Got an encrypted message service? Of course you do! I will send you some product names and sources you can use legally to get them as soon as our call has ended."

"Thanks, Drew. You're the best, brother!"

"Ha! Everybody tells me so. Just not pretty women." He laughed and broke the connection. MacLachlan received his encrypted text a few minutes later and found a chemical supplier in Northern Virginia had both in stock. He had them drop shipped to his hotel in London.

He sent an encrypted text to Anna. It updated her with the new drone information.

The next call was to his longtime friend and sometime associate, Gunny.

"Mack, you ain't been killed by a jealous husband yet?" the raspy former drill instructor voice asked.

"The jealous husband who can kill you or me hasn't been born yet, Gunny!"

"I reckon you're right. How are ya?"

"Great. Hope you are. Hey, I have a little project I could use your help on. A couple of weeks in Europe. Could be dangerous. Would be worth a hundred thousand to you. Deposited up front. Anywhere."

"You've upped your game, boy."

"It's gonna be fast and dirty. I am putting together a dream team of very few operators. No kids on this one. All combat experienced. Marines, Foreign Legion, SAS, and one more."

"Will we get to train together?"

"Not much. Which is why I am selecting from the best. I'd like you to be number two. There's another fellow I've worked with will handle J-2," MacLachlan said.

"Then, he's an old intelligence hand?"

"Yep. Under his country's Communist and democratic regimes both."

"A lotta money, Mack. Sounds like it could be wild."

"Could be. Not as wild as Bosnia, Afghanistan, and others were for you. No army. Just security types."

"Okay. We'll discuss the money transfer in person. Where do you want me? I got reasonable travel funds," Gunny said.

"Can you be in London in three days? Monkey Puzzle Pub around five their time? Best pub there. Maybe anywhere."

"I'll be there with bells on."

"Haha. I'll listen for you, then."

It was probably too early to reach Paul at the night club in Palma, Mallorca. MacLachlan would call him mid-afternoon Florida time. Paul would be in and preparing his staff for a wild night at Shout by then.

MacLachlan went out back and set up steel targets at seven-yard combat distance and others at twenty-five yards. He put non-hollow point full metal jacket cartridges in four Glock magazines and clipped a holster on his belt.

He fired all sixty rounds in quick succession. Most shots were fired two-handed, but he alternated between right and left as strong hands. He practiced drawing for each string of five shots. The steel rang sixty times.

MacLachlan knew pistol shooting was not like riding a bike. It was something one had to practice regularly to stay really sharp. Which is what he had to be. Always.

Each of his Glock 19 9mm pistols was set up the same. Talon grip tape, steel combat sights, with black in the rear and high visibility in the front. He cleaned the one he had just shot. He would wear it to Northern Virginia, where it would resume its place in the small gun safe in his storage facility.

During his brief stay in London, his hands, feet, and head would be his weapons.

The phone rang as soon as he walked back into the cabin.

"Hey, Mack. Sorry I missed your call. The old Toff has kept us running on a situation," Rory Murphy said.

"No problem, Rory. How are you?"

"Busy. But, good. Don't worry, I have not forgotten about my best man. No invitations have gone out. Léa is in the middle of a really big case, so she's still in Belgium. Soon, though!" Rory said.

"Great! I'm arriving in London early tomorrow morning. With no notice, how does your schedule look? I'll understand if you are busy."

"I'm good through maybe an early lunch, but then I have to drive to Oxford on business," he said.

"St. Stephens Tavern around noon?" MacLachlan asked.

"Too much of a luncheon spot for the toffs here at the agency. Even Sir-You-Know-Who. How about I hop a bus and see you at the Grill at Harrod's? Less conspicuous than around Parliament," Rory suggested.

"Half-eleven?" MacLachlan asked in UK fashion.

"See ya there, Mate!"

The only one left was Paul. He would be a good addition for the team.

Schutte called the next day.

"The stand-in CEO got a call. As we both thought the kidnapping of Nisa was, this is related to the pharma deal. The ransom is to fully subcontract the deal. It would transfer over to just one Russian company. The deal is to be one hundred percent secret."

"Why both, I wonder? Think the government is behind it?" MacLachlan asked.

"I don't really know yet. The CEO did a good job of inflating the time to prepare legal documents, especially secret ones. He thinks he bought us a week."

"I have the team pretty much put together and hope we will be in place within three to four days, fully equipped. Does anyone on our side have eyes on the location?" MacLachlan asked.

"I have three guys on the way. They will watch and brief me. Then, they will be sent back. They are surveillance people, not trained operators. I will share their findings with you. Unfortunately, I lost my best men in the firefight."

"Okay, will do. I'm sorry about your losses. It suggests the kidnappers were trained and experienced. I will be stopping in London to finalize part of my plan. I get in early tomorrow. I'll let you know when I arrive," MacLachlan said.

He put his meager kit in the Jeep and left. MacLachlan never second guessed whether an assignment would be a particularly rough or dangerous ones. Even the virtual suicide missions he had taken and returned victorious.

The day he started second guessing would mark the last mission he would take. He promised himself. He was not sure whether or not he mentally crossed his fingers behind his back.

Once he hit I-81 N, he called Paul in Mallorca. He recognized the voice which answered to be the man at the cameras. MacLachlan told him who he was. They chatted in French for a moment or two and the man asked, "Do you want to speak with Paul?"

"I do, please."

Paul came on the line quickly.

"Don't tell me the girl has gotten away again!" he said humorously.

"She has. This time, her mother and father were kidnapped with her. Pros, Paul. Maybe Russians. His company wants me to bring them back. Their location has been pinpointed. After Mallorca, the father planted a GPS locator in the girl's ass."

Paul broke into the robust, loud laughter of a man who has seen the worst and can still find humor in the small things.

"I was thinking...do you have a week or so off to make a hundred thousand Euros?"

"You are kidding, right?" the big man asked.

"I need a team fast. Men who have combat experience. I don't have time for them to train, so they have to show up already professionals. Like maybe a senior non-com in the Legion. And the money is real and I can pay it to any account you specify anywhere. Upfront. Interested?"

"I take it there will be fighting and shooting?"

"You can bet on it," MacLachlan answered.

"Who's aboard?" Paul asked.

"Under me for ops is a tough Marine Master Gunnery Sergeant. He's seen action close to worldwide. We've worked together a lot and known each other for years. For intel, I have a Czech secret agent who served Communist and democratic masters. He's tough and we've also worked together. I am meeting in London tomorrow with an SAS guy who is not available but can refer an SAS man with bonafides."

"When do you need me?" Paul asked.

"Just like with the Legion, my friend. As soon as you can get with me."

"Where will you be?" he asked.

"London tomorrow. I hope to head to the Czech Republic the day after. Some time was bought in the negotiations," MacLachlan said.

"I'll talk with the owner and call you back inside of a half hour, okay?"

"Okay! Hope you can make it. You'd be a significant addition to the team."

Paul called back in five minutes. He was in. They agreed to meet at the Monkey Puzzle when he met with Gunny.

MacLachlan turned east at the intersection of Interstates 81 and 66. Driving through some of the prettiest country the Old Dominion had to offer, his phone rang again.

"It's me," Kate said. "Are you boarding yet?"

"No, I just pulled onto I-66. The flight is around 6:00."

"You will be seeing my uncle?"

"I will."

"Will you keep him safe?"

"I will give it my best. I have some younger combat guys to do the heavy lifting. He should be fine. But you know how tough he is."

"He is tough. But he's retired."

"I know."

"Will you be in his country?" she asked.

"It would be best for you if I told you face-to-face afterwards."

"I don't like the sound of 'face-to-face afterwards', Mack."

"It's righteous, Kate. The mission is to save a family."

"Is Anna going?"

"No. She is not. She is in her home country busy resurrecting her previous business."

"And you don't want me to tell your best friend?"

"Right. The less you know, the better, honey."

"You still call me 'honey'," she said.

"Does it bother you?"

"Just don't stop, alright? And, come back in one piece."

"I will."

"I...I, oh, never mind."

"You what, Kate? It sounded important," MacLachlan said.

"I'll tell you face-to-face when you get back."

"You're engaged? You are pregnant?"

"I have only one ring and you gave it to me. And, I have not been with anyone since you. I believe your last question would be an impossibility due to the passage of well over a year."

"Okay. I won't pressure you. You mean too much to me. I will call you when the dust has cleared and so will Tomás."

She choked a sob and hung up.

Putting the address of the chemical company in his smart phone, he drove straight there. They had a small customer counter. He showed the clerk the short list of what he wanted.

"That will be no problem. We have the aerosols in stock," the man said.

"Can you drop ship them to me in London within two days?"

"We can, though the handling and shipping costs will add another hundred dollars."

"Not a problem," MacLachlan said. He gave the man his hotel and the name under which he was registered. He also gave him a Visa card in the same name.

The whole transaction took about ten minutes.

He drove on to cross the Atlantic and engage in a probable gun battle. He was perplexed and optimistic at the same time.

MacLachlan was getting used to this Atlantic hop. He cleared TSA with his Pre-Check number on his boarding pass to expedite. All he had was a carry-on.

He always kept the GPS trackers off on his iPhone, iPad, and SAT phone. He made sure all were off before boarding and put them in a Faraday bag to make sure they were not emitting anything to anybody.

He settled into a large seat in Business Class and began to listen to a Fred Burton book on Audible. The flight attendant offered him a drink and he took her up on a Scotch whisky. He was generally a very light drinker but thought it would help him sleep. She brought him a wee dram of Glenlivet, which made him like her a lot. The next week or two was going to be very damn demanding, he was sure. He listened to Ghost for a couple hours after dinner, then turned it off when he was getting close to dozing off to sleep.

The lights came on an hour or so before landing at Gatwick. He cleared Immigration and hopped a train to the city center. It was a quick walk from St. Pancreas Station to his hotel.

He checked in and freshened up before requesting the front desk get him a minicab for the ride to the Parliament area to meet Rory for an early lunch at Harrods.

He clasped the tall, muscular Irishman like the brother he considered him to be.

"You look good, my friend!" he said. "How's Léa?" MacLachlan asked.

"Beautiful and busy on a big case. Whatever you have going, it's sure I am I'd like to help. Alas you know my restrictions with the Service." MacLachlan nodded.

They ordered and chatted through the meal in low voices. As both had carefully transited London, they were not worried about tails at Harrod's, but both lived by tradecraft.

"A really rich person in the Middle East has been kidnapped. His wife and daughter are there, too. They are in the Czech Republic. Dumbasses kept their phones, so we know exactly where they are," MacLachlan said.

"How do you know they didn't plant the mobiles in a lorry going to who-knows-where?" Rory asked.

"The daughter had just been taken and retrieved by a friend of yours. She also has a transmitting device implanted in her butt cheek. They correspond."

"Man! Extreme way to approach parental control! I'm guessing you were the friend who retrieved her, so they reached out to you for the big one?" Rory asked.

"Pretty much."

"I have put together a pretty tough team. Some

former Eastern Bloc secret police, a Marine Master Gunnery Sergeant, a senior sergeant in the Foreign Legion. But I'd like a special operator with some hostage rescue training, if not direct experience. You were the first one I thought about. But I knew you would have a big conflict of interest. I figured you might know a guy."

"In fact, Mack, I have an SAS guy for you. Another sergeant. Tough as hell and smart, too. He could be me with a different accent!"

"A Canadian?" MacLachlan asked his friend who thought he was Canadian through most of their early friendship.

"No. An Aussie. He's called Brooksie Strahan. Burly, but fast. Can handle any gun ever invented. Sniper in Afghanistan with a real, I mean real, long range record."

"Think he'd give me a hard week or two for a lot of Euros? If he doesn't have a private offshore account, you should help him with one."

"He came here looking for a job. Hasn't found one yet. Sir Walter is thinking about him. His accent might be a built-in cover."

"Can I see him today, Rory? I need to get in-country pretty quickly."

"You can. I already called him. He can be here in fifteen minutes. I will stay long enough to introduce you, then it's drive to Cornwall and interview somebody."

"Oh, by the way. Since the remaining assassins Anna Visser was supposed to lead us to is dead, is she free and clear?" MacLachlan asked.

"Free as a bird. She's not going back in the same

business, is she?"

"Let me answer by saying the SIS should think of her as a new asset for supplying any sort of equipment anywhere. I think she wants to only work for the good guys. Governments tend to pay quickly without past-due notices."

"Good to know, Mack. You know her as well as anyone. Is she mental? I mean she killed assassin Solange Camu in a heartbeat, set it up as a suicide and disappeared. Trained killer, or psycho?"

"I'd tell you, brother, if I knew. But I really cannot figure her out," MacLachlan admitted.

"Do you trust her?" Rory asked.

"For me, in a heartbeat. She'd take a bullet for me. Maybe for you, too. In business, I'd trust her. For her and anyone she is not dedicated to, I just don't know."

"Mack, I guess you think of Lexi a lot?"

"Every day. It's down from every hour, but I think it's gonna stick at every day."

"Me, too, my brother. She taught me so much. Then, when she killed the diplomat in Budapest and got hurt so badly. The damn diplomatic toffs were on Sir Walter to prosecute her. At the least, fire her. She had no idea how much he stood up for her."

"She did towards the end of our Highlands Blood op. Rory, she didn't have to die. She had a powerful revolver in the car. It should have been on her person. She could have killed Camu in the damn supermarket instead of the other way around. But she let her guard down. Don't you ever do what she did, promise me? Please, Rory," MacLachlan said.

"I promise, Mate. And, if somebody gets me, will you take them out?"

"I will. I would have without you even mentioning it. Shoot my Irish brother and your ass is dead," MacLachlan said.

"Let me call Brooksie," Rory said as he looked at his watch.

True to his claim, Brooksie walked in fifteen minutes later. MacLachlan already picked him out, walking through the Harrod's customers, cutting his eyes behind him and checking for either threats or tails in a manner only noticeable to another trained operator. He moved deliberately but without swagger. MacLachlan grinned at the effect the thirty-year old had on women of all ages as he politely moved through them.

"Brooksie Strahan, this is my mate, Mack MacLachlan. He's my big brother from another mother. Mack, this is Brooksie, my not-so-little brother from Downunder."

The two men shook and appraised one another in the way warriors always so. Both had the advantage of Rory's strong endorsements.

Brooksie looked to be about six-three and two hundred pounds. If he had an ounce of fat, MacLachlan could not detect it. Florid complexion, probably a few tatts under his suit. The suit did not disguise the fact he was either a military spec ops operator or a very together cop. His crew cut and square jaw helped further the image.

Rory left and the two men talked for over half an hour. Brooksie had been in constant combat while serving in Afghanistan. Some was sniping at over half a mile. Other was hand-to-hand combat. CQB. Close quarters battle. He had also been used on an unpublished hostage rescue at home. The Australian SAS Regiment or SASR serves as a counter terrorism element when police SWAT is not enough. It was something all SAS operators are trained to do. Brooksie could not go into details. MacLachlan respected his adherence to his country's Official Secrets rules. Rory had given him a rough sketch ahead of time, knowing both MacLachlan's clearance level and making a managerial decision on need-to-know. His Irish friend told MacLachlan enough to know the op had not been dissimilar to the one facing them outside of Prague.

Overall, MacLachlan assessed him as trustworthy, tough, and very competent. He was, in fact, another Rory Murphy. Just what MacLachlan needed. When MacLachlan told him the fee he was prepared to pay, Brooksie almost fell out of his chair. It was several year's SAS salary for a week or two. Moreover, while the op was dangerous, it was no more so than what he had been doing for seven years.

"Brooksie, I want you to be on your best game when we hit this place. I have not got enough intel yet to know what to call it. Estate? Farmhouse? Warehouse? We are going to deploy a drone to develop useable intelligence."

"I used drones a lot in Afghanistan," the Aussie said, surprising and pleasing MacLachlan.

"You just gave me the best news yet! I don't know one end of a drone from another. Do they all operate pretty much the same?" he asked.

"Pretty much. Now, the big ones with rockets, long range and all take a real pilot. The ones you can actually buy are pretty simple to operate. What kind are we getting?" Brooksie asked. MacLachlan grinned. The pronoun "we" told him Brooksie had bought in to the op and was a co-owner. This pleased the former Marine a lot.

"I gave two model numbers recommended by a guy to my supplier. I am not sure what she will be able to get. I promise you will be the first one to know."

"'She?'"

"Oh, yeah."

"Rory hinted you always have some insanely beautiful woman around. He told me about the Scottish one. I'm real sorry, Colonel."

"She was proof even real pros can break tradecraft and pay the ultimate price, Brooksie. And Mack is fine. There are some guys we may not even know the last names of, so first names are simpler. We are going to rescue a family from kidnappers in a foreign country with illegal weapons. It's safer and simpler to use first names or *noms de guerre*," MacLachlan said.

"Yeah. We use first names and respect rank but don't use it in conversation amongst ourselves in the Regiment," Brooksie said.

"You guys use M4 short rifles like the US, don't you?" MacLachlan asked.

"It's a primary long gun."

"I'm thinking with your sniper experience, having an M4 pattern rifle in 300 Blackout with a suppressor and a night-capable scope might be real prudent."

"I couldn't do the shots I did with a .50 Barrett or even a .338 Lapua. But I could do head shots with what you are talking about at any reasonable flat land distances."

"Are you familiar with 300 Blackout?"

"We didn't use them. I know it can be subsonic for suppressor use. My reading suggests a max range of a tad over 450 meters or 500 yards. I gather the energy is about like a hot 9mm pistol at the muzzle when you reach out there five football fields. So, I'd probably do a controlled pair to the center of mass. Then, one to the head."

"A failure drill or Mozambique, in other words."

"Precisely," Brooksie said.

"I'll amend the supply order. Do you have a Swiss, Belize, or Isle of Man or other private account I can wire the money to?"

"Not yet."

"You can open an account with a couple of Swiss banks here in London. I am not sure it's as private as opening one in Switzerland. It's just a gut feeling. Here's a list of ten banks in Switzerland and my phone number. Why don't you slip over there tonight or tomorrow. Tell me the one you are going to, and I will have the money transferred to it to open your account. I was a young military man once. Tell me if you need an advance to get there, and to cover lodging and so forth," MacLachlan said.

"Thanks, Mack. I lived with no personal expenses to speak of for seven years. I am okay on money. I will catch a flight over tonight or take the Eurostar train to Paris and connect to Zurich. I'll call you sometime tomorrow and let you know the bank name."

"I'd better let you take the train under the channel at over a hundred miles per hour then! I'm glad Rory connected us, Brooksie. I will see you somewhere near Prague in two days. We'll talk in the meantime about directions." They shook and parted.

MacLachlan watched him go and followed at a discreet distance. It did not appear he had any tails. Ditto when he hit the front door and walked to the bus stop. He watched Brooksie wait and scanned the crowd around him. The only interest he saw was glance and some stares from every female young or old who saw him. Nobody suspicious. Brooksie got on a bus. No cars mysteriously pulled away from the curb and followed the bus.

MacLachlan headed back towards the Monkey Puzzle to meet with Gunny.

---

HE GOT to the famous pub early and visited with his friend, publican Gary. He saw Gunny walking in from God knows where. He was not worried about surveillance detection routes, figuring he as a career combat Marine could take on about anybody or anything who wanted to try him. MacLachlan accepted Gunny's philosophy as probably valid. He was big and rawboned. The kind of guy weightlifting cops hated to face. The older guy drinking his breakfast beer at the bar. The man who has been through a thousand brawls and won most. The one who would sucker punch the daylights out of a trained fighter.

He came in and looked around defiantly. Spotting his friend, he called him in a gravelly voice which had terrified generations of recruits and not a few officers going through training under Gunny's tutelage.

MacLachlan met him with the military/cop non-hug and the two sat down.

"So. You sent me enough money to run away from home just to meet you in a bar and talk about a possible assignment, Mack. What's the deal?"

MacLachlan looked around. The pub was virtually empty. Gary had left the table to give instructions to his staff before the onslaught of post-work regulars and some tourists. Keeping it down, he and Gunny could speak freely.

"The deal is a hundred thousand bucks for a week or two work. It will be dangerous. But it's righteous, Gunny. Rescuing a kidnapped family."

"Where are they? How many bad guys? What's their level of training and arms?" the retired Marine asked.

"They are in the Czech Republic. Not too far from Prague. I don't know the physical building description, but we are going to use a drone and get pictures from every angle.

There were at least ten kidnappers. Some may have departed now it's more a custodial situation than operational.

"They came in hard and fast and took down some well-trained security staff with automatic weapons. The security head survived. I've worked with him recently. He strikes me as a pro. He feels they were special operators, but not from an operation like the Russian Spetsnaz top tier. Maybe Spetsnaz from a former USSR country. He bases this on them keeping all the latest and most expensive generation iPhones. Something an LA gang banger would do. The trackers on the phones largely led the surviving security agents to them outside of Prague. Along with a GPS tracker in the butt cheek of the family's wayward daughter."

Gunny raised bushy eyebrows at the last but said nothing.

"Got an op plan, Mack?" he growled.

"We need to see the lay of the land and base the plan on what we find."

"Tell me about the team."

"I am lead. You are ops lead below me. A real experienced Czech former secret agent and his former associates will be intel lead. I have worked with him before. He is solid as it gets.

"An Aussie SAS sergeant and a senior sergeant from the Foreign Legion are assaulters with you and me."

"Sounds interesting. I might have to look 'em over to render my opinion to you. At first glance sounds like a salty crew you've assembled fast. How about materiel? Especially weapons."

"We should get the final result on what was accumulated just after dinner, London time. I'm not worried. It will come down to things which don't matter to this group: Glocks vs CZ-75's, M4s vs H&K MP-5s, and so forth. I requested smoke grenades, flash bangs, binoculars, a sniper rifle. All long guns suppressed. And a drone as a surveillance and delivery vehicle. A couple of transports for people and equipment."

MacLachlan looked out of the window and saw Paul approaching. He was a military man, not a spy. Though careful, he was walking like Gunny did. No SDRs. Just a confident in-your-face stride.

"Here comes the Legionnaire."

"Damn! He's a big boy. If it comes to a fight, you fight him instead of me," Gunny said.

"I'm glad he's on our side. After intros, take a long head call and I'll talk business with him. I am paying everyone the same. It's high enough it shouldn't upset anyone. But folks are leery of talking money in front of strangers."

"Copy. At my age, a head call would probably be in order anyway," Gunny said then broke out in laughter like it was a joke instead of truth.

Both men rose and greeted Paul. After handshakes, they sat, and the server took dinner orders. MacLachlan would rather eat pub style dinner here than a gourmet French dinner. It suited him far better.

"I'm gonna excuse myself from you ladies for a few minutes and wash my hands," Gunny said. He arose and walked to the Gents.

"A good opportunity to discuss the stipend for this week or two," MacLachlan began. He offered the same thing he had just told Gunny. Paul was a cool guy, but he could not help raising his eyebrows.

"What are we going to have to do for a hundred thousand? Kill a nunnery full of sisters?" he asked under his breath.

"Nope. Just bad guys. I doubt more than ten. We have to extract these three people. The father, mother and the daughter who was taken from your club. It's got to be surgical, and they cannot be hurt. The bad guys may be low tier Spetsnaz. Hit hard and fast and get the hell out of the Czech Republic. Several of the team members we will meet there are former Czech secret agents. Having insiders will help."

"The Czech secret police during the Commie days were bad dudes," Paul said, staying in English though Gunny had not returned.

"These guys served under both types of regimes. They helped me exfiltrate one person a bit over a year ago. Don't let the wrinkles fool you. They are hard, deadly men who will get the job done no matter what it takes," MacLachlan said.

"So. We have war fighters and spies and you, who I suspect is both?" Paul asked.

"Yes. Seems like a good combination, huh?"

"Not what I expected, but the more I think about it, the more it appeals to me."

They saw Gunny walking back, eyeing a female server.

Paul grinned.

"His last girlfriend—maybe she's still current—is below forty," MacLachlan said.

"Man! He's who I want to be!"

"Paul, I have no doubt you will, brother," MacLachlan said, clapping him on the shoulder.

MacLachlan had two extra rooms reserved at his hotel for Gunny and Paul, since Brooksie had left for Zurich to set up a private bank account for his anticipated transfer. MacLachlan would transfer funds for Gunny and Paul tomorrow morning as soon as the banks opened.

Drinks were drunk and the "there I was..." stories were told. Towards ten, the three hailed a taxi back to the hotel. The master gunnery sergeant and the legionnaire traveled lightly. Each had a carry-on.

## 4

MacLachlan called Anna at her apartment. He got a voicemail. He called her office and she answered.

"I have your order filled," she began. "It will be in a storage facility in Leipzig by late tomorrow afternoon. I will give you the passcode to get into the facility and the one for the unit now. As soon as we hang up, I'll email the name of the place and the address."

"You were able to get everything okay?" he asked.

"Absolutely. A lot of the military and police units have transitioned to the SIG MPX, so I found some gently used police Heckler & Koch MP5s on the market. All had suppressors. We Europeans don't like a lot of noise. I found similar deals on CZ-75 pistols and holsters. The quantity of ammunition you requested is there in metal containers. I found you Safeguard Clothing Kevlar vests to be worn outside. I got black in the number and sizes you specified. Both types of grenades. I threw in three real ones of the fragmentation variety for good measure. You will love the drone. It has arms on it where a bomb bay would be. I got you two Steiner binoculars and the cars are a Sprinter and a Toyota Landcruiser. Both are dark gray and have darkened windows.

"I saw an opportunity for a hunting rifle with a scope and suppressor. Maybe you could use it for sniping. It's a classic 8 x 57 mm Mauser 98 with a black fiberglass sporter stock and new barrel. It was a deal, so I threw it in for free. Everything else is packed in Pelican boxes. All distinctive containers are in heavy cardboard packing cartons and sealed with heavy tape. Everything was delivered to the storage unit in Leipzig. It's one hundred sixty miles from Leipzig to Prague. Pick up the cars at the Europa Car office."

"You are beyond believable," MacLachlan said.

"Let's see what you say when you see the bill," was her only response. She told him the amount.

"I will wire it to your bank first thing in the morning."

"Without seeing the goods?" she asked.

"I trust you. Besides, we've slept together."

"That was pleasure. This is business."

"Right," MacLachlan said. She gave him the two combinations. The name and address of the storage facility in Leipzig arrived in the promised email within minutes of the end of the phone call.

MacLachlan called Brooksie before brushing his teeth.

"It's Mack. Did you get your arrangements made?"

"I did. I was just getting ready to send you an email on the encrypted messenger system you recommended. It will have the bank name and account number."

"Good. I will delete the number once I get the confirmation from my bank saying the money went through without a hitch," MacLachlan said.

"Give me a second to look at travel options on my laptop." Brooksie came back in two minutes. "I can take a flight from Zurich to Leipzig. It gets in midday."

"Good," MacLachlan said. "Hang at the airport and wait for a call. Dark gray Toyota Landcruiser or Mercedes Sprinter van. Same color."

"I'll be there waiting for your call. All the other guys in?"

"Yes, except for the ones who live in-country."

"Good, mate. See you around lunch tomorrow."

Before turning in, MacLachlan called Studrich and advised him of the team's arrival the following day. He asked if the former Czech agent had any ideas about a base, given the coordinates of the hostages. Tomás said he would look into it first thing in the morning.

---

MACLACHLAN, Gunny and Paul all took different flights to Leipzig the next morning. He emphasized the need for stealth in their travel and arrivals. He felt Brooksie would not need the hints. SAS operators dealt with appearing and disappearing covertly regularly.

When he arrived at the airport, he texted each man to meet him at the rental car area. The vehicles were already checked out by Anna or Adele. They just had to pick them up and drive away.

By one o'clock, the whole team other than Tomás had driven to the storage facility and were inside the unit inspecting their equipment.

Tomás called him and said he had located a possible base. It was a farmhouse which was placed on the market by a friend of his. The friend said it could be used privately for a week or so with no paperwork. In his country, the former secret policeman was one who always "knew a guy".

The four operators drove in from Leipzig and Tomás and three former Czech secret police, or agents as they were variously over the years, arrived shortly after. He introduced them to the others by first name only. They were Andrej, Filip, and Jakub. The three looked like Eastern European secret police officers. Seasoned, but still capable of extreme violence. Very fast extreme violence.

MacLachlan and Tomás walked through the house. They would need cots, sleeping bags and towels. There were enough restaurants within five miles to cover food needs with take-outs. The house did not have much furniture, but it did have electricity and good ceiling lighting.

"We don't plan on being here very long," MacLachlan said. They unloaded their gear and moved the vehicles around back and into a barn.

MacLachlan checked the latitude and longitude for the farm and compared it with the known location of the hostages. They were less than four miles apart, or almost six and a half kilometers.

"You guys get settled in and Brooksie and I are

going to put the drone together and drive a little closer and get some video of the location. We'll have a planning session when we have decent layouts to show you," MacLachlan said.

The drone came together quickly with Brooksie's experience. It fit in the back of the Sprinter van, so they took it rather than the SUV.

They parked the Sprinter in the woods and put the drone on a field a mile away from the location.

Brooksie lifted the drone off and practiced hovering. Using a small computer, they dropped the drone and raised it. They found this one had a range away from them of approximately four miles. The ceiling was irrelevant. They wanted to come in high and silent, then drop it to where the video camera could record details. Details such as window security, cameras, guard posts and whether there was any sign of hostage life visible through the windows.

On the first run, Brooksie brought the drone in at a height of several hundred yards, then dropped it into a hover fifteen yards from the center of the roof. They shot video of the roof, then he moved it three hundred sixty degrees around the building. They shot overall details. No people were visible, though there were several vehicles parked around the old two-story estate house.

Presently, a man carrying an AK-47 came out. He was wearing fatigues.

Brooksie lifted the drone out of his view.

The man made a circle around the house, met a second man from the other direction. The first man checked the three outbuildings. From the open doors, they appeared to be a garage, a small barn and a storage building.

It did not look like any of the Faheems were being kept outside the main house.

"Not much protection. I cannot believe they have these blokes patrolling by spread so far apart and there is not continuous around-the-clock patrol," Brooksie said.

"They are either confidant about being secure here or very stupid," MacLachlan responded. "Stupid people do not pull off a kidnapping of a well-guarded billionaire, Brooksie. Maybe stupid people merely serve as hostage custodians here. If so, it makes our job easier."

They got the tag numbers of each outside vehicle. MacLachlan wrote those down, despite having them recorded. Perhaps the former Czech agents on his team could find out information about them. MacLachlan would have one disable the vehicles. If he could not access rotors, he could simply slash each tire.

Brooksie flew the drone around the ends of the house once the guard finished his patrol. Both men wanted to see the eaves of the house as a possible entry point. Maybe have one or two men ascend to the roof and rappel to the eaves to make entry. They dismissed the idea after studying the live feed from the drone.

The night was cool. It was already down to 10C. MacLachlan saw from the drone feed what he could not see in the waning light. Smoke coming out both of the chimneys! The flues were open, paving the way to drop the sedation and smoke bombs in. Otherwise, they were going to have to put both through windows. The upstairs would be tough.

Before dark, the sky turned a bright orange, then muted into a dark foreboding red.

"Mack, it's a blood sky. It forebodes people dying here tomorrow. I never saw a blood sky before an op before. It gives me a shiver, mate," Brooksie said.

"It is pretty remarkable. I feel the blood spilled will be theirs. Not ours. We have the advantage of surprise, and we know our experience. An SAS man, two Marines, a Foreign Legionnaire, and four tough ass Czech agents who survived Communism and a democratic government. They may be some sort of second-class Spetsnaz, but we have the time in battle on them. We will prevail, my friend."

The op plan they talked about certainly appeared possible. The chimneys were open below the smoke dispersers on top. Brooksie would have to hover and spray between the disperser roofs and the bottom of their supports.

Brooksie circled the house about a hundred yards off and they focused the video camera on the doors and windows. MacLachlan took notes. Brooksie would dump the gaseous benzodiazepine on them, followed by a couple smoke grenades down the second chimney a few minutes later. He and Brooksie would have to take the empty chemical cans off and load the smoke grenades on, so the time between would give the gas a chance to permeate through the house.

They had noted there was no HVAC equipment on the roof. Nor was there any around back. But there was what appeared to be a coal chute. Apparently, there was no air conditioning, but solely a coal-fired furnace, likely with radiators. The deployment of sedation and smoke should work. If it didn't or one or both type dispersal devices did not work, MacLachlan told Brooksie, they would be no worse off than they would if they just hit the house like most assaulters would. By kicking in the door, rolling flash-bangs and shooting their way in.

MacLachlan took the joystick to familiarize himself. He flew the drone back towards them and out of sight of the target building. He practiced hovering, landing, and takeoffs for five minutes and gently brought the drone to the ground by the van. He needed Brooksie to have a backup when they commenced the assault. Time did not allow for much practice today, however. They needed to get back to the team and formulate their strategy.

Gunny had distributed the weapons. The Czechs were pleased with the issue of CZ-75s. The handgun was to them as the 1911 Colt is to longtime gunners. And how the Glock 17 is to later shooters. Iconic.

Tomás was pleased to see the sporterized Mauser. It was a rifle every man of his generation from this part of the world knew well.

MacLachlan and Brooksie arrived back at the house. MacLachlan had been thinking about an assault plan and what he would share with team in the remaining hours of light today.

He called Schutte to see if there were any new developments before he began a briefing. The kidnappers had been silent.

MacLachlan had worked with the Czechs on his team a bit over a year ago. It was when he went in without sanction and rescued Kate from an art depository run by and created just to provide funding for Hezbollah. He knew the Czechs all spoke English. So did Paul.

"Gather around, men. We have videos of the target site. As you watch, Brooksie and I will start at the top and work our way down to where we'll spend our time.

"The roof is slate. It's steep and slick to walk on. The eaves seem to be covered over with solid framing. Not a good choice for entry.

"We have seen two men walking sentry patrol. It appears they start on opposite sides of the house and pass each other. This seems to happen hourly. Nobody else. You will see the vehicles. That many trucks suggests a full staff inside.

"Next, the windows. We have to assume the hostages are being held upstairs. Once the bad guys are aware of our attack, they might use the windows as sniper ports. It's a worrisome possibility because we might hit a hostage while attempting to shoot a sniper.

"I am thinking about trying something a bit different. We have some chemicals in the supply order. They are sedatives in gas form. They will not put the people inside to sleep, but they will make them drowsy and throw their response times off. Both should prove advantageous to us. Brooksie will deploy it with the drone. He'll shoot the gas straight down one chimney. We'll bring the drone back and load smoke grenades to drop down the second chimney once the folks inside get sluggish.

"Murphy of Murphy's Law always comes along

on these raids. So, even if it either does not deploy properly, we'll be no worse off than we would have been without it.

"Tomás, should it still be dark here at 0430?"

"Very dark, Mack."

"Do you and the rest of you guys feel it would be a good time to hit?" Tomás and the rest of the men all nodded as MacLachlan moved his eyes around the room.

"Gunny? Paul? Brooksie? Okay, it's a plan."

"Here's what I was thinking. There's a big bush near the front door. I will move in and hide behind it. Whenever the guard appears, I will take him out. Gunny and Tomás will have the Steiners. Once they see the front guard go down, Tomás, Paul, and the three Czechs cross the front and around to the back.

"Tomás, designate one man to take out the guard in the back and one to disable the cars however you can quickly. If you slash tires, slash all or several on each vehicle. I'll be covering you at the front door and Brooksie will have the sniper rifle ready for long shots.

"Once the guys are all out of sight and getting in position to hit the rear door, Gunny, Paul, and Brooksie move out and I will move around back. I'll whistle and we hit both front and rear simultaneously.

"The mantra for the hostages is just like a body-guard job. Cover and evacuate. Get the three into the van and back to the farmhouse. Put them in the safest position in the center of the house and establish a strong, armed perimeter until we can exfiltrate them.

The remaining part of this team will be doing clean up operations.

"Any questions?"

"What about brass?" Paul asked.

"Really good question, Paul. If we remember where we shot, once everything is quiet, it would be great to remove evidence. But the lives of the man, woman and teen girl are primary. If we have to run and leave brass, so be it. We will try to return the weapons we fired, and maybe ones we didn't, to our source. Or dispose of them after they've been wiped. We cannot jeopardize the mission for the cost of a few carbines or pistols.

"When a couple of us go into Prague and pick up cots and sleeping bags, we'll get some disposable gloves. We'll also get some rags and gun oil. Once we strip and oil the guns tonight, we will put gloves on and wipe them down. Then, load up. We don't want our prints on either cartridges or firearms. So, be conscious of not touching them afterwards with bare hands," MacLachlan said.

"How about chow?" Brooksie asked.

"Something quick. What are your preferences between fish and chips for a choice and pizza for another choice?"

Everyone opted for pizza as long as beer was available. MacLachlan was not worried about a bit of beer before an op. He would hold the purchase down to a couple per man. He knew these guys drank beer like water. Two beers the night before would not affect their abilities at all.

There was a working stove at the farmhouse and pots and pans. He would get a big to-go carton or two of coffee and they could reheat it in the wee hours of the morning.

Donuts or croissants would have to do for breakfast.

MacLachlan and Paul slipped into town and found a large grocery and department store with everything they needed but the food. They filled the Sprinter van and got pizzas and cold beer.

MacLachlan briefed them again as they ate.

"At 0430, Brooksie will deploy the drone. He will put the chemical in the chimney first. He will bring the drone back to his position, rearm it with the smoke bombs and send it to deploy them in the other chimney. Same way. He will bring the drone back and begin scanning the area with the sniper rifle.

"Tomás, his guys and I will move out at 0430 also. He will designate a team member to disable their vehicles. As soon as we hear the smoke grenades go off. I will neutralize the guard in the rear. The Czech guys will take care of any bad guys who rush out the rear door.

"Paul will move out the same time we do and neutralize the front guard. Brooksie will leave his sniper nest and he and Gunny will join Paul to be at the front when within minutes of the smoke popping. Any hostiles coming out the front door are their fair game. They will assault the front as soon as the door is clear. We will do the same in the back.

"The front team will clear the first floor and wire tie any captures. Scan for the hostages, though I suspect they will be on the top floor.

"I will go up the stairs first. Remember the fatal funnel aspect of stairs, men! Tomás and his team will follow me. Our job will be to neutralize any hostiles up there with speed and extreme prejudice before they harm the hostages. I am hoping the sedative gas will slow their responses and the smoke with disorient them.

"My information is the sedative gas will dissipate quickly. The smoke will still be there. Don your gas masks before going in. They should work for any lingering gas and certainly for the smoke. Do a check on them before hitting the sack tonight. Remember, don't touch your weapons or ammo or the masks without the gloves on. If you have, wipe them down.

"Once we get the hostages, we will take them out the way with the least gunfire. They will go in the van with the Gunny, Paul and Brooksie. They will protect them at the farmhouse, and I will haul ass back here and help the local guys clean up our mess. We will return to the farmhouse as soon as we've finished. I will call our control tonight and let him know we are hitting the estate tomorrow. He will arrange hostage transport. It will probably be a corporate jet.

"Once their exfiltration is set, Gunny and I will take them to the airport.

"I want Paul and Brooksie to return the weapons, ammunition and other gear to the storage facility. Lock it up. Here is a slip of paper with the entry code, the room number, and its code. You guys take different flights to somewhere other than home. Return home by a series of cutouts. Use taxis, trains, buses, flights to muddy your path. Use cash. Your deposits have already been made, so you should all be pretty flush.

"Gunny and I will do the same. Our local friends

here will merely return from their golf or fishing or whatever outing old friends take. We were never here, right?

"I will run through this once more tomorrow morning. We will leave here at 0400.

"Questions? None? Okay! Somebody, hand me a beer. I'm parched from all this talking," MacLachlan said before quaffing a Starobrno beer.

Later, Gunny commented to his old friend as they sat with Tomás. "This feels just like the night before my op in Granada as a Force Recon with the 34th MEU. It was the blood red sky which reminded me. What a righteous mission! Those young American med students sure were happy to see us!"

"I bet they were, Gunny!" MacLachlan said.

"This is a righteous mission, too. Not like attacking a hill because somebody in the brass wanted it on his watch. This is saving a family. Rich or not. They are civilians. They didn't sign up for this crap, Mack. Guys like you both and me...we chose the violent path."

"We did. I have to tell you, Gunny, I've come back from too many missions I did not expect to return from. I know you and Tomás have, too. I wonder how many of my nine lives this cat has left. I keep trying to retire. But I keep having people shake money for some job in my face. Unless it's real personal, like bringing back Kate from this very country, I don't plan on accepting any more jobs."

"Fine words, Mack. However, I know you. You will. You have too many tough years left. You will run and gun until you just cannot do it any longer. I could almost be your father. Yet here I am. You will be too, my friend. Unless you marry my niece and she makes you settle down," Tomás said.

"Tomás, I've about given up on marrying your niece. Her call. I was close to marrying a Scottish intel agent some months ago. But she was killed by one of a pair of international assassins."

"I guess they are dead now."

"Deader than hell."

"Your kill count is growing," Gunny observed.

"It is, unfortunately. Hard to carve notches on the grips of a plastic pistol," MacLachlan said.

---

THE TWO VEHICLES departed the base farm at 0400. They reached the staging point MacLachlan and Brooksie had chosen at dusk the evening before. Brooksie immediately got the drone in the air for a quick look around the estate. All was quiet. The two guards were not present yet. He kept the drone in a stationary hover as the two teams deployed.

MacLachlan and the Czechs went first. They had farther to go to get around back and one man had to immobilize the accessible vehicles. After a couple of minutes, Gunny and Paul started. The schedule was a bit skewed.

Brooksie watched as Gunny and Paul approached the house. He saw a guard unexpectedly come around the left corner and head toward them.

The guard had not seen the two operators when Brooksie dropped him at a hundred meters with the silenced Mauser rifle.

Gunny and Paul could not hear the suppressed

rifle shot, but saw the man fall. Paul ran over, H&K at the ready and checked the man. Head shot in bad light. With a rifle he was unfamiliar with. One without a night scope. The kid was good.

As he and Gunny approached the front door, Brooksie dropped the drone into a low hover beside the top of the right chimney. He deployed the Benzo-diazepine gas into the opening and returned the drone to his feet.

During this several minutes, MacLachlan and the Czechs had their own challenges. The two guards had stepped out of the front and rear doors simultaneously. The team at the rear stepped back silently as the guard paused to scan the area.

MacLachlan leapt forward and punched him in the throat. He spun the man around and sunk his fighting knife into his kidney, then withdrawing it, stabbed the man in the middle side of his neck. The blade severed his carotid artery. The man was dead within a quarter of a minute.

MacLachlan dragged him over to some bushes in the yard and hid the body.

He got back to his team in time to hear the "Pop" of the several smoke grenades. Brooksie had experimented and found a way to fasten the firing mechanism to the arms of the drone to fire them as they were released into the depths of the chimney. The weight of the grenades falling pulled the trigger against an immobile object.

Two went down the hole and the house was becoming full of the smell of smoke, if not smoke itself. This was as planned. MacLachlan knew the terror of awakening without access to full senses, and smelling smoke in the dark would trigger the fear and disorientation he sought.

The door opened outwards. It could not be kicked in, so a suppressed shot from the MP5 took the lock out.

The five men, MacLachlan in front, went in SWAT-style in a stick or straight formation, one hand on the shoulder of the man in front.

Inside, they fanned out.

Immediately, all hell broke loose. A couple of men stumbled down the stairs, guns at ready. The first one aimed at MacLachlan who stepped aside.

Tomás shot him with a three-shot suppressed burst. He fell down the steps. MacLachlan shot the two behind him and stepped over them to get to the top and prevent a captor from executing the three hostages. The four Czechs followed him. At the top of the landing, MacLachlan took a left and motioned for Andrej to follow. Tomás took Filip and Jakub with him to the right.

They reached the end of the hall, hearing shots downstairs. Some suppressed and some loud cracks.

MacLachlan heard a lock being unlocked in a room down the hall from him. He stopped. A man burst out with a sawed-off shotgun and shot MacLachlan in the center of mass. He fell to the floor, dropping his MP5. Andrej fired a three-shot burst and killed the shotgun wielder. Covering the door, he knelt by MacLachlan who was trying to get up.

"I'm okay. The Kevlar vest caught the whole pattern at this range. Thank God! I just have the wind knocked out of me."

He got to his feet slowly and unsteadily and Andrej took the lead and cleared the now-open bedroom door.

There were three iron beds in the room. Faheem, his wife, and Nisa were handcuffed to their beds. Faheem was in boxer shorts and a ripped undershirt. The two women were naked. It was obvious they had been sexually assaulted, whether to make Faheem talk or for entertainment, MacLachlan did not know.

Nisa looked up and recognized him. She smiled at him for the first time since he had known her.

"Colonel MacLachlan. I knew it would be you," she said. Faheem was obviously incensed with anger. His wife seemed in a stupor.

"Andrej, watch the door. I have not heard a shot for a while, but we don't know the status at the end of the hall or downstairs."

MacLachlan took the worldwide standard handcuff key out of a pocket inside his right boot and unlocked them all, Faheem first.

"You are the man who brought my daughter back?" he asked with neither appreciation nor friendliness in his voice.

"I am. We can talk later. As soon as we know it's clear downstairs, I need to get the three of you into a van and to a safehouse until you can be evacuated by jet."

Not knowing if the still silent wife and mother spoke English, MacLachlan turned to the girl.

"Do you know where they have your clothes?"

"No," Nisa said, back to her laconic speech pattern.

"I assume they were not going to surrender you naked after the ransom was paid," MacLachlan said.

"The clothes did not matter to them. They were going to continue to pleasure themselves with my wife and daughter, then kill us once they got their demands fulfilled," Faheem said.

Nisa had already covered her mother with a sheet and was beginning to fashion a sheet covering for herself.

Tomás called MacLachlan in a low voice to signal he was approaching and to not fire. He had Filip and Jakub behind him.

He took one look at the damage to the front cover of MacLachlan's Kevlar and steel plate holder.

"Looks like you had a match with a shotgun," he said.

"I did, but Andrej won," MacLachlan said, nodding to the dead man on the floor.

"Do you know the status downstairs?" MacLachlan asked.

"No. Filip, carefully go down. Call for Gunny, Paul or Brooksie by name. Check on them and also bring Mack and me a casualty count," Tomás said.

The youngest of the Czechs, though still retired, left quickly.

He returned quickly with Gunny in tow.

"We killed five. Add the two guards is seven, this one is eight," Gunny counted.

"I got one at the door," MacLachlan added.

"Okay, nine."

"We got one down the hall for ten," Jakub said.

MacLachlan turned to Faheem.

"Is ten it?" he asked.

"Perhaps. I counted ten after we were dropped off by more professional men. Then there was another. He may have left. These are scum."

"Let's scare up some clothes for Mr. Faheem and something the women can wear until we can get them properly attired," MacLachlan said.

Once the former hostages were clothed, they were surrounded by Brooksie, Paul and Gunny. MacLachlan led them out of the house to the Sprinter. They saw the carnage their rescue had wrought as they descended the stairs and went through the estate to the rear door.

They went around the building, past the disabled vehicles, and between the estate building and the securely locked garage. Brooksie sprinted ahead to get the van and bring it up to the side of the building.

They waited for the van.

All of a sudden, the garage door opened, and a black SUV came out, throttle to the floor.

His pistol caliber MP5 slung, MacLachlan drew the CZ-75 semiautomatic pistol and fired three successive controlled pairs into the driver side windshield. Gunny and Paul ushered the Faheems away from the path of the large oncoming vehicle. It was a Mercedes.

MacLachlan stood his ground and fired another pair into the large hole he had put in the glass in front of the driver. He saw the driver slumped, but the SUV still coming, he dove to the side just as it passed, brushing him.

The Mercedes crashed into the stone side of the building at twenty miles per hour and the driver was thrown out. He slammed into the wall headfirst and slid down to the destroyed hood of the vehicle. It was obvious MacLachlan had mitigated him as a threat to anyone. Ever again.

MacLachlan got up, reloaded, and holstered the pistol. He unslung the rifle and ran to the garage. He reached it just as Brooksie arrived, driving fast. The Aussie slid the Sprinter around, lifting two inside tires a couple inches off the ground in the turn.

It took MacLachlan mere minutes to clear the garage and return as the team was loading the Faheem family into the van.

They expressed neither appreciation nor awe at their rescue or at having their lives saved so dramatically just now.

Brooksie and Paul looked at them, then at their team leader. Both shook their heads almost imperceptibly and with extreme disgust. These people were not shell-shocked. They were cold, self-obsessed asses.

The only two things which mattered to MacLachlan was they were safe, and their company's deposit had cleared. He was not in this business for accolades.

He spoke with the Czech team with cleanup ideas for a moment before he mounted the Sprinter. He sped off with the Faheems, Paul and Gunny. The affable and highly talented Brooksie was at the wheel.

He called Schutte during the short trip and reported the family had been freed with no injuries. It was not the time to mention the abuse the women had suffered.

"Do you want me to send two top operators on

the plane to cover them until they are transferred to the protection of your men?" MacLachlan asked.

"Yes. I would appreciate the added coverage," Schutte said. "I will be leaving the hospital before you arrive at the executive terminal. I will be on the plane when it arrives in Prague. As I told you, my best operatives were killed in the attack. A couple of yours would be most appreciated. You can come yourself if you wish. The plane will be larger than the usual corporate jet."

"I have to supervise the cleanup here. My job has been done. I'd like to give you an oral debrief in a few hours. Can you receive calls on this larger plane?"

"Yes. Let's do it in two or three hours."

"My men are carrying pistols and suppressed MP5s. Can you cover them carrying those arms in Dubai?"

"Oh, yeah! Not to worry. Where to you want the weapons shipped back to?"

"Either Prague or Belgium. I have a dealer in the latter you can ship to pretty easily. She's a good source for you also."

"Good. Give me the information during the briefing later today."

"Do you want to speak to the principal?" MacLachlan asked.

"Not at the moment. Tell him I will speak with him at length on the plane in several hours. I have to scramble to get a plane sorted and in the air right this moment," Schutte said and rang off.

"Mr. Faheem, Schutte will speak with you on the plane. He is getting out of the hospital to come on the plane to pick you up in Prague. Currently, he has to spend his time obtaining a plane and getting it underway as soon as possible."

The billionaire stared at MacLachlan and said nothing.

"Mother and I will need some medical attention due to the treatment we received," Nisa said.

"You will shut up, girl. I will arrange whatever needs to be done for my wife and daughter," Faheem snapped.

MacLachlan saw his men were appropriately stone-faced. The only giveaway was the color of Brooksie's knuckles as he gripped the steering wheel tighter in otherwise unshown anger.

MacLachlan thought, *The sooner this asshole and his two cold women are out of sight the better*. He knew his men's thoughts mirrored his own.

They arrived at the farmhouse and got out. Paul and Brooksie cleared it before the Faheems went in. MacLachlan showed them to bedrooms and the bath, where there was a stack of clean towels bought the night before.

He took the three men aside and spoke quietly.

"Gunny, Schutte wants several men to accompany the Faheems on the plane to Dubai. It will add to the security at the airport and en route to their home. Schutte's best men were killed in the assault where the Faheems were taken.

Are you guys up for a trip to Dubai?" he asked.

"I'd like to pass, Mack," Gunny said.

The other two were happy to go. The mission had only lasted a couple days. They had scheduled a week or two for the op. Neither had seen Dubai.

"Leave your weapons with Schutte. He will take

care of them. It would be a bit shaky to try to get them back to Mallorca or London," MacLachlan told them.

MacLachlan sought Faheem. The man had cleaned up and was sitting in one of the few chairs.

"This place is a dump."

"This place is a safe house nobody knows about, sir. Anywhere nicer would have been too public to allow us to make our weapons ready. We have only had it a couple of days and will abandon it once we have removed all evidence we were here.

"I will leave here in a short time and return to where you were held captive.

"We shot or knifed ten men to release you. We need to destroy as much evidence as possible because we came into the Czech Republic legally, but we were unauthorized to do an operation like this. We used illegal weapons with deadly effect. All of us could face life imprisonment."

"I am sure. But you were paid well," Faheem snapped.

"And, what good is money when you are behind bars for life? Risks are inherent in my business like yours. So, I mitigate them to the greatest extent possible. While we have an open dialogue, who kidnapped you? What did they ask in return for your release? I gather not money."

"Don't you know?" the billionaire asked.

"I'd like to hear it firsthand from you, the victim."

"We were kidnapped by elite Russians. Former special operations troops. They were hired by one of the two pharmacy firms I outbid in the COVID-19 and subsequent vaccines contract for the Middle East and Southwest Asia. It is called Petrovitch Pharma CJSC.

"This brings up another project I want you to do, if you are interested," Faheem said.

"Go ahead."

"I want you to go to St. Petersburg, Russia and strike the firm. Let them know they cannot have their way to have me sign the contract over to them. Destroy their building. Kill their people at work if you have to. Let them know. I will authorize a seven-figure stipend for you to do this."

"You realize, Mr. Faheem, this is a suicide mission?"

"Your problem, MacLachlan. If not you, someone else."

"I know my industry. There are lots of people who would seek the contract. Very damn few could bring it to fruition. And most of those would die trying."

"You seem innovative. Give it a try for the money," Faheem said.

"You'll have my answer via Schutte before your plane lands in Dubai," MacLachlan said. He turned, briefed the team on site and left in the Sprinter for the estate.

He found the Czech team had moved the bodies to one place, using a wheelbarrow found in the garage. Tomás was eyeing a fairly new tractor with a power take-off controlling a front-end shovel.

"We could use this to bury them somewhere on the property which is distant from the house. If the police had occasion to look, they would find bodies. I doubt they would search the whole property. Especially if we clean up the blood. Or, if we drop some drugs around and make this this look like a drug war. We play it like a drug war, we just leave the bodies lying where they dropped," he said.

"Can you or your guys come up with the type 'evidence' to give it a drug war spin?" MacLachlan asked.

"Have another couple thousand Euros?" Tomás asked.

MacLachlan hesitated. He had paid these guys for several day's work more than they had earned for several years work for the government. But, Tomás had saved his life. Twice actually. And he was Kate's uncle. Andrej had saved MacLachlan just now, also.

"Give me a second."

He went to his carry-on and counted out two thousand Euros. He had learned early on in this business one always needed some emergency cash.

He counted it out on the table to Tomás. The man nodded and handed the money to Filip. He told him something in Czech. Filip took off, using an intact car he found located in the garage. MacLachlan suspected the Mercedes E-Class was going to be a spoil of war also. Probably Kate's uncle's spoil.

He chalked it up to years living in a Communist country where one had to order a car years in advance and take whatever make, style or color came in. Years of wanting but not having except by working the system. It had to have an effect on how one looked at money and possessions.

As with most things, MacLachlan just looked at the bottom line. Tomás and the three ex-secret police friends had done everything he had asked of them and done it professionally. The hostages were on their way home soon. The Czechs had come up with a way their fellow police investigators would "buy" the shootout and make invalid assumptions not involving MacLachlan or his team. He was all for such an ending and did not give it any further thought.

He realized he had a larger issue to resolve. Should he take the secondary assignment and go to Russia—a country where he was not particularly welcome—and exact another man's retribution on a major corporation? Was it as much a suicide mission as it looked on the initial assessment? Was it worth risking for a million Euros? He certainly did not need the money. He had already grown tired of the luxury life.

He had gotten rid of the exotic Jaguar. He was tiring of the mega wealthy neighbors in what used to be Old Florida. MacLachlan was ready to put the Casey Key property on the market. Its ties to the beloved grandparents who virtually raised him there were clouded when their original house was blown up by people hired by Hezbollah. The new one was just not the same. It simply felt different now.

His direction in life was less clear, too. Lexi was dead and buried in Scotland. Kate. Well, what about Kate? He did not know any more than she did.

MacLachlan loved his cabin in the Virginia woods. And the wee cottage on Loch Fyne in Straithlachlan. Maybe a modest place in Marathon or Key West would be better than the memories at Casey Key.

He had secretly funded an old lover's cancer research in Brazil for years. Maybe, whether he made it back or not, an anonymous contribution of one million Euros to her effort could bump the research over into a cure for the horrific disease. It would be a nice legacy, even if no one but he knew about it. Better than fading away like an old soldier.

Maybe it was the blood sky last night leaving him feeling morose. Maybe it was a direct hit of buckshot in the kill zone of his chest. He would be dead, but for the Kevlar and steel plates he wore.

MacLachlan decided to take the assignment. He would make Tomás his check-in contact. If he did not check in, Kate would know. And, if she knew, his friend Will Grafton would know. Will would contact his parents if things went south. He would contact the banker friend who was successor trustee of his estate. Everyone who mattered would be in the loop.

Schutte called and gave him the address of the private airport outside of Prague. He told MacLachlan the time of arrival. MacLachlan advised him of the offer to wreak retribution on the Russian Pharmaceutical Company in St. Petersburg.

"You are crazy! He's giving you a death sentence. Probably himself too. The Russians have long memories. Hurt them, and they will hurt you worse. I'd tell him no. Hell no!"

"If I give him the name and account number of a charity fund I help, can I trust him to actually send the money to it?" MacLachlan asked.

"Yes. He is a cold fish and a jerk. A megalomaniac. But his word is golden. As a backup, you can give it to me also. If you take this suicide assignment."

MacLachlan gave him his friend's account and

name. The information pretty much verified his decision to go ahead to St. Petersburg.

---

HE WALKED the house and the property once Filip got back with a variety of drugs and needles. They left most in the upstairs rooms where the hostages had been kept.

There was no need to give needle marks to the dead men. A postmortem would conclude they were not users. Let it look like they were paid to hold drug users, now departed. Perhaps taken by the gang who came after them and killed their captors.

Tomás and his friends admitted they did not know what spin their successors would put on the crime scene. They stated emphatically, however, the policemen would take the easiest way to a quick solution. It would be the one which would make them look good with the least amount of work.

All four used the MP5s for any shots they fired and elected to keep the CZ-75 pistols. MacLachlan had no issue with their decision. He may want to access the men quickly in the future. Having them armed would be a benefit.

He called Schutte to update him on the scene at the estate.

"Hi. Yeah, the boss gave your retribution assignment to me to handle when you accept. The fee is low seven figures. He wants you to make a big dent in the company's ability to manufacture anything. He is ambivalent regarding deaths incurred in the process. Unless you need a LOT of money in addition to what you already earned, I'd pass on it. I don't see any way you would survive taking down a major corporation in Mother Russia."

"I will tell him I will take it. He can pay half now and half when he receives proof of success. Proof will most likely be in the form of a newspaper article.

"I will not move on the op for several months. For a couple reasons. We are coming up on the end of White Nights in the St Petersburg area. The White Night's eighteen hours or so of daylight would not help me infiltrate, do the op, and exfiltrate. The night is my friend.

"Second, as you can well imagine, Russia is not like swimming the Rio Grande. It's hard to break into and you don't just get a bus ride back home. You get shot or imprisoned in or out. It takes a serious op plan, a bulletproof cover with perfect credentials, and a plausibly deniable reason to be there. I need some time to put it all together. Half fee in the cancer research private account now. Half in the same place when he gets verification the job is done," MacLachlan said. He then texted him the numbers.

"I will talk with him today once the plane is aloft. I believe I can convince him it all makes sense. It surely does to me. Watch for half deposited tomorrow. It will be the next day before full credit is extended by this bank in Zurich you gave me. I will only call you if we get additional collateral intel which I believe will help you hurt Petrovitch Pharma CJSC," Schutte said.

"Sounds good! My intent is to hurt their building and not persons. I am not an assassin. Well, unless it's an official thing and national safety is involved. Certainly not on personal vendettas."

"I figured you weren't. The boss wants them hurt from a business standpoint. He does not care one way or the other about their people. Except maybe the ones who kidnapped him and repeatedly raped his wife and daughter," Schutte said.

"It appears to me, somebody at the competing pharmacy corporation, maybe in your capacity, hired some top-level Russian mercenaries to do the grab. The rapists were the guards. They were all low-level and are all very dead. So, he's vindicated as to the rapes. I hope the big bosses will be punished by my actions relative to their headquarters or manufacturing plant. I need to do some research, but I think the latter would be the most effective target to cripple them for a long period of time. It certainly would send a message, too," MacLachlan said.

"I agree. Most corporate headquarters are leased space in high rises. Lots of people to be hurt and lots of police to respond and be pressured to solve the case and get the person who did it. Maybe a remote factory-type situation would have slower response and less concern. I don't know, though. These seem to be the two largest pharma companies in Russia. They make a lot more than COVID-19 vaccine."

"Yes. The other things they make worry me, too. I do not want to destroy half the medicine making capability for a large country. I'd like to strike the COVID-19 manufacturing area. But, finding out where it is would likely be impossible. Unless I can ID one of their scientists and have a talk with him. Do you think your pharmaceutical folks could help with any of this?" MacLachlan asked.

"Hmm...they might. Let me snoop around a bit. First, I will seek where the manufacturing building's located. Second, the scientists' names. I will get back to you when I find something. Since you are going in the early fall, we have some time, right?"

"Right. This has to be done very carefully or not at all," MacLachlan said, almost thinking aloud. "I've got a couple of final things to inspect here. We made the crime scene look like some drug gang members were being held here and were rescued by their gang in a firefight. There are drugs lying around. Several of my team members are intimately familiar with such things and are convinced the planted scene will send the local gendarmerie plodding off the wrong direction.

"So, I will talk with you later. If there is any issue with your boss, let me know," MacLachlan said.

"I will. You have been talking with me on the plane. I am already a third of the way to Prague. Later, then." Schutte killed the connection and left MacLachlan free to wrap up and get back to the base and dismiss the men.

---

FILIP AND ANDREJ finished planting evidence and went to the garage area. The E-class Tomás had now firmly claimed as his had not had the tires slashed. It was a virtually new car these career tough cops could license so nobody would know Tomás was not the original owner. Filip claimed a van and they took good tires and put them on to replace the ones slashed at the onset of the assault.

With one final look-through, they began a three-car convoy back to the farmhouse.

MacLachlan sought out Faheem and took him aside.

"Mr. Faheem, I have decided to take your assignment. I have given my initial thoughts to Mr. Schutte. He will convey them to you on the plane. There is no reason to go into them here. The fewer people who know what we are planning, the better."

"I agree. Go there and ruin them! The bastards who did this and defiled my wife and daughter! They should lose their company and burn in hell!"

"The ones who abused your wife and daughter are already burning in hell, sir. We killed every single one of them. You saw the bodies. We have rearranged the evidence to make it look like a totally different scenario happened there. Nothing should come back to you or us now," MacLachlan said.

"For what you are paid, I would not expect any blow-back," Faheem said in his normal, self-obsessed, rude way.

MacLachlan gave him an unreadable look and said nothing. If he died on this operation, it was not going to be for Faheem or his bratty daughter. It was going to be for a damn large contribution to medical research. Nothing more.

If he made it back, he was going to either spend time training for the US Intelligence Community, or if working with Kate was too disconcerting for either or both, he would just retire and travel for fun.

These "ifs" were a new and concerning thing for

MacLachlan. He never considered his own mortality when accepting, or even fulfilling, a mission. He wondered why such a thing floated into his psyche now.

Could it be he was unhappy about his recent losses? Kate. Lexi. Or, with a sure suicide mission at the behest of a jerk he neither liked nor respected?

Perhaps he should renege on the mission. He would ponder it in the next hour before he put the Faheems on the plane. He had not felt at his peak for some time now. He knew the loss of Alexandria Campbell had to be part of it. And certainly, Kate turning away from him almost two years ago. The loss of those two successively had not helped his drive and enthusiasm. He had not been operating at his normal peak for several years. He just did not care much anymore. He sure as hell was not going to take the case, no matter how lucrative, for the Faheems. Any of them. But he needed a really demanding case perhaps only he could pull off. Maybe this suicide mission was it. And, if he didn't make it back, he would have gone out in a blaze of glory and maybe, just maybe, his last effort would find a cure for the horrible disease. He knew what his decision was. And he sure as hell was not going to change it. He would ride into the storm guns blazing.

---

WHEN HE ARRIVED at the farmhouse, it had been sanitized by Gunny, Paul, and Brooksie. The latter two were excited to make the trip to Dubai on the plane.

Gunny privately briefed them on what MacLachlan had experienced with his contacts with Faheem and the daughter so far.

"Billionaires, lads, are a different sort of animal. They think they are above everyone else, have no concern about your welfare or even your life. All they care about with respect to you is what you can do for them. You see, it's only about them. Nobody else. Yeah, some give to charity. It gives them a tax write-off and makes 'em feel good. Just don't expect any conversation with them on the plane. Stay vigilant and keep any contact down to emergencies and other things which are absolutely necessary."

MacLachlan thanked Andrej, Filip, and Jakub for their assistance and wished them well. They and Tomás would not accompany the van and Land-cruiser to the small private airport. He motioned Tomás aside and mentioned he wanted to have lunch with him after dropping the two operators and family at the executive airport and taking Gunny to Prague's Václav Havel Airport. Tomás happily agreed and they set the lunch for two hours hence at a pizza place which was one of the Czech's favorites.

"Okay, men," MacLachlan began before Paul and Brooksie got in the front of the Sprinter and he and Gunny mounted the Toyota.

"The most dangerous place in executive protection is loading or unloading the principal into or out of a vehicle. We have to watch dismounting the Sprinter and cover the family in a tight circle all the way onto the plane. Keep your MP5s at low ready until the doors are closed on the plane. Schutte and perhaps one or two of his men will be in the plane.

He's our primary contact, so look to him for direction. Follow Gunny's earlier instructions to the letter.

"It's been great working with you both. I look forward to seeing both of you soon. In the meantime, be safe!"

They all shook hands, then mounted up and departed for the small private airport.

When they arrived, the Faheems were surrounded and moved into the main building. Schutte pre-arranged for their plane to be the only one coming in, so the building did not have passengers or other visitors to see all the guns.

The plane arrived. It was not a Lear. It was a 737-passenger jet. It taxied to the gate and docked for a fuel replenishment. The door opened and stairs came down. A security man with a new SIG carbine stepped out and glanced around. MacLachlan went out and approached him, MP5 slung in an unthreatening manner. The next person out walked with a cane. He was a medium-sized man, balding and with a salt and pepper mustache and goatee.

"Schutte?" MacLachlan called. The man nodded as he came down.

He slung his carbine and stuck out his hand.

"Johan is fine at this point, Mack," he said as they shook.

"Your principal is ready to ride. The giant of my guys is Paul. He's a former senior non-com with the French Foreign Legion. The younger one is Brooksie. He's very recently out of the Australian SAS. Both are first rate."

"Half of your vendetta stipend had been deposited in the cancer charity in Brazil. There has to be a story about it. Perhaps over a beer when you return and the other half is sent," Schutte said.

"I look forward to telling you the story. It's one filled with dedication and hard work for the good of mankind."

Schutte's man was joined by another almost twin at the top of the plane's stairs.

Johan Schutte limped with MacLachlan into the small terminal building.

The Faheems nodded curtly at the man who had almost given his life trying to protect them.

Once again, MacLachlan thought, *I hope they are paying Schutte a helluva lot to put up with them*.

Paul and Brooksie shook with Gunny and MacLachlan and they formed a circle around the Faheems along with Schutte at the lead and began the twenty-yard walk to the plane.

MacLachlan hung back and unslung his MP5, watching.

He had a feeling. This was ending too easily.

He heard tires screech and saw a large black Mercedes careen around the building. *We should have walked the perimeter, damn it! We broke trade-craft!* MacLachlan thought.

Schutte was moving slowly. So, Paul and Brooksie ushered the Faheems at speed to the stair. Both of Schutte's men came down and added to the phalanx, rifles shouldered.

Back windows came down and guns appeared. MacLachlan opened up before they shot. He filled the GLS with full auto rounds from the MP5. He could see the rear seat man on his side fall. He saw, or rather heard, the passenger side rear door open and a man stumble out.

MacLachlan ran around the car, ignoring the fact a fast reverse would have killed him.

As the man who tumbled out tried to gain his balance and level a short Russian AK-15 at him. MacLachlan fired the MP5 from his hip and struck the receiver of the AK. It went flying.

MacLachlan tackled the man, and both went to the pavement.

As they went down, the Mercedes squealed the tires and took off around the building with nothing but the driver and a dead shooter in the rear aboard. Paul and Brooksie fired at it.

The man got on top of MacLachlan. He heard the jet engines rev and the stairs raise, passengers and guards inside.

The man had his hands around MacLachlan's throat. Gunny was running his way to assist. MacLachlan punched the assailant's face with an open-hand palm blow. His nose was devastated. As his head rocked back, MacLachlan hit him with a throat blow with his fist. Gunny arrived and the two men checked the other for weapons. Finding no weapons on his person, they dragged him to the stairs. Schutte had lowered them and was motioning them forward. His two men raced down the steps and walked the man up them, handcuffing him behind the back as they ushered him up the stairs and into the plane. He would be unofficially deported to Dubai where Faheem's money would supersede his rights. Within hours, MacLachlan would know who the hit team was.

He needed to get out of Dodge. Gunny was already in the Sprinter. He drove the Toyota at highway speed to the airport to avoid police notice.

He dropped the Toyota at the rental return and, by text agreement, met Gunny in the short-term parking to see where the van was and pick up the keys.

"You're not flying back from here, Mack? I would have thought you would want to get out of the Czech Republic quickly," Gunny said.

"I need to meet with Tomás in an hour and visit. We are old friends and hardly had a chance to talk. I have another contract in Europe, so I am staying. I'll cache the equipment and switch vehicles today or tomorrow.

"Thanks for coming over and working on this one, Gunny. I couldn't have done it without you."

"Well, with Paul and Brooksie you sure could have. They are fine operators. I understand Paul runs security for a night club on Mallorca?"

"He does. It's where Nisa Faheem was kidnapped the first time. He and Brooksie are both great guys. This new op is much further north. I am going to get a camper van and drive up. I'll transfer what I need at the storage unit and leave from there. It's a long-term gig with a lot of research first. I may find a campground somewhere and spend the rest of the summer relaxing," MacLachlan said.

"This is my last operational contract. I am getting too damn old for this silliness, Mack. With the outrageous amount of money you just paid me for a couple day's work, I will flat out retire permanently to my little spread in Texas."

"I'll see you when I get back to the States. Be safe and thanks again, Gunny!" They shook and parted.

MacLachlan left in the Sprinter and drove to Leipzig. He transferred everything to the storage facility in which he had found the gear from Anna. He put the drone, the grenades and flash bangs, one MP5, the Mauser and two CZ-75s aside. He moved a large quantity of ammunition over beside them. Included were a cot and sleeping bag, some of the vinyl gloves and one Kevlar vest with additional steel plates inserted. He would pick these up later for the Russia trip.

He drove the Sprinter into town and met Tomás at the pizza joint after a half hour of surveillance detection routes and stationary watching for tails from diagonally across the street.

"Thanks again to you, Andrej, Filip and Jakub for the help. Nothing pays off better than knowledgeable local guys. And you all are!

"But I wanted to mention another topic. Tomás, I'm going on a solo mission to Russia. I wonder if I provided you with a SAT phone and a year's subscription, if you would monitor call-ins every day. If I don't call in by the prescribed time, wait three hours and let Will Grafton know. I will give you his 24-hour number. Will Grafton is Kate's boss and would let her know, as well as my folks, and the successor trustee of my estate."

"Sounds like you think you might not make it back from this one, Mack," the tough former secret police agent said.

"I'm just covering my bases. As you might guess, this is related to the op we just had. It's kind of the epilogue to the story. It's dangerous. I am not doing it for the principal. I am doing it for a worthwhile charity."

"Mack, what on earth kind of charity would be so important you'd go on what sounds like a suicide mission for?" Tomás asked.

"One where the fee might find the cure for cancer. I have a friend who is both a medical doctor and a botanist. She, like other scientists, feels like the cure for cancer and many other diseases, lies unknown in the jungles of the Amazon. She has been working there, studying plants for the better part of twenty-five years. I have been silently contributing to her efforts. She has no idea who her secret benefactor is.

"Only my banker and now, you are aware."

"Is she very important to you, Mack?"

"Yes, but only as a friend. She has a male research doctor she considers her partner. Has for years. I'm just the guy who drops her a card every now and then."

"You must really believe in her, Mack, to put a lot of your income into her research."

"I do. She is becoming internationally renowned. If I can help just a little, it will be worthwhile."

"What would Kate think of you risking your life for charity?" Tomás asked.

"It's hard for me to figure out what Kate thinks lately. She is totally wrapped up in her job. She is brilliant at it, so I hate to interfere. I offered her the ability to retire and travel the world. She'd never have to worry about money ever again. I even gave her a ring. But nothing. I am through pressuring her. I had given up enough to fall for an MI6 agent who was closer to my age. But she was killed when we were chasing down two international assassins."

"Does Kate know about her?"

"Yes, they met at a briefing and the two women and Will Grafton had lunch with me. They actually seemed to get along well. I know Kate is gracious, but I considered the ease with which she accepted Lexi to be a bad sign for us.

"I guess the bottom line is I have pretty much given up on finding a partner to keep me warm at nights. I may get a dog instead."

Tomás snorted with disapproval.

"I think you believe you are too old for my niece. Which is unfathomable to a European. Man or woman. Only Americans worry about such things. Silly!"

"If I thought she wanted to raise a family, I might be. But, not under our circumstances. No, it's all in her court now. She has refused my offers. I have made all the offers I can or will for the foreseeable future, Tomás," MacLachlan said.

"Perhaps I should have a favorite uncle talk with my niece."

"As you wish. But you Czechs are almost as stubborn as we Scots are."

"Not quite. And we don't drink as much either!"

MacLachlan grinned at his friend, before observing, "Czechs are the champion beer drinkers in the world."

"So, what time do you propose calling me? I am no spring chicken and I need my beauty sleep," Tomás said.

"It's your choice."

"How about eight PM Prague time?"

"Eight? Won't eight disrupt your beauty sleep?" MacLachlan asked.

"Don't be a smartass. If you keep this up, I won't put in a good word for you with my niece."

"Okay. Eight in the evening Prague time. Give me three hours after before pulling the alarm."

"When will I get this satellite phone?"

"I suspect in a couple of weeks. I am not going until they stop having daylight for eighteen hours a day. So, probably around September or October."

"What will you be doing until then?"

"I am going to buy a campervan and drive to Helsinki. I want to take the drone and a couple of the guns we used this week."

"I sure liked the Mauser. It brought back fond memories."

"Wasn't it a Mauser eight by fifty-seven you used to kill the Romany who set up Kate's kidnapping?"

"Yes, and I field stripped it and discarded the pieces in several locations. I miss the old girl," he said referring to the Mauser bolt action.

"Well, I have the one we had for our op this week in the van. It's yours. I guess we have to go to your garage for me to give it to you?" MacLachlan asked.

"If it's in a rifle case, you can give it to me on the street. It's a hunting rifle. The Czech Republic has some of the finest gun manufacturers in the world. We are a free country."

"It is. The Sprinter is a block down on the left. If you want to drive down, I'll give it to you," MacLachlan said.

Ten minutes later, MacLachlan gave Tomás the Mauser and a hundred rounds of 8x57 Mauser cartridges on a main drag on the edge of city center Prague.

He called Anna once he left Tomás.

"Hi! How are you? Adele working out well? Business good?"

"Fine, yes, and yes! Is your contract fulfilled?" she responded.

"It is. The family is back aboard a plane heading home as we speak. I have a couple questions about some gear."

"Fire away if it's stuff we can talk about over an open line," she said.

"I was wondering if it was okay, we turned the Landcruiser in to the airport rental in Prague. I want to do the same with the Sprinter."

"Prague is where we rented them. Adele, who is a doll, and I drove them with the gear down to Leipzig ourselves, and rented and loaded the storage facility."

"I left a preponderance of the gear there. I need a few things for an upcoming contract. Would you have preferred I brought everything back here?"

"Not necessarily. Can we bring all back in the Sprinter if you leave it for us in Prague?" she asked.

"Definitely. I will find a safe place. Want me to mail the keys to you?" he asked.

"Please, unless you can leave them for me to get from someone you trust. Is there anything you need for your new contract?"

"There are several things. I am going to do some research first. I will not be leaving until late September, so we have plenty of time. I will send you an encrypted email with a couple of things I know about. I will need to keep the drone. Don't worry about crediting back the items in Leuven. Put them in inventory and resell. I do not believe anything will be dirty. Maybe the MPs," he said, intentionally leaving off the rest of the model nomenclature.

"I have a solution for such situations once I know they have been used," she said.

He knew she would re-barrel them and destroy the forensically damning original barrels.

He called Tomás back to ask about a safe parking location. He said to leave it and the keys at his place. He would put it in the garage and give the keys to Anna and Adele upon their arrival.

MacLachlan had some serious shopping to do tomorrow. He rode through several motels and found one with what he sought. A concrete wall in the parking lot. He would back the Sprinter against it and block access to the rear doors. With the large drone on top of the gun and ammo boxes packed flat, it would be very difficult to remove anything through the doors. Especially since MacLachlan parked under a high-power sodium lamp.

He went in, one CZ-75 secreted in his belt under his shirttail. There was a room for the night, and he took it.

His plan was to find a camper rig tomorrow for the slow trip to Helsinki. He would use it as a mobile base of operations. He would pay cash and either sell it at the end of his mission or give it to Anna for her company.

After the pizza for lunch, MacLachlan was not particularly hungry. He turned in early.

He was starving the next morning and had a big breakfast. Afterwards, he drafted an encrypted text to Anna asking her to attempt to locate a current issue Russian battle carbine with a suppressor and a Russian shoulder-fired rocket launcher. He asked for at least four rockets. He specified two explosive (HE) and two with incendiary capability. A lot depended on what he found out about Petrovitch Pharmaceutical CJSC. If he could get in close enough, he could lob a rocket through several windows of the laboratory building at off-hours.

*An overhead fire sprinkler system might be a hinderance. Perhaps a high explosive first to disrupt the fire system would be the way to go,* MacLachlan thought.

He took the Sprinter over to Tomás' house and they put it in the garage, and he left the keys with Tomás.

"My plan is to find a new or slightly used camper trailer and a used tow vehicle.

I could pull it around while I'm killing time, sleep in it, and use it for the trip to the far north for my op. I think a camper would be ubiquitous. Like hiding in plain sight," he told his friend.

"Why don't I take you around to look for one? You could buy me lunch. Besides, I'd like to drive the new E-Class a bit, now the registration has been fixed so nobody will ever question its ownership. One of the benefits to my contacts from the past." MacLachlan took it to mean during past car theft ring investigations he had developed some contacts who owed him favors.

They went to several recreational vehicle dealers.

The one he chose was a small teardrop type camper trailer, or caravan, as it was called in Europe. It had solar panels added. According to MacLachlan's measurements, the drone would fit, unassembled. MacLachlan found a used Volvo V50 wagon with all-wheel drive and the larger 2.4-liter diesel. It already had a trailer hitch and light package. At 96k kilometers, it was hardly broken in for a diesel. It had a few dings, which was what MacLachlan wanted in a car he did not wish to stand out.

"It's nerdy enough nobody would suspect it was an attack vehicle," MacLachlan thought aloud.

One call and sufficient Euros were transferred to both the caravan and car dealers to buy each free and clear.

He assured Tomás he would be receiving the SAT phone by special delivery in the next week, fully paid for a year. He emphasized the check-in calls would not begin until he had cleared the border, which Tomás knew to be Russia.

By mid-afternoon, he left the CZ with Tomás, then bade his friend adieu and left for the next adventure.

---

HE HEADED NORTH to Liberec and found a place to camp with a nearby shower, restroom and laundry facility. It also had a good Wi-fi signal.

He studied routes on his computer and decided when it was time to head to Russia, he would go north until he got to Estonia, then take the car ferry at Tullin fifty-four miles across to Finland.

At the campground, he found some of the peace he knew he had been missing.

He picked up a pipe and some mild tobacco along the way. He had some Czechvar beer in the camper's small refrigerator and had purchased an awning, folding chair, and small folding table at the dealership.

MacLachlan sat in the chair enjoying the cold beer and a cheese sandwich made with local bread and cheese. After, he lit his pipe and thought about his grandfather, an inveterate pipe smoker. The warm breeze was quickly inducing some much needed drowsiness, so he put the pipe aside after one bowl of tobacco and allowed himself to doze off.

For the next two months, his greatest danger would be traffic. He put the notifications on his smartphone back on until the op began.

He was awakened by the vibration of a text coming in.

It was from Grafton.

"Where in hell are you? Are you up for a security course like we talked about? One is available in three weeks in Northern Virginia."

"Not available. Touring Eastern Europe towing my new camper. Taking a nap currently. Out," was his response.

Fifteen minutes later, another text came in. This one was from Kate.

"Uncle Tomás said you two just had lunch together. What's up in the Czech Republic? Will says you have a camper. What? Mack MacLachlan has a damn camper?"

Since she was just being nosey, he responded laconically then turned the iPhone off.

"Yes. Nothing. Yes."

It gave him a disproportionate pleasure, no matter how childish his action was. He went back to sleep.

Next, his SAT phone rang. He forgotten to turn it off.

"Are you driving through a bad cell zone? Your iPhone is going directly to voicemail," Kate said.

"Nope, dear. I turned it off. I am enjoying a warm Czech breeze and taking a nap."

"Why are you being so evasive?" she asked.

"I'm not evasive. I'm off the grid."

"Do you have a job?"

"Not currently. I am unemployed for a while. It would be nice to have a travel companion. This is a nice little camper or caravan as they call them over here. But it's built for two."

"I thought you liked to rough it with the snakes and bugs," she said.

"I'm beginning to like having an awning and folding chair. And a bed in a little trailer I can lock at night. Especially since I don't have any sort of gun with me."

"Is this really you?" she said, causing him to grin broadly.

"I am not really sure anymore, honey. I am trying to figure out who I am and who I want to be when I grow up."

"Mack MacLachlan never said anything like so touchy-feely in his life. You will be meditating next and talking about your Chakras."

"My what?"

"You need to come home. Run the Shenandoah. Catch a snook in Florida. Be you."

"I am seriously considering selling the Casey Key home," he said, shocking her.

"You are kidding, right?"

"I am dead serious. You won't come there because of the memories of having to kill a Hezbollah leader with a knife in our bedroom. It's not the same house I grew up in, just a copy. I don't like my posh egomaniacal neighbors. Why not sell it?"

The phone was silent as Kate searched for an answer. The only thing she liked in what she heard was the mention of "our bedroom". She could not come up with a response, so she changed the subject.

"There are only good memories on Cedar Creek. Except for Lexi, I guess," she said.

"Except for Lexi," he agreed.

"Do you miss her?"

"I do," he said.

"Do you miss me?"

"I do," he said again.

Another pause. Kate had taken herself somewhere she was not ready to go. Yet.

"Since the response to your last question seems to be escaping you, I will go back to my nap. I'm glad we had this talk. I think," he said pleasantly as he broke the connection. He found, however, he was unable to resume the nap. He stared at the blue Czech sky. He was unfocussed in several ways.

Four thousand four hundred miles away, the beautiful redhead sat at her desk holding her phone long after the end of the conversation. She studied it as if it might give her an answer. Perhaps, like her, it did not even know the question, much less the answer. She sat the phone back in its cradle. And stared at her computer screen instead. It did not have the answer either.

---

MACLACHLAN, having come down from the adrenalin rush of close quarter battle, set up his lightweight folding table. He placed his Mac Pro laptop on it and adjusted the settings for the campground's Wi-Fi.

He began work in earnest, searching routes in and out of the town of Petrovia, where the manufacturing and research facility for Petrovitch Pharmaceuticals CJSC was located. He looked at road maps and satellite maps showing terrain. He looked for places to base and wait.

MacLachlan decided to leave the camper in Helsinki and buy or steal an old work truck. He had already asked Anna to have her identification counterfeiter prepare him additional credentials, including passport and work papers for a Russian workman returning after a building project in Finland. The man already had a photo of MacLachlan with a beard. He had to be a Russian because he did not speak either Finnish or Swedish, the two primary languages of Finland. Many Finns spoke English, but English was the last identity the Russians would look past without handcuffs.

He studied Petrovia itself. Its weather, people, density, and primary exports. The city's largest employer was the site he was going to disable.

MacLachlan really hated to put people out of

work. He hated the fact he might harm the production of much-needed medicines, too. All for the revenge of a man he personally thought was not worth a bullet.

Hopefully, his fee would contribute heavily to the Brazilian cancer research his friend appeared to be bringing to a successful conclusion. If not, it was all in vain.

He put all of his research on a flash drive and hid it in a small plastic bag wired under the passenger seat of the Volvo. He then wiped it off his computer.

Anna called a week later with two bits of information.

"Adele and I flew to Prague and went to your friend's house. We picked up the Sprinter and are driving it home to Leuven now. We will inventory the items once we get to my highly secure little warehouse. The second thing is I have found a source for a suppressed Russian AK-15K. It would be their equivalent of the M4 the US and many other countries use. It's 7.62 x 39 mm like an AK-47. The next thing will thrill you! I can pick up a Russian RPG7V2 and hyperbaric head rockets. The hyperbaric design mixes more air with the HE and causes a big rolling explosion which is both damaging from a HE standpoint and an incendiary one," Anna said.

"Perfect! I will take both with two HE, and two hyperbaric rockets. I will research the range and operation on YouTube. I have not fired a shoulder fired rocket in over twenty years. Thanks. Go ahead and obtain them and I will give a delivery address in Finland when I can."

He walked over to the Lužická Nisa River and tried to decide whether he wanted to fish it.

"Oh, why not?" he said and went back to the campground store and rented a rod and reel and bought the recommended bait.

Later, he had a nice fish. He took it back to the store and the old man behind the counter told him it was eminently edible. He had steamed broccoli and very fresh fish for dinner.

He went for a ten-mile run, by his best estimation, the next morning and felt better. He was getting better by the day. Better from whatever it was bothering him.

He plugged in the flash drive and did more research. The trouble with working like this was not being able to print. He wished he had purchased a small, portable printer in Prague. Perhaps he would get one in Liberec. Without further thought, he got in the Volvo and headed to town. Finding and setting up the small printer was not difficult.

He was working and printing well before dinner.

After a week, he checked out of the campground and drove north into Poland. MacLachlan found a campground at Lodz online and drove to it. He checked in and unhooked his trailer, set up his awning, and put out his table and chair.

The woman who checked him in was both attractive and flirtatious. MacLachlan was appreciative of her attention, but was just polite, smiled at her and went about his business. He was not in the market for another woman anytime soon. He had felt the same way before Lexi walked into his life, too. So, maybe his resolve was... flexible.

His research plan for the day centered around the CEO of Petrovitch Pharmaceuticals CJSC, his family, and its board of directors.

He learned a lot after Internet searches, using the three basic Boolean operators: *and*, *or*, and *not*.

He found the CEO was a man called Dima Novikov. He found a number of images of Novikov and his wife and family in newspapers and magazine articles. He seemed to be quite the popular figure. MacLachlan printed them for memorization and planning. He would destroy them before crossing into Russia in two months. He spent a week in Poland before moving on to Lithuania for another week.

He had not had any trouble driving through borders between any of the countries so far.

He felt as if he was transiting Eastern Europe naked as he had left every gun behind in Prague. He had safe deposit boxes with a gun, knife, passports and cash in major cities, like London, Paris, Tel Aviv and others. But none were near where he was driving.

Though he was going within the EU, until he sneaked into Russia, border guards could do a full vehicle inspection at any time. It was simply not worth jeopardizing a million-dollar contract for one handgun.

MacLachlan had never been to the country. It was a Baltic state which was largely populated by natives, with a few Poles and Russians. It was primarily Christian and had joined both the EU and NATO in 2004. It had become the first Baltic state to declare its independence from the collapsing USSR. The country had a high per capita income and a favorable level of freedom for its inhabitants.

The capital of Lithuania, Vilnius, was likely the mathematic center of Europe.

He expected to like it even before he arrived because of how it had grasped the Western World.

He set up his camp and fixed some coffee. With the solar panels, he was guaranteed enough electricity to run the computer, charge the phones and make coffee even camping without an electrical hookup. He had a hookup here, though, and took advantage of it to make a cup of Czech H káva, a thick, strong coffee.

Even MacLachlan, connoisseur of black coffee, had to put cream in this chest hair raising brew. He sipped it as he trolled the Internet, seeking additional bits of information about his target company or its CEO and his family. He had no intention of hurting the man or his family but knew too much information was always better than too little. He took notes on his Word for Mac program, eschewing the word processing which came with the laptop. He looked at the calendar on his smart phone.

He should plan on getting to Helsinki in less than three weeks. He would spend some time there, possibly seeing his young hacker friend, Elias. He used the pseudonym, Commander Zero, on the web. Mostly the dark web.

It occurred to MacLachlan Elias may have some less-than-scrupulous friends or relatives who sneaked in and out of Russia. Maybe hitching a ride for a fee would be a possibility. He could drive, using the GPS on his phone or the Garmin he carried everywhere he went. He would wait and see what Elias Koskella recommended. He knew he could trust the kid. Virtually everything Elias did, and everyone with whom he interacted, could land him in a Finnish prison. He had not made it to the ripe old age of nineteen by talking indiscreetly.

Despite the possibility of facial recognition software at border crossings, MacLachlan felt traveling the way he was doing with virtually no credit cards, using cash, sleeping in the camper was a discreet way to travel. The tracker on his phones were turned off again. Agencies could still track them if he was a specific target. He had the Virtual Private Network turned on, so his computer showed him jumping all over the world.

It was certainly not the fastest way to travel, but under the radar generally.

Towards the end of the first week in September, MacLachlan leisurely pulled into Tullin, Estonia. He spent the night at a campground, or holiday park.

He received a call from Schutte.

"Mack. The scientists have nothing from their Russian counterparts. They were not even allowed to respond to our calls. I guess it's due to the kidnappings and the loss of the contracts. The Petrovitch folks have their knickers in a twist," he said.

"I'll play it by ear," MacLachlan said. "Thanks for trying."

## 5

The next morning, his wagon and camper were carefully guided aboard the ferry to Finland. The fifty-four-mile trip would take a couple of hours. He squeezed out of the door and walked up to the upper deck. Getting a to-go cup of pressed coffee, he watched the dark waters. The waves were much of the way towards the height which would have delayed the ferry.

MacLachlan focused on the horizon to lessen the chance of seasickness. It happened to the most experienced seamen at one time or another. Usually, when it was least expected. And, least needed.

Other than the large ferry pitching its way across, the trip was uneventful. As Estonia and Finland were both EU members, the arrival was just another border crossing.

With a little help from the Internet, MacLachlan found a waterfront caravan park and rented a space for a month. It was far longer than he planned to use it but was part of his cover. He backed the camper into a spot in the trees and hooked to water and electricity. He immediately took advantage of the Wi-Fi to check the status of White Nights in St. Petersburg. He did not wish to fulfil the contract until he could operate under the cover of darkness and escape in the same.

His campground was a half hour drive from downtown Helsinki.

Once settled, he sent an encrypted text to his young hacker friend, Elias.

"Zero, your buddy from Florida. Lunch tomorrow? Pick a quiet place in your hometown" was the entire text.

He received an immediate response with the name of a restaurant and a time. MacLachlan acknowledged with "Roger".

MacLachlan ventured into Helsinki for his first time the next day. He put an address several blocks from the restaurant into his phone and found a parking space. Except for meetings, he eschewed parking garages. Too many cameras. Too difficult to make rapid and unseen escapes. And far too many "fatal funnels."

He followed his usual routine. Get there forty-five minutes early. Park several blocks away. Walk the area, stopping at display windows to use them as mirrors. Walk as if he was going somewhere specific, then snapping his fingers as if he had forgotten something. And, quickly turning and walking back in the direction he had come and watching for panicking tails scurrying to not be seen. Lastly, he found a coffee shop and took a window seat. It was across from the target restaurant. He ordered a rich Paulig Juhla Mokka coffee and watched the sidewalk and street.

MacLachlan did not see anybody particularly suspicious walking by, nor the same person more than once. Tails could be drunks, bag ladies, homeless, businessmen. Anybody. He looked for someone who appeared to be on a mission. Looking for him.

He saw a plethora of Nissan and Toyota taxis. He watched to see if the drivers and passengers were dressed differently. In a sophisticated city like Helsinki, he expected most drivers to be in open collar sports shirts and most passengers to be in business suits. The ones he saw were.

Five minutes before the agreed upon time, he saw Elias enter the restaurant. His tradecraft was horrendous. He walked straight up to the restaurant and did an exaggerated scan behind himself before going in. Tails would have probably given themselves away by breaking into laughter.

*Maybe there is method in his madness,* MacLachlan thought.

"Nah," he grinned on second thought. He arose from his window seat and walked to the restaurant and greeted his friend.

"I bought you a small gift," he said as he put a small white noise machine on the table and slid it over to Elias.

The kid was probably a millionaire by sixteen from illegal hacking, both for himself and contractually for people like MacLachlan.

However, one would think MacLachlan had given him a new Porsche.

Elias dropped his voice, and in a *sotto voce* said, "Spy equipment, right?"

"A white noise generator. It makes a conversation more difficult to hear or record. Kind of like running water to accomplish the same ends," MacLachlan said.

"Wow, Mack. Thanks! Should we leave it on here?" he asked.

"It would be prudent. I checked out the outside thoroughly, but not the inside. The key is not bringing attention to oneself."

"What are you doing here, Mack? I bet it's not a vacation."

"No, it's not. The trip up from Eastern Europe was though. This will be my jumping off point for the biggest city east of here."

"You mean," but MacLachlan raised his finger to his lips quickly, stopping him.

"Yes. And I wanted to pick your brain on some things man-to-man. This is not the best place. But you seem eager to learn tradecraft, so I'll show you the types of places we can chat safely. Interested?"

"Yes!" he said with great enthusiasm.

"Let's eat lunch first. Then, some tradecraft," MacLachlan suggested.

Elias ordered a meal befitting his girth. MacLachlan, who probably burned more calories in a day than the younger man in three days, ate more reasonably.

Afterwards, they took a walk. They found a park, with a bench conveniently located in the middle. All the people there had been there well before them. MacLachlan taught Elias how to circle the park and check for threats and surveillance before deciding on a location to speak. They came at the bench from different sides of the park. MacLachlan arrived, by plan, five minutes early and unfolded a newspaper and began to read. He spoke no Finnish and was just glad he got the paper right side up.

Elias arrived and sat on the far end of the bench. Guys just did not sit close. They nodded politely as he asked if he could share.

Their chat appeared to be one of polite strangers.

"Where might I find a trucker or delivery person who makes runs from here to St. Petersburg? Someone unlikely to be stopped beyond a normal search at the border?"

"I have a second cousin who delivers fresh fish from here to St Petersburg in a refrigerated truck."

"If I paid him a goodly amount, with a finder's fee for you of course, could he take fewer fish? I may have some questionable items to hide under them."

"A lot of risk, Mack, costs a lot of money."

"Haha. I'm not as rich as you, Elias. But I would pay him appropriately. You've never seen me shirk my duty in paying."

"No. Never. Always paid well and in advance," Elias agreed.

"Can he keep his mouth shut? Our freedom depends on it, Elias. The natives of the country in question are not gentle when threatened."

"He can. As to their temperament, Mack. We are next door neighbors. We are well aware of the dangers."

"Does he make his runs in the day or at night?" MacLachlan asked.

"Night. He picks up the fish when the boats come

in to dock around eighteen hundred hours. By the time they are loaded and iced, he leaves at twenty hundred. He gets into the city's fishmongers around midnight. By car and with no stops, it would be two and a half hours. But between driving an old truck and up to several agricultural inspections, it takes longer," Elias said, his covertly activated new toy wafting white noise into nature.

Elias stopped talking. MacLachlan was watching for "tells" and said, "What is it you want to tell me but aren't, Elias?"

Elias turned red and gulped.

"How did you know?"

"Not my first rodeo, cowboy."

"Did you ever know any cowboys?" Elias asked, changing the subject.

"Years ago, I was High School All-Around Cowboy in Texas," MacLachlan said truthfully. "But, more importantly, share what you are holding back on your friend."

"Could be my cousin imports some other things to St. Petersburg."

"So, he's a smuggler. Drugs?"

"Oh, no! Just cigarettes. Maybe some blue jeans. Never drugs."

"Does he hide them under the fish?" MacLachlan asked.

"Yes."

"The biggest thing I have to hide is a drone. Folded up. I may not take it depending on my research."

"That might be tough, Mack. How big is it folded?"

Holding his arms, MacLachlan showed Elias the length, width and depth of a box which would hold it.

"Though it is not illegal, a drone would raise questions in a fish truck. I am pretty sure it would not fit in the fish ice chests anyway."

"I would pay him to leave the cigarettes and jeans at home on my trip," MacLachlan said.

"A thousand Euros would cover his losses. Not his risk, of course. Risk costs a lot more," Elias said.

"I know. It always does. I am prepared to cover him fairly. You, too."

"When do you want to go, Mack?"

"As soon as nights are as long as days. End of September?" he responded.

"Maybe middle of October this year. Ulvar says he hates smuggling in the damn daylight!"

"Ask your cousin if he's interested. Don't mention money yet except to say I'm willing to pay to cover his risk. Only identify me as someone you have dealt with and trust. No names. Swear him to secrecy. Just so you will know, my intention is to destroy something, but not hurt or kill anyone knowingly. As you know, operating on the dark side, there is always a possibility of death. It comes with the turf, Elias."

"I know, Mack," he said, believing he spoke the truth. The reality is he made a lot of money sitting on his butt in front of a computer. The only people he ever shot or whoever shot at him were in some version of Mortal Kombat on his computer.

*His self-image is not unrealistic, and it's a balloon I won't pop,* MacLachlan thought to himself. *He's a brilliant asset who could be turned into an operator with some good tutoring and a bit of Marine Corps conditioning.*

"One thing guys like us should do sitting in the open like this is look for a way to evacuate while seeking cover along the way. Cover is good when it hides you or part of you, Elias. It's better when it's a barrier which is capable of stopping bullets coming downrange at you. The key when bullets start flying and you don't have immediate barriers is movement. Move erratically. Move as soon as you shoot, then keep moving.

"Remember what the great boxing champion Muhammad Ali said, 'Float like a butterfly, sting like a bee.' Your floating is your movement. Most people cannot shoot well. Especially under stress. So, take advantage of it and make yourself a harder target to hit."

Elias was drinking every word intently. This is stuff which could save his life one day, he knew. He had done a lot of deep Internet search on MacLachlan. Including the Dark Web. The guy was a legend. And the legend was teaching Elias how to be like him!

"How's Anna?" Elias asked as they were walking back and MacLachlan was showing him surveillance detection routes on foot.

"Last I spoke with her she was fine. Her new business is doing really well."

"You only see her for business now?" Elias asked.

"Pretty much. Business is her driver. She's really dedicated to get it going again."

"Is she happy with the computer system and its security I set up for her?"

"As far as I know she is. Have you called to check in and see if she needs anything further? Might be a good idea."

Elias lit up at the prospect. MacLachlan wondered why someone as intelligent as this computer genius had not thought of it before. Naïveté was the probable answer.

"Elias, let's stay in touch as I move around the area. Let me know what your cousin says. We will plan for me to ride with him once daylight and darkness are equalized in St. Petersburg. Since he's going back and forth on a regular basis, he may be the arbiter of the decision for when I will go," MacLachlan said.

They parted. MacLachlan stopped by a fish market after chatting about the cousin and his fish and contraband delivery service. He picked up some haddock fillets and some fresh bread and vegetables at the grocery next door. On his next trip into the city, he would look for a theatrical store and get some face camouflage makeup.

He went back to the campground, or holiday park, and put his groceries away to cook later.

"Anna? Is this a good time to speak?" he asked.

"Yes, Mack. It's fine. How are you?"

"I'm fine. Are you alright?" he asked.

"Wonderfully busy. I may be able to retire at forty!"

"Good! Have you gotten the materials from the printer?" he asked, referring to his new passport, driving license, credit card and peripheral identification materials such as insurance cards.

"I have them in hand. Want me to send them in the box with the 'scientific' equipment you ordered?"

"That would be most appreciated. I will need everything within three weeks. How will you get it to me?"

"I've been working on it. Nothing is really great. As a licensed weapons importer, I can ship firearms about anywhere. In Finland, they would have to go to a licensed gun dealer or government agency. You are neither. For a surcharge of one thousand Euros, Adele as my agent, or I could deliver them by train. I really would not be obligated to prove the end user," she said.

"Let's do it by train then. Could you oversee shipping the drone on the trip back for the surcharge?" he asked.

"Sure. You pay the shipping, which should not be horrendous, and I will oversee it."

"You said you have the printed material in hand. How about the 'scientific' equipment?" he asked.

"I have it all in my warehouse awaiting delivery to you. If we do it this way, we can call it what it is: military grade firearms and munitions. They fall within the scope of my license. You will be the buyer for a nonexistent security firm. The shoulder-fired goody will be conveniently listed as 'riot control gear'. You will get a security firm-legal carbine and a surprise pistol in the firearms carton. The Russian rifle will be broken down, so it and the pistol will be easy to ship in a non-gun looking box."

"Great. What's the pistol?"

"Very special. Just for my Mack! It's the new MPL striker-fired Makarov replacement. Unlike the

Putin bodyguard guns in 9x21mm, it's a standard 9x19 like in use all over the world. But it is rated for +P+ high velocity ammunition. And, you have a box of it with hollow points. There is also a bonus for you. A KGB-replacement FSB identity card with your bearded photo on it. I hope your Russian is as good as a native's!" she said.

"It's pretty good. The benefit to Russia is it's so damn big, some are virtually Europeans and on the other side they have Chinese neighbors. There are a lot of dialects to claim lightyears away from wherever you are when questioned.

"The FSB ID is a sweet idea. It could literally get me executed on the spot, though."

"Or immediately buy you time out of a really tight situation."

"True. Do you know if it's printed on edible paper?" he asked, tongue-in-cheek.

"Sure it is. The plastic laminate is edible, too!"

"I am so screwed, Anna." All he heard on the other end was her musical giggle.

"I would remind you we are a full-service logistics company. But I have to send Adele with your order. And, you better not!"

"No worries, Anna. At all."

"Do you have a safe place to keep the things?" she asked.

"Yep. My camper trailer at the campground."

"Is a camper trailer at a campground the same as a caravan at a holiday park?"

"Very similar."

"So exactly the same?"

"Pretty much."

"You know. The drone is not a prohibited item. You could go to any shipping service and they would pack and deliver the drone. You could send it to your house in Florida."

"Makes sense. I may have use for it at home. I think I'll do it. Thanks," he said.

"Give me a second to check with Adele and let her do some computer planning."

"Okay."

Anna came back in two minutes.

"Can you meet her at the Helsinki Central Station day after tomorrow at noon?"

"I'll be there."

"She will too. Bye!" she said as she hung up.

He shipped the drone to Florida the next day, with himself as the recipient. Its absence immediately resulted in more space in the cramped camper.

He parked the Volvo near the station and did his SDR's two days later around eleven. He entered the impressive station with its large architectural arch.

Checking the arrival board, he walked to where one met incoming passengers from the Brussels train.

It was not difficult to pick Adele out of the crowd, even amongst the handsome Finns. She was truly model quality. A beautiful arms dealer, who worked for Anna, the original beautiful arms dealer.

She gave MacLachlan a big hug and a kiss on both cheeks. He remembered Anna's admonition and steeled his resolve to behave.

"We need to pick up the items I shipped," she said in French. He responded the same.

What was apparently the pistol and its ammo was

in a small box she could carry. The taken-down rifle, rocket launcher and four rockets were in a larger box MacLachlan carried. It was more awkward than heavy. He loaded all into the back of the Volvo wagon and pulled the tonneau over them. As he got into the car, she gave him a manila envelope with all his forged credentials. He would look at them back at the camp.

"Adele, what is your schedule? Going back tomorrow?"

"No, Mack. Midnight train tonight," she responded.

"How about come out to the campground and I'll fix you dinner and bring you back easily in time for your departure?"

"It sounds good to me!"

Thirty minutes later, they were unloading the Volvo at the campground.

"Aren't you going to check the items?" Adele asked.

"No, I'll do it tomorrow. If something is missing, there is nothing you can do about it tonight. I will call tomorrow and sort it out with Anna," he said.

He opened a bottle of wine from the refrigerator and let her pour it while he prepared Haddock fillets in lemon sauce and green beans with bacon. He had a baguette of bread from the grocery and some country butter for it.

They ate at a picnic table on the site.

"Tell me how it's going and what you think so far, Adele."

"I love it. I have started the University of Leuven. I switched my major to International Business. I think it's going to expose me to the skills I need to help Anna run the business."

"I don't doubt it at all, Adele. There is a temptation in the particular line of work you are in to skirt the law. The consequences are very grave. Perhaps you could be the voice of moderation and help keep the ship afloat?"

"I will try. I am already seeing it will not be easy, Mack."

"Just help Anna where you can. What her former employers did was totally illegal. I guess you know by now, I killed the male, and she killed the female just before I pulled the trigger on her."

"I never knew the details, but figured it was something similar."

Adele pursued queries on the details of MacLachlan's contract. He was sure Anna had put her up to it. Finally, he decided to meet her questions head on.

"Too much knowledge about what I am going to do might make you or Anna or both co-conspirators or worse. Let's leave it at me going to Russia to effect a payback for the Faheem kidnappings. I do not plan to harm a single soul. My target is property. Nothing else."

"What is your probability of making it out of Russia okay after you do whatever it is you plan to do?" she asked. MacLachlan thought it was a question showing great perception for someone so young and inexperienced in spec ops.

"About thirty percent of making it out, therefore seventy percent of not coming back."

"Are you serious, Mack?" Adele asked.

"Very, Adele."

"Why would you take such a contract? Does Anna know the odds?" she asked.

"I have taken ones like this before. So-called suicide missions. I always make it out, though sometimes with new scars. And no. Anna does not know."

"Yet, you told me. Someone you hardly know."

"I told you because you asked. There is a man in Prague. His name is Tomás Studrich. I will be making check-in calls to him from Russia once a day. They will start when I leave Finland. If I miss one by three hours, he will call certain people in government. Anna is not one. If you want, you can be a person Tomás can call."

"Of course, Mack. But, why not Anna?"

"Anna feels like she needs to protect me, Adele. She shadowed me around both Scotland and Florida after our dear Lexi was killed. She is very good at tailing and surveilling. Very good. But she is not a trained operator. I am afraid if she thought I was in trouble in Russia, she would try to come and help me. I don't want her hurt. Ever."

"You would trust me to do this, Mack?" Adele asked.

"I have done this sort of thing since before you were born, Adele. I have become fairly good at reading people. Yes, I would trust you. Just as I trust you to keep this to yourself unless you get a call from Tomás. If you get a call, you cannot tell Anna where I was. You have to protect her from trying to help me. If a call comes, it will be too late anyway."

She leaned over and took one of his hands and held it as she cried softly. She felt very drawn to this man who was at once gentle and very deadly. His very presence made her feel safe.

MacLachlan put his other hand over hers and they sat for a while. Her tears dried, leaving mere tracks on her cheeks. He was taken with her sincerity and emotion.

"Don't worry, little one. I am very hard to kill. Russians have tried it, Hezbollah many times. Others. This will just be another adventure. You will see. I will stop by Leuven and take the two of you out to dinner on the way back through. Or fly you all to my wee cottage in Scotland, or the cabin in Valley of Virginia. Or Florida before I sell it."

"It would be wonderful. I liked it when you called me little one. It was so endearing. You are a very special man, Mack. Anna says you make the world a safer place."

"I think she believes it to be so. But I also think she lets her feelings for me exaggerate my capabilities," he said.

"Do you love her?" Adele asked.

"Of course. I love you also, though we hardly know one another. Anna and I have a love born of friendship and trust. It's not a little cottage with roses and wee bairns frolicking about in the garden type of love."

"I love her, too. And you. And this exciting lifestyle. It's right out of a book or movie. And I'm living it with bigger than life people. So, I am going to take whatever classes in university or like Anna did to learn the skills necessary to be one of you."

MacLachlan nodded and smiled at her. *What's not to like with this one?* he thought.

"How old are you, Adele? Twenty-one?"

"I tell people I am eighteen sometimes and twenty-one others. Really, I am twenty-four. I started college late," she said. "May I ask one more question before we head back to the train station?"

"Sure," he replied.

"Is what you are going to do related to Nisa or her family?"

"Adele, this is the kind of thing where what you don't know cannot be used by investigators. You can pass any interrogations if you are totally unaware. Whether it is or isn't related to the Faheems, I don't want you in a compromised position if Interpol or someone comes knocking at your door. Anna either. My lack of an answer is not distrust of either of you. It is purely for your safety."

"I understand, Mack."

"We better go back to the station now."

They drove to the Helsinki Central Station, and he pulled up to the curb.

"Thanks for the talk and the delicious meal!" she said then surprised him by leaning over and kissing him on the lips. He got out and walked around and opened her door for her. She kissed him again and walked away. Like a cowboy at the end of a movie, she did not look back. Anna was training her well.

MacLachlan checked the deliveries as soon as he got back. He examined the new Russian Army issue carbine and pistol and their ammunition. He left the rifle broken down for storage. He looked at the shoulder fired RPG7V2 rocket launcher and the four rockets. From reading the Cyrillic lettering on the cases, he determined two were regular high explosive and two were the hyperbaric rockets.

He measured the disassembled rifle and the RPG7V2. He would buy a backpack tomorrow which would be capable of carrying all the weaponry on his back. The total weight would not exceed forty pounds, he figured. He would not know exactly how he would get to the pharmaceutical company manufacturing site until he spoke with Elias's cousin. Would he take him? Probably not. Maybe a motor bike. He had used one years ago to transit Russian-controlled East Germany on a mission. He could buy one small enough to take in the truck, dump the weapons after use and ride back across the border to Finland.

He opened the envelope with the passport, driving license, credit card and various other cards needed to make a wallet look genuine. He also looked at the FSB card in his Russian cover name like the rest of the credentials. He smiled and tried not to think about his life, no matter how short, if he was arrested with it in his pocket.

MacLachlan came away from this day duly impressed with the young French woman. Even at the slightly older age, she was mature, and her thinking showed insight and breadth. He smiled. It was a shame she was not twenty or twenty-five years older.

All these smart and truly beautiful women, and none to enjoy life with. He likened it to the old "water, water, everywhere, and not a drop to drink", line from Coleridge's Rime of the Ancient Mariner.

He wondered if he had struck at the root of what had been bothering him.

"No, he was MacLachlan. Something like this would not throw his equilibrium off." Or so he told himself, proving how naïve a worldly, well-adjusted human could be in matters of the mind...and, heart.

Having dismissed this line of thought, he carefully hid the credentials, guns, launcher and rockets and sat out in his folding chair and smoked his pipe. He stayed out in daylight until almost midnight before retiring to the bed in the camper. Helsinki had its own version of White Days, like St. Petersburg. He was anxious to get this contract fulfilled, but there was absolutely not a thing he could do to expedite it. The almost constant daylight would add greatly to the risk of an already high-risk mission.

He ate an even healthier diet than normal and ran five days a week.

MacLachlan was not sure yet how circumstances would affect his exfiltration from Russia, so he wanted to be ready for the most extreme cases. He expected the temps to range in the low 40 F. range by the time he got there. He picked up worn work clothes at a second-hand store in Helsinki. He had some lightweight hiking boots which were well broken in and passable as work boots. Like his dress shoes, this pair also had a lightweight titanium toe cap, making them lethal for head kicks and painful for all others.

While he still had some weeks left before leaving, he researched the latest information on re-entering Finland. His Russian passport would require a visa, which he did not want to draw attention by requesting.

He called Anna and asked for a passport and driving license from Canada. The forger should use his bearded file photo and the name Guy Vachon from Montreal. He knew there would be a surcharge for speed and was prepared to pay it.

He received it and an invoice for five thousand Euros a week later. As were the other credentials from this man, these were perfect.

MacLachlan used the new Canadian credentials when he purchased a Dual Sport Honda XR 650 L dirt and road bike. It was several years old, and the finish was faded and scarred. Just as he wanted it to be. The mechanicals seemed perfect, and the mileage was reasonable. He did not want something shiny and too new looking.

He picked up a helmet from the used bike dealer and a simple black jacket of factory distressed leather.

The days passed and the daylight got shorter. When it became almost what he was used to in the US, he contacted Elias about meeting with his cousin.

The three men met for lunch in the restaurant Elias chose the first time. Elias had his new white noise toy and energized it immediately.

MacLachlan resolved to feel out Ulvar Koskella a bit before getting into details.

"We will have to discuss details in a more private location. The gist of the matter is I'd like to ride with you on one of your fish deliveries and carry a motorbike in your truck, as well as two packages of these dimensions," MacLachlan said and handed a slip of paper with the dimensions of two boxes. One for the guns, the other for the rocket launcher and four rockets. He did not disclose what the contents would be to Ulvar.

"These items are things to sell, but not drugs or money. I want to be taken to within thirty-five kilometers of the town of Bavinck. Do you know it?" MacLachlan asked, deliberately choosing a town his research showed to be about forty kilometers south of the main route to St. Petersburg. Petrovia, unmentioned, was thirty kilometers in the opposite direction on the same road.

"Yes, I know the intersection where I could drop you. It is about the distance you mentioned," Ulvar said in English.

"Will I be bringing you back?" he asked.

"No. I will ride the dirt bike back. I will not have any sort of contraband with me by then. I understand it is not difficult for one with my country of origin passport to enter Finland without a visa," MacLachlan said without mentioning what his country of origin was.

---

MACLACHLAN CALLED Ulvar Koskella the day his calculation determined the Helsinki area daylight and darkness were the same.

"What's your schedule, Ulvar? And what do you think taking me, a little contraband, and a dirt bike to the intersection heading to Petrovia is worth?"

Ulvar thought he was highballing the amount. The figure he mentioned was several thousand Euros less than MacLachlan was prepared to pay.

MacLachlan did not want to jump at the amount too quickly and make the smuggler think he could have gotten much more. Finally, MacLachlan agreed. Ulvar wanted the money in cash before they left. He said he did not want to get captured with such an amount on him. MacLachlan agreed again.

The next day, he hit several ATMs and obtained the amount. He put a rubber band around the wad of Euros.

Tonight was the night.

MacLachlan dressed in the old work clothes he had purchased. Purchased carefully. The trousers were faded black jeans, the shirt was an old dark gray work shirt, and the cap was a navy-blue stocking cap. He had the Russian credentials in the pocket of his new, but factory aged black leather jacket. The re-entry Canadian passport and license were in his work boots under the inner sole. He had a small, fixed blade Morakniv knife in his pocket. A knife which every man in Scandinavia had several. They were inexpensive, razor sharp and lasted some time beyond forever. He added a pair of non-prescription tortoise-shell glasses. He had been careful to get gun oil and dirt under his short fingernails and in the creases of his hands.

MacLachlan did as he ordered his team to do in the Czech Republic. He did not touch the rifle, pistol, launcher, rockets, or ammunition without gloves on. The "work" gloves were really tactical gloves. They were thin, but with a cut-proof mesh liner. There was an area built out slightly over each knuckle. Each slight protrusion was filled with lead powder. The palms could handle grabbing the blade of the sharpest of knives. The lead knuckles would make one of MacLachlan's devastating blows even more damaging. He was just upping his edge with the gloves and titanium boot toes. This was a solo op in what, to an American operator, may be the most dangerous place one could be.

With the armaments and some dark replacement clothes in his new backpack he strapped on, MacLachlan fired up the Honda dirt bike and roared out of the campground.

He rendezvoused with Ulvar Koskella at their planned pull-off. In the darkness, they loaded the weapons into the back of the truck. Ulvar covered the two boxes with layers of heavy plastic and duct tape. He dumped several buckets of crushed ice on top, then fish, then more ice. They put the bike between the large metal fish lockers and secured it to eye bolts on the inside walls of the truck with bungee cords.

MacLachlan balled the leather jacket up and stuffed it into the backpack to replace the now-missing weaponry boxes. It was not as filled out quite as much as before, but he and Ulvar were the only ones who knew.

Ulvar restarted the diesel of the beat-up Iveco truck, and they pulled out onto the main highway.

The game was afoot.

MacLachlan used a burner phone to make his first check in call to Tomás. In a bit over two hours, Ulvar pulled over to the side in a dark, wooded area. The truck was not visible from the road. Anyone seeing it would assume the driver had pulled over to relieve himself or take a nap before driving into town and unloading his cargo.

First, the bike was out. MacLachlan donned the leather jacket and tactical gloves. Ulvar removed the RPG-7V2 box first, then the one containing the guns and ammunition.

MacLachlan shook hands with Ulvar and thanked him. He watched the Finn pull off onto the main road and out of sight. He was now alone in Russia with highly illegal weapons. Alone and on a suicide mission. MacLachlan gave it a glimmer of thought and then dismissed it from his mind. He was in full operational mode now, concentrating only on the mission and getting the hell back to Finland afterwards.

MacLachlan wiped the two parts of the AK-15K carbine but left them separated. He put them in the backpack with the screw on suppressor. He then loaded four thirty round magazines with 7.62x39 cartridges. He dropped those in the backpack. He did the same with the RPG-7V2 and rockets. The last wipe down and loading was the new Kalashnikov Lebedev 9mm pistol. He put the pistol in its inside the waistband holster and the three loaded 16 round magazines in his left jeans pocket. MacLachlan ripped the labels off the two boxes and tore the boxes apart. He put the cardboard in the brush and burned the labels.

MacLachlan started the Honda 650 and drove onto the highway, soon to turn left and proceed north to Petrovia. The bike had a phone clip on the handlebar.

MacLachlan dialed in the address of the Petro-vitch Pharmaceuticals site on Google Maps and settled in for a quiet ride. The off-road bike was much quieter than his dark green Mustang. But, then again, most things with engines were.

He was riding slowly. He realized how cold it was getting. Riding the bike instead of being inside in the heated truck cab was significantly colder. Temperatures were usually around the low to mid-forties in this part of Russia now. It felt a lot colder.

MacLachlan looked at the burner phone for the time. It was just eight PM. Much too early to attack. He would have to conduct surveillance first but thought more like three AM would be more appropriate. But many variables could, and probably would, affect his plan.

He drove the bike off the road and hid it under a tree. He did a Man Overboard press on the Helsinki-purchased Garmin GPS to be able to find the bike in the woods in the dark. He left his iPhone and original GPS at the campground. Their history would tell the Russians far too much about who he was and from where he came.

With the backpack on, he proceeded down the road, staying at least fifty feet off the road into the woods. He walked carefully and quietly without his high lumen flashlight on. Most of the vehicles were going against him. *So, away from the Petrovitch site,* he thought to himself.

"It seems like they are ending a shift without another starting. There should be an overlap in cars arriving roughly equaling ones leaving. So, perhaps there is not another shift tonight. Which would be perfect!"

He knew he would have to wait until attack time to make sure.

He heard a heavy engine and rough tires on the tarmac.

Turning, he saw an army truck passing him and going towards the Pharmaceutical building. From what he could see in the dark, the troops looked sharp, they were not lazing around in the back of the truck.

If he had a list of what he did not want to see tonight, the truck would be at the top of it. It had a whole patrol in it by his best estimation.

"Damn! I really don't want to spend a rocket on them, but to get out of here alive after sending a rocket or two in a window, I may have to."

The truck did not look like an armored personnel carrier. Just a five-ton with dual rear wheels and a canvas cover over a flat bed. One of the HE rockets would scatter pieces of it over quite a debris field.

His plan had been to use the suppressed carbine to open a hole in each window he planned to lob a rocket into. Now, maybe not. Trained troops deployed outside may hear and recognize a suppressed shot and begin responding before he could fire several rockets. He would watch and try to see where they based in the building.

If they set up a perimeter outside and used the truck as a comms point, he would have to take out the truck early on. Anyone in the building, like a chemist working late or cleaning crew, would not respond to explosions or shots with the trained alacrity of a soldier.

MacLachlan hiked quietly to the perimeter of the grounds and set up in a copse of trees to watch.

The soldiers did just as he expected. They fanned

out around the building. Luckily, none were assigned to patrol inside the surrounding wood line. Where he was.

Nor did they mount a mobile patrol. It appeared they took stationary positions every couple hundred yards.

*Bad tactics!* MacLachlan thought. Some of those troopers will be dozing by two or three o'clock. He suspected a sergeant or lieutenant would patrol around the perimeter and check on his guards.

There was a bank of lights on in the southeastern quarter of the building. They were on the third floor.

They could have indicated two things. The section was the one being cleaned first. Or, it was the laboratory, which was his desired target. It was also the location most apt to have chemicals which would exacerbate the effect of his rockets.

MacLachlan knew he was making a lot of assumptions here, but they were based on all he had to go on.

His hide in the copse of trees was a five-minute sprint away from the dirt bike. More importantly, it was seventy-five yards from the lit windows. It was about the same from the military truck.

It was pretty definite now. He would have to take out the truck to have any chance of getting away.

He looked at his phone for the time. He shaded its glow with his hand. He left the stainless Rolex Oyster Perpetual watch at the campground, hidden in the trailer. It was ten o'clock.

The optimum time for a sneak attack has been considered around four or five AM. The Apaches knew it and used it with great advantage. The more recent determinations called it the Third Phase of Deep Sleep. It was non-rapid eye movement (REM) sleep. It often occurs before dawn.

It he waited for the non-REM period, the last part of his escape to Finland would occur in daylight. He knew from many years of experience night was his friend. Unlike many, he operated virtually as well in the dark as in the light.

He decided to bump his attack back several hours. He would begin at two AM, not four-thirty or five. What he would give up in slower enemy response, he would gain in escape and evasion. Or so he hoped. Deadly ops were a throw of the dice. You just never knew, as Will Grafton often said.

He continued to watch the site and the soldiers. The rifle was assembled and loaded at his side. The rocket launcher was also. No one else drove into the compound, nor did anyone leave. The personnel appeared to be stable for the night.

MacLachlan decided to take a quick rest. He set his phone alarm to vibrate at two AM. Rifle over his lap, he leaned the backpack against a tree. He laid back against it and was asleep in several minutes.

He felt the vibration in his pocket. It seemed like he had drifted off minutes ago. It had been over an hour and a half. But it was worth it. He felt rested.

It was one o'clock. He pulled the RPG-7V2 to full firing mode. He armed it with a HE rocket.

Knowing the device had blowback, MacLachlan moved away from the tree, leaving open space behind himself and the rear of the rocket launcher.

He took careful aim at the military truck. It was an easy target. Shooting fish in a barrel.

He fired the HE rocket and watched its flame and trail as it soared towards the truck. When it hit, the five-ton truck raised five feet in the air and exploded.

MacLachlan immediately rearmed the launcher with a thermobaric warhead. He fired into a lit window, rearmed and fired another thermobaric rocket into a lit window seven windows down.

The damage was readily apparent. The floor of the building was fully afire. He could see the ceiling collapsing in giant chunks of burning material. There was no fire suppression system working. Either one had not been installed, or as he hoped, the blast destroyed it.

Soldiers around the building had sprung into action two minutes ago when the truck blew. They were running around sans officers or non-comms to direct them.

The soldiers represented a threat to MacLachlan and he knew it. He raised the AK-15K and dropped ten before anyone knew they were being sniped by a suppressed rifle.

He took a series of fast cellphone photos and a video with his high-grade burner phone. He sent them to Schutte via encrypted email.

Still wearing his gloves, he strapped the backpack on, slung the rifle and began to run as fast as he could in the dark and between trees. He had the RPG in one hand, the remaining HE rocket in the other. The burner phone, now of no further use to him, was in a jacket pocket. He would either make it to Finland by the check-in time tonight or be in Russian custody. Or dead.

He went straight to the Honda dirt bike without

having to use the GPS. He started it and slowly rode it down the edge of the two-lane highway to and from the site. Never, never rush away from a scene of a crime you have committed. MacLachlan had committed a big one. He had probably killed fifteen Russian soldiers outside and destroyed their vehicle.

He may have killed scientists inside and had a building well headed for collapse due to immolation.

After a mile, he slowed and threw the burner phone as far as he could into the woods. It had no PII, personally identifiable information, on it nor a single print. It did have the evidentiary photos of the building, but the emails had automatically been deleted.

MacLachlan drove on at approximately forty miles per hour. He still thought in miles and yards whenever it was just him. The Marine Corps had not changed to kilometers until well after his active duty.

He saw a glow off the trees in front of him and turned to look behind.

There were two vehicles closing fast. He cut the light on the front of the dirt bike and pulled off the road to the right at a curve.

He dumped the bike and pulled the RPG out and armed it with the last rocket, an HE.

The two vehicles came around the curve. They stopped. It was obvious from the straight road there was no vehicle ahead. So, it must be in the woods here.

MacLachlan listened and quickly assessed the situation with his fair Russian. These two carloads of soldiers were unhurt at his rocket attack and rifle fire. Perhaps they were around back. There was a senior sergeant or officer commanding them. The cars were conscripted from the lot.

These guys, as MacLachlan had noticed before were moving into position and handled their weapons like operators. Not like grunts. Maybe Spetsnaz. Worse, they were acting like Alphas or Vegas. The Russian version of Tier-1 operators.

MacLachlan did what he had to do. He fired an HE rocket almost point blank into the front car. It lifted up and flipped over, parts becoming shrapnel creating a large debris field. Shrapnel landed all around him. It did much worse than just landing for the men on the road.

Four men remained standing and three started raking the woods where he was with selector switches on full auto. He knew most were wounded and admired their tenacity.

MacLachlan rolled behind a big tree and tried to make his six feet one inch and almost two hundred pounds much smaller.

One bullet hit him in the left shoulder. He thought it was a through-and-through. It was dead-ened and did not hurt. But boy howdy, it sure would soon. Real soon. He knew. He had already been shot there.

He returned fire with one hand, raking the muzzle low and cutting off one soldier at the shin level. He fell screaming. Another salvo of shots came his way, but he had already moved ten feet, rolling on his bloody shoulder. He was on his last rifle magazine. He knew he could not run with the rifle, using it with one hand. He was down to the pistol. He left the rifle behind the log he had jumped, or maybe fallen, over.

He was not sure which and did not give a damn right now.

He pulled the pistol, and trigger finger on the frame below the slide, began to run.

He could hear the leader, whatever his rank, giving orders and spurring his men on.

MacLachlan ran as fast and far as he could. The others kept up but did not gain. Whether not gaining was by choice or not was not clear to the American.

He had brought several of the Prague hostage rescue contract flash bang grenades and the last smoke grenade in his pocket. They were primarily for when SWAT breached closed space and needed to disorient. He figured tonight or after dawn, he would use them creatively on these guys. He decided they were good. They stood and shot under fire. They did not flinch. They were disciplined.

The leader had two choices as MacLachlan saw it. Leave one man with the severely wounded one and pursue him with just one. Or leave the man to administer his own first aid or bleed out. Which would leave three total coming after MacLachlan.

From the voices, it appeared he chose the second option. He had mission-focus discipline.

MacLachlan had a small Quik Clot pad he could put on the exit wound in his shoulder. He could not take the time to do it until he was either farther ahead or well hidden.

He sprinted across an open space in the woods.

Maybe it was time for an ambush. He had to reduce the odds against him.

The three men came to the edge of the woods. He

could hear low voices discussing their options, but not discern what they were saying.

It quickly became apparent. They spread out and began to cross twenty or thirty feet apart. Harder targets.

MacLachlan, on two knees, hurled a flashbang grenade like a fast pitch in a game of hardball. If one was going to play this game. It would have to be hardball.

The grenade slammed into an operator and exploded with a flash and terrific concussion.

MacLachlan heard a scream but had already dropped behind a downed tree. He swung the large pistol towards the farthest man and fired a fast controlled pair at him.

The man went down as MacLachlan rolled away from his firing point which was immediately filled with incoming bullets.

With a quick assessment, MacLachlan determined the officer or non-commissioned officer was still his biggest threat. The degree of threat afforded him by the man hit with the flashbang was still unknown. Flashbangs were designed to scare and disorient, not to be anti-personnel. Yet one exploding as it slammed into you had to deliver heat and shrapnel. And the trooper caught it dead on the center of mass. At the very least, he was wounded and slowed.

MacLachlan stood behind a tree and turned and ran. Ran for his very life.

The leader said something to the flashbang recipient. MacLachlan could not hear what, nor the response. He ran on.

He estimated they had covered several miles. He

had not heard the primary and sole person chasing him speak into a radio or cell phone. Unless he missed it—and he thought he had not—the man had no reinforcements on the way. He was sure fire engines and more people, police or military or both, were en route.

But they would not know one or two of their own were chasing the perpetrator through the woods.

MacLachlan was running parallel to the road into the site. He was already several miles away from his two-wheeled source of transportation. And several hundred miles away from the Finnish border. Things were not looking good for a happy retirement.

He saw a glow in the sky. Like the raid near Prague to free his client and his family, there was going to be a blood sky.

MacLachlan did not interpret what, if any omen, it offered. He was not concerned by such things. The sky was the color of blood. So what? He ran on, hearing the sirens of fire trucks in the distance.

Why would they run sirens on a deserted two-lane road to nowhere? Go figure.

He pulled the plastic water bottle out of his jacket pocket and took a swallow.

He doubted his pursuer had water. He also doubted he had an energy bar like MacLachlan did.

He could not feel blood trickling down his back anymore. It was either just seeping or had stopped bleeding. Odd for a probable thirty caliber wound at high velocity, he thought.

He had been hit by the same round almost two years ago during Kate's rescue. She had killed the shooter, a Spetsnaz Alpha, albeit former. Very former.

The redhead's rounds had rendered him dead well before he toppled forward and hit the deck.

Kate. He did not have time to ponder about her now. Her uncle was another matter. It was thirteen hours from his next check-in. He wondered where he would be then.

The wound did not seem to be holding him back anywhere near as much as he expected. Maybe it was a glancing wound instead of a through-and-through. He hoped so. He would try to find out once he stopped to rest.

The damn Russian was still after him. He was close enough MacLachlan could hear him running through the trees and brush periodically. He suspected the senior man would be a tough one to ambush.

MacLachlan heard a helicopter coming. He hoped it was not equipped with FLIR. He would be located and targeted immediately if it was.

And it was. It was Russian Army green and hovered overhead. Guiding his pursuer directly to him. MacLachlan assumed a responding emergency vehicle had stopped for either the guy he had shot in the legs or the flash bang victim and had been briefed. It really did not matter.

What mattered was it was daylight with a blood red sky, and he had an army helicopter overhead. And a very tough special ops soldier closing in.

He moved towards the road, then stopped in a deep gully under some trees.

The Russian was coming. MacLachlan could hear him. Then, see him.

He was around forty-five, tall and muscular. He

had a pistol in hand. It was not the Kalashnikov Lebedev. Nor a Makarov.

MacLachlan shot him twice in the center of mass. He went down hard.

Then, he got back up, really pissed. He was wearing a vest.

MacLachlan shot at his right kneecap with a controlled pair as the man was aiming the strange pistol. This time he went down and did not arise. Even a man this tough could not hide the pain and anguish of having a +P+ round strike him.

The man's pistol was too far to reach.

MacLachlan approached carefully, well aware of the helo hovering above.

As he approached, the man pulled a fixed blade knife and lunged forward. MacLachlan went down on top of him. He grappled with the man for the seven-inch blade knife and got ahold of his wrist with two hands.

MacLachlan's shoulder felt like it was on fire now.

He relinquished his right-hand grasp long enough to swing his elbow into the Russian's jaw. Nothing.

So, he throat punched the man, who began to make the expected croaking noises.

MacLachlan took the knife and stepped back as the man began to recover.

He had an idea to use a bit of disinformation and muddy the water.

MacLachlan withdrew the cred wallet with his perfect fake FSB identification and held it so the man could see it.

The Russian showed total confusion. He knew what the ID was. He had a similar one.

MacLachlan held his finger to his lips for silence. The man nodded, still confused.

MacLachlan kicked him in the side of the head with the titanium-toed boot and sent him to slumber land. Or hell. MacLachlan did not know which. He also did not have much time. He noticed his first shot had missed the knee altogether. His second was a bit off but hit the popliteal artery.

His honor would not let a worthy warrior bleed to death, so MacLachlan spent a minute which could be potentially fatal for himself. He fashioned a tourniquet above the bleeding artery. He made a big red T with blood on the man's forehead to catch the attention of paramedics a tourniquet was deployed.

He took out the single grenade left. The smoke grenade. He pulled the pin and tossed it nearby. It immediately drew the helo.

MacLachlan left the unconscious man and staggered towards the road.

An unmarked Russian Lada sedan pulled off the road near MacLachlan's position.

He again pulled the FSB credential and held it high as he approached the car, saying "FSB" in Russian.

Two plain clothes officers, likely from the agency themselves, got out of the car and approached him, guns drawn. The helo was seeking a landing zone to check on the man down. To see whether he was the fugitive or the Spetsnaz.

Tired and almost staggering, MacLachlan

approached the men who were now beginning to focus on the credential identical to their own.

From ten feet, MacLachlan took advantage of their diverted attention and performed his fastest draw ever. He killed both where they stood.

MacLachlan slid into the still running sedan and did a bootlegger turn and headed away from the action.

He knew the car would be sought. He had to exchange it for another. Very soon.

A marked police car approached, lights and siren going.

MacLachlan slid the Lada into a position perpendicular to the lane, effectively blocking the police car. He flipped the light switches on the Lada and blue emergency lights began flashing in the grille and upper center of the windshield.

MacLachlan stepped out, FSB creds held high and yelled "FSB!" in Russian. Something local cops would listen to.

They got out and approached him, hands on undrawn guns. Big mistake.

He drew and killed them both. He dragged both over to the Lada and pushed one of them in and closed the door.

MacLachlan put the other into the rear seat of the police car. He got into the Hyundai police car and turned it around. In the best Russian police fashion, he took off away from the attack site lights flashing and siren screaming.

He put "nearest hospital" into his browser and followed the directions.

Twenty minutes later, he was pulling into the Petrovia Regional Hospital.

He killed the siren as a nurse and several orderlies came out to meet him.

MacLachlan flashed the FSB card and falsely identified himself again. He said he needed to call in, using garbled Russian and walked off.

The hospital had a parking garage. It was the shopping center he wanted. He picked an old Zil. He knew older cars were the easiest to hotwire. And, he had neither a screwdriver nor pliers. Easier was not only better, it was mandatory to his condition and circumstances. He suspected this faded out, dinged up car would not attract the attention of anyone but a junk dealer.

Two minutes later, he had thrown the backpack into the rear seat and was driving painfully on the main road towards the border and Helsinki.

———

WHEN THE ROAD sign read "5 Km to Finnish Border", MacLachlan pulled the decrepit Zil sedan to the shoulder.

He raised the hood. It did not have emergency flashers. Walking behind an inevitable McDonald's, he dropped the pistol, remaining mags, and FSB and Russian credentials into two different dumpsters. He walked to an area behind a nearby building and dug a small hole with the Morakniv; he wiped the knife and pulled the gloves he had had on for hours off. He buried both and kicked dirty, oily soil into the hole and stepped on it to trample it down.

He was now "clean".

MacLachlan walked the remaining way to the border and crossed as a backpacker on holiday. He used his Canadian passport. "Everyone loves Canadians," he grinned. He surely did love them. Being a Canadian by fake credential had gotten him in and out of a lot of bad places with a smile over the years.

Well into town, he called for an Uber and rode to the campground in style. Not much style. At least he was cramped into a subcompact but not walking.

He had to painfully peel the shirt away from his bullet wound. He washed it thoroughly. It was a through and through wound.

"Very damn lucky!" he said aloud. Putting the jacket back on, he walked to the camp store and bought a pint bottle of the cheapest vodka he could find.

Outside, but out of sight of other campers, he poured the entire bottle down his shoulder. The pain was excruciating. The benefit, he hoped, was worth it.

He called his Czech friend and advised he was fine and there would be no more check-in calls.

MacLachlan slept fitfully during the night. His shoulder began to hurt and burn. It became hot to the touch. Heat signaled infection to him from past experience.

He called Tomás Studrich back the next morning in a great deal of pain. Pain multiple aspirins would not begin to touch.

"Tomás, I am back in Helsinki. Is the doctor who took such good care of me when we brought Kate out of the Hezbollah art depository two years ago still around?"

"Why do I think you left something very important out when you called me yesterday? Are you shot
or stabbed?" his friend asked.

"I am shot. A little bit."

"There is no such thing as "shot a little bit".
Where is this little shot you have?" Tomás asked
impatiently.

"My left shoulder. It is a through-and-through.
Overnight it became very painful and got hot around
the wound. I doused it in vodka to kill the germs."

"You should have doused it in hydrogen peroxide
and drank the damn vodka, Mack."

"The vodka was so cheap and strong you could
run your car on it."

"Maybe my old car. My new Mercedes is a diesel.
Anyway, let me call my doctor friend and see what he
says. I will call you back soon," he said and hung the
receiver of his 1960's dial phone up, leaving
MacLachlan with his iPhone still pressed against
his ear.

He looked at his old friend of over thirty years,
the Rolex, and saw he could take three more aspirin
and did so.

Tomás called him back an hour later with good
news.

"My doctor who treated you before has a medical
school friend. He practices just 32 km outside of
Helsinki. Can you get there on your own?"

"I can. I have a nice diesel Volvo wagon. All-
wheel drive, too," MacLachlan said.

"Screw your mode of transportation. He will be
at his surgery for another two hours and is expecting
you. I will text you his name and surgery address.

Whatever he charges will be the standard rate. My friend says tripling it is appropriate in these circumstances. I haven't heard of anything big where you just were. At least it has not hit in Prague's news. But I assume you are a wanted criminal there."

"Not necessarily. Someone is, but I am thinking it won't be me," MacLachlan said with more than a modicum of belief.

"Go program your computer-like telephone with the address and get underway. I don't know what Helsinki rush hour is like, so don't mess around."

"Thanks, Tomás. No need for Kate to know about any of this, right? It will just worry her."

"Of course there is a need. She loves you. She just has no idea how much. You should tell her sometime before you are in a wheelchair and being fed baby food."

"Okay, thanks again." MacLachlan hung up first this time. He knew exactly where the Czech's next phone call was going and there was nothing he could do about it. Furthermore, he bet he was paying for it on the new SAT phone and subscription he had given Kate's Uncle Tomás.

---

"I AM SENDING you a special email, Niece," Tomás said on his brief call to Kate two minutes later. It was his way of saying it was too sensitive to discuss without encryption.

"Is everything okay?" she asked.

"More or less. Your boyfriend has been quite busy. Are you aware?"

"No," she said truthfully, "I am not." But she had a grave suspicion. Her uncle had already severed the connection.

Early this morning, her tactically trained analyst on the Russia desk briefed her on an attack on a Russian pharmaceutical laboratory in Petrovia, just outside of St. Petersburg.

The lab building had been rocketed. A Spetsnaz vehicle and fifteen or twenty troopers had died in the attack, which included a firefight and pursuit. Chatter suggested a rogue FSB agent had done it, but no motive could be found. Her analyst had dug deeper and determined the company had just lost a possibly multi-billion Euro contract to a Dubai-owned company. She only knew vague facts, but Mack had her uncle assist him in recovering a rich guy from Dubai in the Czech Republic not long ago. It had to be related.

"Rogue FSB agent, my eye! Rogue security contractor, more likely!" she said aloud in her sound-proof office within a large Sensitive Compartmented Information Facility or SCIF.

At the same time, the rogue was driving painfully towards Kerava, Finland listening to Johan Schutte on an encrypted call.

"First off, the remainder of our deal has been taken care of. I am sending you an email of our deposit of the second half to the cancer research fund. Secondly, my boss is thrilled with your work. Russian papers say the laboratory building was virtually destroyed by a rocket attack. The COVID research wing was decimated. Eight scientists were killed as well as most of a patrol of Spetsnaz on scene and in a running gunfight. There is an unconfirmed rumor an FSB agent coordinated the attack for a reason as yet unknown. He and a team estimated to be at least twenty in number have escaped, though there is a large manhunt underway now," Schutte said.

MacLachlan laughed harder than he had in months. The laughing hurt his shoulder like a hot blade going in.

"Priceless. Hey, how is the illness you were suffering from when I saw you last?"

"It is still painful, but not debilitating. How are you after your recent trip?"

"I fear, Johan, I picked up a case of the bug you caught. I'm on the way to a private clinic now to get it addressed. Nothing major. A couple of aspirin and the doc will call me in the morning, I suspect."

"Take care of yourself. I hope your friend in the jungle discovers something world-changing, Mack."

"Me, too, Johan. Until next time," and he disconnected.

MacLachlan arrived at Kerava and quickly found the surgery. He went in and was seated only a moment before being walked into an examining room.

A nurse helped him take his shirt off and used something which felt like hydrochloric acid to re-clean the wound. It made the vodka seem mild.

"Gunshot?" she asked.

"Maybe. There were some people target shooting where I was hiking," he lied.

The doctor came in and ushered the nurse out.

"Well, let's take a look. Do you know the caliber and type of gun?"

"I think it was an AK. Probably .30 caliber, 7.62x39."

The doctor measured with a small ruler.

"I am guessing .22. Maybe 5.56 NATO or the Russian variation. If I am right, it's why you walked in instead of being carried in. A .30 would have made a bigger hole in your shoulder."

"Do you think it will prove debilitating?" MacLachlan asked.

"It will be stiff for quite a while. I would recommend physical therapy starting within a week. It needs to rest a while right now.

I am going to stitch it up. It will not need plastic or corrective surgery beyond stitching. You are very lucky. What did you do before any first aid?"

"I ran about fifteen miles," MacLachlan said.

"Were you scared or was someone chasing you?" the doctor asked.

"Both."

"I see," he said, though he really did not. "Did someone drive you here? You may not feel like driving after the stitching. I will give you some pain deadener, then something to sleep."

"I will drive myself. I didn't feel like running fifteen miles either. Sometimes, you have to do whatever is required, Doctor. Please avoid narcotics. I'd rather have the pain than have my ability to react affected."

"Are you some sort of policeman or something?" the doctor asked.

"Or something. It doesn't matter. Lots of us have dangerous occupations. Doctors, too. How dangerous is an emergency room? Pretty dangerous I'd say. I just like to be alert."

"We can do it. No narcotics. Just paracetamol-based," he said using the generic European name for Tylenol.

"Thanks. I was going to head south towards the Czech Republic with my wagon and caravan. Do you recommend I wait here a week, then start physical therapy here?"

"I absolutely do. You should plan on staying here for at least another month. One week to let the stitches settle in and three to start PT on your shoulder. Otherwise, you may have trouble with it for the rest of your life."

"Do you have a physical therapist you can refer? I am at a campground—a holiday park—about a half hour east of Helsinki," MacLachlan asked.

The doctor scribbled something down. The only thing MacLachlan could read was the phone number.

"What's her first name?"

"Neea."

"Okay, I will call her from the car."

"I really advise calling her from a hotel room in Kerava. We have plenty. Take the meds I am going to give you and go to bed. If you feel up to it in the morning, eat breakfast and drive back to your caravan. If not, spend another night and rest, rest, rest," the doctor said. "It is what you need the most to recover properly."

"You're the doc. I will look for a room."

"My receptionist will get you one. She will make up your bill for today. The medications in the bag the nurse is preparing are all manufacturer samples. Gratis."

"On the bill. I would like to come back in here and pay you in Euros."

"Cash always simplifies accounting," the doctor said.

While the nurse was preparing the white paper bag of prescription meds, MacLachlan went out and waited until the receptionist finished his bill. He turned his back, tripled it in Euros and went down the hall. He handed the bill and the cash to the doctor, thanked him and walked to reception after the nurse gave him his bag of meds.

On the way out, the receptionist gave him a note with the name of a small hotel and directions to it. It appeared, without studying it, to be down the street from the surgery.

It was almost too close to drive, but MacLachlan wanted to park in the hotel lot.

He presented himself at the desk and was given the key to a nice room. The bath and toilets were shared and down the hall. At this point, he did not care a whit.

There was a chemist down the block. MacLachlan went in and purchased a toothbrush, toothpaste, a comb and the current copy of the Helsingin Sanomat. It was a morning paper, so a bit behind. He wanted to see if there was anything about the fire at the Petrovitch Pharmaceuticals in Petrovia. There was not. At least in pictures. Not speaking a word of Finnish, he left the newspaper in the toilet for someone who did.

MacLachlan dutifully took his meds and went to

bed. The mattress was fair, the sheets and pillowcase smelled great. Possibly dried on a line in the sun like his mother used to do on the ranch in Texas when he was a boy.

He slept deeply without dreams. The meds took the edge off the pain in his shoulder.

Studrich would say he should have killed the Spetsnaz. From his uniform, he turned out to be Brigade V or Vega for Vympel. Equal in training to Alpha, V guarded special sites, and was used for paramilitary and covert ops. Having Vympel guarding the pharmaceutical site made perfect sense. But what intel did they have to send them there? He feared he would never know.

The Vega operator was a warrant officer and a warrior.

It was out of respect MacLachlan put the tourniquet on his leg, marked the T for Tourniquet in blood on the Russian's forehead. They locked eyes and MacLachlan squeezed his enemy's shoulder before leaving. Popping the final smoke grenade from the Faheem rescue was risky. But it was the right thing to do. The smoke would bring the helo directly there to help the wounded warrior.

Enemies? Maybe. But it did not mean they should not respect each other. MacLachlan had seen the surprise and appreciation in the man's eyes before he left. He was pretty sure the warrant officer bought the FSB identity. Who else would help him instead of putting a bullet in his brain?

MacLachlan laid there, thinking about this. He finally got up. He felt the shoulder through the new dressing. It was still warm, but not burning hot like yesterday. He would still have to take the antibiotics for the next seven days. The paracetamol painkillers, too.

He went down the hall, showered and shaved his beard off. He would get his usual short haircut later in the day. He would not look like the man who went to Russia and back.

Putting on yesterday's outfit, he walked down to the small restaurant in the hotel and had a rye bread and salmon sandwich and a couple of boiled eggs with strong Finnish coffee.

He felt at least fair. Fair enough to check out and drive back to his camper. By 0930, he was making coffee at the camper.

MacLachlan knew, if he was a cat, he would be on his fifteenth life. Surviving this op was surely a gift from God.

Even he did not know how he walked across the Russian border to Finland as a Canadian hiker. Especially with a rifle wound in his shoulder.

He resolved this would be the last contract he would take other than training for the Community. Of course, he had made the same resolution several times in the last couple of years. This time he really meant it. Just like he had those other times.

He would find a nice, sexy, age appropriate (whatever "age appropriate" means) woman who wanted to be retired with a halfway decent guy and travel, never worrying about money again. How the hell hard could it be?

Well, so far, impossible. He did find one. But she was shot to death by an international assassin. Maybe there is another Lexi out there. She would be worth seeking with the doggedness he used to escape the Russians over the past few days.

He draped an SPF infused fishing shirt over his wounded shoulder and sat out shirtless with hiking shorts. He may end up with a weird suntan, but the warmth felt good. It and the meds made him drowsy and, eschewing OPSEC, he allowed himself a nap.

The physical therapy began a week later. The older Finnish woman reminded him of the Marine drill instructor who helped train him as a young officer at the Quantico officer training school years ago. Tough, gravelly voiced and very effective.

At the end of several weeks, she cut him loose. She made him promise to get another PT to work with him when he got home. Wherever home was.

He figured he should head to Florida first. His trust banker had looked into the value of his property on Casey Key grandfather had left him and sent a vague evaluation of "several million". Maybe more in the great seller's market for upscale Florida waterfront.

MacLachlan did a fast Internet search for private islands in Florida. There were several on the market, but so far up in the millions they may as well have been on the moon.

He went to several recreational vehicle dealers in Helsinki and found a fair price for the travel trailer. He took the offer without quibbling.

A Volvo dealer gave him wholesale for the wagon, and he accepted it. He took an Uber to the airport and booked a two-stop flight on KLM to Miami. It left early the next morning and arrived at Miami dinner time.

With the comfort and rest business class would afford him, he would be up for driving the almost six hours back to Casey Key after arriving. He sent a text in the clear to the couple who looked after his house. When he sold it, he would do something really nice for them after cutting off a good part of their income. He would work some sort of retirement compensation.

If he could risk his life to give a million Euros, or over 1.2 million dollars to charity, he could facilitate a comfortable retirement for lifelong friends upon whom he depended to clean and repair his property.

He called his trust banker and asked him to explore ways and costs of retirement for two friends. Knowing MacLachlan and his financial situation of tax-free stipends in the general hundred thousand range for years, some much higher, and a low-cost lifestyle (okay, the odd exotic car excepted), he was comfortable he could craft something.

Once the Florida decision was made, he was eager to get it done. Since the house and everything in it had been demolished by a bomb, there was nothing left with sentimental value to him. He had some guns and items of his grandparents in the gun safe. He could transport those to wherever he moved in the Bronco. He would let the safe go with the house. The cost of moving it from a second story would exceed the cost of replacing it.

He slept most of the flight home and took a shuttle bus to his now-dusty Bronco. He had prepared for the several hundred-dollar parking fee and paid in cash.

The twin-turbo engine started at the first crank,

its massive 415 pound-feet of torque engine sending out exhaust which rumbled pleasantly.

MacLachlan aimed the SUV north, hit the Alligator Alley portion of I-75 and set the cruise control on eighty.

The gun safe installed between the front buckets had his Special Deputy US Marshal badge and supporting USIC creds, his Intelligence Community SACS badge, and a Walther PDP Compact he was testing as a new everyday carry, or EDP, pistol. He also had his standard three magazines stashed in the safe.

He pulled into his lane on Casey Key around dawn and performed his usual security checks before going in and turning the alarm off.

After a recuperative nap, he went out for breakfast. The refrigerator was cleaned because of the duration of this trip. He came back and put his personal items into the gun safe. He taped notes to the portraits and other paintings which would not go with the house. He had several suits in the closet and some fishing clothes. They could be packed later. He put his Hells Bay flats skiff on its trailer. He would drive to the Keys in the Bronco towing the skiff and leave the Mustang to pick up once things were more settled.

He drove the Mustang around Casey Key and looked for the realtor with the largest number of "SOLD" signs on top level homes. It was one woman who stood head and shoulders above the rest. He called her and arranged a meeting later in the day.

At the meeting, she did an appraisal with local comps and the amount even exceeded what he expected. His grandfather's ten-thousand-dollar investment in the 1930's had done really well.

A bit saddened, but knowing he was doing the right thing for his well-being, MacLachlan signed the sales agreement. He decided to not deal with viewers and had her place a lockbox on the door with the proviso she had to be present at every showing by another realtor.

When she asked his business, he simply said "investor" and left her wondering.

They shook hands. As she was leaving, she gave him the card of a mid-Keys realtor named Kelly from her firm and highly recommended her.

MacLachlan hitched the skiff to the Bronco. He put his clothes in and a couple of long guns.

Next stop, Florida Keys.

## 6

The trip to the Keys pulling his skiff was as fast as it would have been without trailing the lightweight boat behind.

As soon as he passed the funeral home which he had hired to take care of Alexandria Campbell after her murder, his mood plummeted. It was just damn wrong for her to die unarmed in a supermarket after the life she had led. He missed her a lot and always would.

He drove to Marathon and pulled into a seafood joint for dinner. Having an SUV or pickup with a boat on the back put him in the majority in the dirt and shell parking lot.

He went in, tanned and wearing a Columbia shirt and tan shorts. He left the beard and the salt and pepper beard fit in too.

MacLachlan ordered a blackened grouper sandwich and a side order of conch fritters. He washed it down with a draft beer so cold it hurt his teeth. The further south on the island chain he went, the more his mood improved. He found a motel with a launching ramp and booked three nights. He moved in by hanging four suits, some titanium toed dress shoes and a half closet full of informal wear.

The next morning, he arranged for physical therapy at a storefront place, then went for a run south on US-1, the Overseas Highway. With the mile markers Keys natives relied on, he ran five miles south and five miles back.

MacLachlan did this run more for exploration than exercise. He saw a For Sale sign on the Florida Bay side. The Keys have the Atlantic on the east and Florida Bay, or the Gulf of Mexico, on the west.

MacLachlan ran down the road and came to the end. There was a big lot. Big by Keys standards at least. It was on a short canal shared by only one other house. The canal ran out to Florida Bay. It had possibilities and he memorized the mile marker for his talk with Kelly.

He went back to the motel, checked on the boat, then cleaned up for the realtor meeting. She picked him up in a Caddie SUV. She was forty-years old and highly professional in appearance and demeanor.

MacLachlan explained he had homes in Casey Key, the mountains of Virginia, and Scotland. He told her the amount for which her colleague in Sarasota County had appraised his house on Casey Key.

"What are you looking for, Mr. MacLachlan?" she asked.

"Waterfront. Probably bayside. Bulletproof against hurricanes. As much privacy as can be expected in the Keys where everything is so close together," he said.

"Well, there is a private island about twenty miles from here. Less than a mile offshore. But it's sixty million."

"Too much by far. I may call this my primary home, but I won't spend enough time here to warrant spending over what I expect to get for the Casey Key place."

"Okay. How about size. Most of the ones meeting your requirements are six or seven bedrooms."

"Nope. It's just me. There is no one else on the horizon. I am thinking three bedrooms, one of which will be a study or office. A kitchen, dining room, family room and maybe a formal living room. I'm not real set on a living room though. Two or three full baths. A garage. I want the place on stilts. The parking can be underneath, and the garage can be for storage. Kayaks and the like. Plus, the trailer for my skiff you saw me checking when you pulled in. I will need parking for two cars. When I am gone, only one will be here," he said.

"My colleague told me your home in Casey Key is a Florida cracker style. It has Cyprus siding and a shiny metal roof. Are you looking to replicate a cracker house?" Kelly asked.

"I really like the style. But I am more interested in hurricane protection here in the Keys where big water is on both sides and hurricane-prone Cuba is close."

"Would you consider building exactly what you want?" she asked.

"Perhaps. It presents more opportunities and a lot more variables. Like time, especially. I'd like to be on top of what's going on. I do have some out of state commitments coming up periodically."

"I have a good architect and a good contractor. They would be working for you and your best interest. Plus, I'd stay engaged. Would you like for the four of us to meet this week and talk about options? Of course, before meeting we'd have to find the right lot and maybe option it."

"I'd like your opinion on one I just saw running. It's about a mile from here," he said.

"Okay, point the way!"

They were parking beside it in minutes and she looked up the price. Though high, it was not over the top in his estimation.

"This was one of the lots I was thinking about. The others are oceanside. Maybe better views, more wind, and less shallow water fishing opportunities. I noticed it was a flats boat, not a deep-vee offshore boat on your trailer."

"If I want to go after Mahi-mahi or big grouper, I will hire a guide with the right boat and tackle and some good GPS numbers. I'm more of a shallow water guy as you astutely surmised."

"My husband feels the same way. We eat a lot of mangrove snapper tacos. And return a lot of snook and bones to the water," she said.

"Good for you. I do the same. Let's walk this and get your read on it," he said.

"I'd place the house here and have it face in this direction," she said pointing out into

Florida Bay. You could put your boat lift here. I'd put a concrete block house here. With a water-facing sleep porch. I'd put a sundeck on top for total privacy.

The bedrooms and other rooms as you said. Put hurricane shutters and three lock hurricane doors on all portals. Park underneath. Cars and boat trailer. You would have one motor vehicle and the boat on a lift at risk when you were gone. One motor vehicle only when you were here and evacuated. We'd really need to hear it from the architect and contractor, but I am pretty sure it all could be done for under what you will net on Casey Key."

"It sounds like we should meet with your two guys," MacLachlan said.

"Yes, except both are women. Okay with you?" she asked.

"Of course. I am looking for talent, not gender. Please set it up as soon as possible. I need to get back now. I have a physical therapy appointment at one of the privately-owned PT offices in a storefront on US-1," he said.

"Oh? Recent surgery?" she asked innocently.

"No, just an accident biking recently," he said.

They parted. As she drove the Escalade towards her office she thought about her new customer. He looked very dangerous and was quite affluent. She wondered if he was an organized crime hitman. She may not have been too far off, depending on her perspective. Many people considered governments and big corporations to be organized crime. MacLachlan had not been a hitman for the latter until this last contract. Until people started shooting back. He then turned loose the dogs of hell and hit back hard.

He received a call from his trust banker back at the motel. The banker was able to set up a retirement for the husband and wife who took care of his Casey Key house. It equaled what he paid them monthly. But now they would not have to do anything. They could really be retired. Or, whatever they wanted.

He called them and got both on the speaker. He explained about deciding to sell the house. Then, very quickly shared what he had set up for them. They were thrilled and appreciative. After chatting with them a while, he called his Sarasota realtor and told her to put up the sign. He had explained he wanted to break it to the couple first with good news.

He arrived at the physical therapy office and spent forty-five minutes. He left with his shoulder hurting, but the therapist predicted it would.

A Mahi-mahi fillet and a salad seemed to take his mind off the shoulder. He was not sure whether it was a late lunch or early dinner. Either way, it would be his last meal of the day.

The next call was from Will Grafton.

"Slickmeister! It's me not in the clear." A non-too subtle message this was business.

"Hey, Will. How are you?"

"Finer than frog's hair. You back from wherever you were?"

"I am. In Florida Keys getting ready to build a smaller place and sell the one you have visited. It got to be too much. Fishing is better here anyway."

"Hmm... Does Kate know?"

"Nope. She wouldn't have a vote. She forfeited voting privilege. Just leaving PT, had dinner and going back to the motel. What's up with you?" MacLachlan asked.

"Busy. All sorts of crazy kimchi going on. Rogue

FSB guy blew up a pill plant near St. Petersburg. Russia, not Florida. Big gunfight. One dude killed a bunch of Spetsnaz dudes."

"Do tell? Must have been a pretty tough FSB guy."

"The toughest. Kate thinks she has identified him."

"Oh, I doubt it very much, Will. Nobody knows how many people are in the FSB. Not even them."

"Uh-huh. You said PT. I'm guessing you don't mean physical training."

"No. Physical therapy. I fell off a damn dirt bike. Busted up the bike and my shoulder," MacLachlan lied to his best friend to protect him. His destination fell into the "need to know" category. And Grafton didn't need to know.

"Where was this?" Grafton persisted.

"Where you ride dirt bikes. In the dirt, of course."

"Why do I think you're yanking on my leg?"

"Obviously because you have a leg spasm. And Kate put two and two together and got a brain fart."

"You are really selling Casey Key?"

"I really am. Nothing there has my grandparent's feel since Hezbollah sent the Cubans to blow it up. Everything is new.

"The place I am going to build in the Keys will be blind. Blind trust. Neither realtor has any idea who I am. Using different names."

"Oh. Think somebody is coming after you?"

"Yeah. An old mentor in Germany years ago taught me someone's always coming after me. Look at the Cubans. I was sitting out in the sun playing my bagpipes and there they were. Bombing and shooting."

"That mentor is really smart. Good-looking, too! And you killed every one of them in a matter of minutes. Cold. Unprepared. Except for your rifle and pistol and a lot of ammo by the lawn chair."

"Yep. Sure did. Lucky day for me, huh? Bad day for them."

"I can see you are not going to add anything to our knowledge base, Mack."

"Will, I don't have anything to add. There is no way Kate, even with her brain power, can identify some Russian you say the Russians themselves can't identify. No way."

"Who said she figured out it was a Russian. She thinks it was you!"

MacLachlan did not respond. Damn her magnificent mind!

"Oh, Mack! I have one more tidbit. Did you know the Faheem home in Dubai was hit this morning? Everybody killed. Family, staff, security."

MacLachlan's blood ran cold, but he knew he had to hide it from his friend.

"You know I just rescued them from kidnappers, I take it."

"Of course, I do. You also used Kate's uncle and his underworld gangster cops. And some tough motor scooters I don't know other than your relic friend Gunny."

"You mean the Gunny who is your age? The one who has a girlfriend Kate's age?"

"Don't go changing the subject."

"Just saying."

"Where did you get the other two? They sound pretty good."

"The younger one is looking for a job. Sir 007 across the pond is dilly-dallying about hiring him. If you moved, you could get a good man you can depend on."

"Background?" Will asked.

"Aussie SAS. Sergeant. He could be your body-guard and muscle."

"The director says I need at least one guy. Not a detail."

"Brooksie Strahan could be your man. There's not a weapon made he cannot handle. And he's built like you used to dream of looking reading Charles Atlas ads in your comic books, Will!"

"Who? The short white guy with big arms?"

"No. You are thinking of Popeye, the Sailor Man. Atlas was 5'10." Pretty tall for his generation. The first Mr. World, as I remember."

"Moving on, how do I get in touch with this Strahan fellow?"

"He's in the UK, last I heard. You will have to fly him over for an interview. I will text his contact information to you."

"How about the other fellow?"

"You'd have to pay a lot to drag him away from being head of security for the most popular night club in Mallorca. Former senior sergeant with the French Foreign Legion. Giant of a guy. Tough and impressive. I doubt he would leave, but your call."

"I'll check the kid first. How old?"

"I think slightly north of thirty."

"Send me the details on him. And keep me in the loop next time you get a wild hair."

"I would never put you in a loop which would compromise your position, Will. Never."

Grafton paused on MacLachlan's last, then killed the connection.

"It was the Slickmeister who played superhero in Russia. Kate was right. I gotta have her keep a lid on it. If they killed a billionaire in retribution and his whole household, they'd take him out in a heartbeat." He picked up his phone and hit one of the ten speed dial buttons. This one was near the top. The people whose numbers preceded it were far above his high pay grade.

---

"KATE, NOW PLEASE."

She was there from her office down the hall immediately.

"Close the door." He waited.

"I have been playing 'who can fool the smarter black man' with MacLachlan. Sometimes he forgets who taught him everything he knows, Kate. He can lie his way out of a noose as it's tightening around his neck.

"He did not know the Russians visited Dubai and the Faheems. I could feel him pause. He admitted he knew we were aware of the hostage rescue.

"He figures, correctly, your uncle told you, and you told me."

"Is he pissed at me?"

"Did he tell you Casey Key is on the market and he's moving to the real Keys?"

This caught the brilliant redhead off guard.

"No!"

"Then, I guess he's pissed at you. Selling his grandfather's home he grew up in is a life-altering event. He has a lot of history there. As do you."

"This is your day to catch the two people you are closest to in the world and make them speechless, isn't it?" she asked.

"Indeed."

"So, how are we going to handle it?" Kate asked.

"We are going to try to keep the most dangerous man alive, well, alive!"

"I guess if we ever doubted it, him going into Russia, blowing up a major research center, taking on a bunch of Spetsnaz and living, proves it," she said thinking aloud.

"Unlike you, Kate. I never doubted it. Now. Who did you share your suspicions with?"

"Maria on the Russian desk. She may have had her analysts tracking a few things down."

"Get her and her whole team in here now."

The timing was perfect. Both shifts of the analysts supervised by tactically trained senior analysts were still in the building. There was an hour overlap to allow for briefing the incoming analysts on what had happened during the outgoing analysts' shift. Kate picked up Grafton's phone and hit the speed dial for the Russian Desk.

"Yessir?" Maria answered.

"It's Kate. Is your whole team of both shifts still here? Good! Everybody in Will's office right now!"

Maria had been at the airport when they spotted a man they thought was a movie star or senator and Kate claimed him. It was their first view of MacLachlan, coming into town to teach the capstone course at their tactically trained analyst school.

She led four women and two men into Will Grafton's office. Kate closed the door. Everyone but Grafton looked nervous. Even scared. His expression alone was enough to cause fear.

"Kate," he said, "have you spoken about your suspicion about who the rogue FSB agent really was to anyone outside this office?"

"No, Will. Just Maria and you."

He turned to the eight people other than him.

"Avoiding an international incident and saving the life of an American hero is at stake in this office, right this damn minute. I want everybody here to pick your brains and answer me truthfully and completely. Do you understand?" All nodded.

"Kate came up with the proposition only one man alive could pull off the attack on the Petrovitch Pharmaceuticals CJSC in Petrovia, Russia after Maria advised her of the news and chatter it was done by a rogue FSB agent.

"She thought the man was Mack MacLachlan, who I recruited into the DIA many years ago. He did not stay long. He became a highly cleared and trusted contractor for virtually every agency represented by this office. His specialty has been coming back after pulling off impossible suicide missions. For over twenty years.

"I have spoken with Mack. He is a Congressional

Medal of Honor winner. I have known him since he was a young Marine officer.

*"Hear this and hear it well! It was not him. If the word got out he did it, he would die and we would have something which would be close to the Cuban Missile Crisis. And JFK is not available to bail us out! Do you read me loud and clear? I want to know who you have shared this erroneous intel with! And what was said by all parties. If I detect a hesitation, the FBI will take over the questioning!"*

Will Grafton looked around the room, locking eyes with everyone present, including Kate. There was no humor, no niceness. Just a look which terrified everyone there, including his number two.

He started with Kate and then to Maria. He went through her analysts.

The consensus was the speculation the rogue FSB agent was MacLachlan had stayed within the room. In the discussion associated with analysts speaking, Grafton got the feeling none of them other than him and Kate believed an American could have pulled off such a stunt. They did not believe even one FSB agent could. They felt it was a team and the Russian hierarchy was spinning it.

"Maybe these people aren't as smart as I have been crediting them to be," Grafton thought to himself in his relief.

"Okay. I want you to think of anyone you don't remember right now who you or anyone might have told, or might have overheard a conversation it was MacLachlan, then call Kate. I mean immediately! Call the emergency switchboard no matter what time it is and get Kate. Do you read me?"

He dismissed all but Kate and Maria.

"Maria, any of your people holding back? I was serious as a heart attack about calling in the FBI to interrogate people."

"I believe them. They don't have a clue about the capabilities Mack has. I do, but even I do not believe an American could have infiltrated Russia, impersonated an FSB agent to other FSBs, knocked down a building, killed a bunch of the finest special ops soldiers around, and escaped. No way. Not even Mack."

"Thanks. You can go. Kate, stay over for a minute."

Maria left and Kate again closed the door. It was not unusual, meetings with Will Grafton were always behind closed doors. Even if the director happened to drop in. Especially then.

"So, I probably lied. If anyone Russian or American could pull it off, it's Mack. The Faheem tie in is too convenient. The fact he's hurt makes it more plausible," Grafton said.

"Hurt! You didn't tell me he was hurt! Shot? What, Will?" Kate almost screamed at her boss.

"When I spoke with him I all but asked him if he did it. He played me. I taught him how. He was somewhere in the Keys looking for a new place to live. He has put his grandparents' Casey Key home on the market. He's going to build a smaller house somewhere in the Florida Keys. I have no idea where."

"Hurt! How is he hurt? I can worry about the damn house he did give me a clue about later. Tell me!"

"He said he fell off his dirt bike and hurt his

shoulder. The doctor told him he needed PT for a while. He was evasive where this happened. I could not even say the country in which it happened, Kate."

"Was he shot?"

"I don't know. But whenever he has an injury, it usually has a bullet or two involved. Sometimes a knife.

"I need a week off! I am going down and look for him. Call him and get a triangulation on his cell phone. I'm serious, Will."

"Look, Kate. When I asked him if you knew about selling the house, he told me you lost your vote some time ago. I'm guessing it was when he gave you the ring you have on right now and then you left him high and dry alone in Florida."

"I had just killed somebody in our bedroom in a knife fight. Correct my last. It wasn't somebody. It was a higher up in Hezbollah, damn it! I had to deal with it, Will!"

"Happened two years ago. You look pretty together to me, Kate," Grafton noted.

She did not have a response. How could she? He was right. She had been stonewalling MacLachlan because she wanted to prove something to herself for a couple of years before giving it all up to become a housewife. Then, Lexi appeared, and it was obvious she had lost her chance as Will just verified.

"Permission for leave denied, Kate. If this thing blows to hell, I am going to need you here. National security trumps personal matters every time."

"Then, I hereby resign!"

"Resignation not accepted. You signed a national security agreement and took an oath. I am holding you to it. Your love life, hell, even MacLachlan's very life itself, is way down the priority list compared to an international incident of this ramification.

"MacLachlan would say the same thing. He swore, as I did, to die for his country. He won a damn Congressional Medal of Honor, Kate. He would give his life to save his country in a heartbeat. Assuming he did this attack, for the life of me I cannot understand it. It is totally out of character for the man I have known for so many years. He must have had one helluva reason. A reason I can promise you, neither of us will ever know."

"What should I do?"

"Go home and have a glass of wine. If you call him, don't ask anything about Russia. We don't know if anyone is tapping him, or if so, who. Don't let your curiosity get him killed. You'd never forgive yourself. And I'll never forgive you. Now, get outta here. But stay available, okay?"

Without saying anything, she spun on her Christian Louboutins and left. Five minutes later, she was driving in tears. She had no idea why. She went home, some fifteen minutes away and uncorked a bottle of good wine. She had a glass and sat staring at the ceiling.

Kate fell asleep on the sofa. Her glass was upside down. One of the nine hundred dollar a pair shoes had red wine spilled in it. She never called MacLachlan. Sometimes, no decision is the easiest decision. Even if it was not the best one.

AS SOON AS Grafton had terminated the call, MacLachlan called Johan Schutte's number in Dubai. It rang until it went into voicemail.

He immediately got online and found the corporate number for the entity which had wired his funds. It was, he remembered from talking with Schutte, the head office of Faheem's group of corporations. Schutte would work for it instead of a subsidiary.

"Hello, I am calling from the United States. I have been trying to reach Johan Schutte on his line with no success. Can you ring me through to him?"

"I am sorry. But we had some violence here and unfortunately, Mr. Schutte was a casualty," the woman said in a measured yet sad voice.

"You say 'casualty' do you mean wounded?" MacLachlan asked.

"No, I am afraid Mr. Schutte did not survive the attack on the Faheem residence."

MacLachlan, sick to the very pit of his gut, hung up the phone. Schutte was a good man. A good man working for a piece of excrement. He thought for a moment about trying to attend his funeral, whether it was in South Africa, Dubai, or anywhere else. But he knew the Russians would have watchers there. He had pulled off the impossible. There was no need to stick his face in theirs now. He sat for a long time thinking, then began planning.

MacLachlan had a relatively important, if not busy, day planned. No PT appointment, but a meeting with his realtor, the architect, and contractor.

His first realtor meeting was to transfer money and sign a binder to hold the lot they saw yesterday. The way property was moving in the Keys, Kelly highly recommended a right of first refusal. If he decided not to meet someone's higher offer, he would lose his ten thousand dollars. If he agreed to buy at the contract price, the ten thousand would go towards the full price. He had the money sent in by one of his blind trusts. His trusteeship was in a false name, for which he had ample identification. The realtor even knew him by a cover name.

MacLachlan did not know how worried Will and Kate were. He, however, was being his usual careful self. He was convinced the Spetsnaz from Vega Brigade was his only witness and believed MacLachlan was really FSB. He had no reason to believe otherwise. MacLachlan was armed exclusively with Russian arms and ammunition, and he only uttered a few words in Russian. Certainly not enough to give one a reason to question his authenticity.

He was scheduled to meet with the three people about the house and lot first at the lot, then at Kelly's office.

He slipped the skiff in the water and started the Mercury outboard. It was a racing model rated at sixty horsepower, which he felt was far short of what it really was. He picked a likely salt flat and cut the engine and tilted it up. Taking the 21-foot pole, he poled the skiff onto the flat. The water was warm and around a foot and a half deep. He tied a Lefty's Deceiver fly on and began casting. He played more of the light line out with each cast.

He was looking for fish as he cast. He saw a shadow and cast in front of it.

It hit explosively and took off. It was a redfish and

a large one. The fly line was emptying fast. The fish turned and MacLachlan retrieved a bit of line.

He fought the fish with a smile on his face for ten minutes, then the line snapped, and the fish won. The hook was one which would rust through in a day and leave no harm.

He wound in and tied another leader on and another fly. He figured discretion was the better part of valor and poled off the flat to head back to the motel. He had to back the Bronco and trailer in, drive the boat on and flush the engine before going to his meeting. It had been a hot, sunny day so a shower and crisp dress shirt and slacks were in order.

The architect and contractor agreed with Kelly's placement of the house and of the boat lift. The contractor gave him the card of a boat lift installer she frequently used. She suggested putting the boat lift in as soon as power was run at the site. MacLachlan agreed. It would give him a place to keep the boat instead of a motel parking lot.

They agreed on preliminary plans and approximate prices and the professionals left to develop bids. Kelly went to her office. On the way to Marathon, MacLachlan had passed the supermarket where Solange Camu had gunned down Alexandria Campbell in cold blood. She killed a witness for just being there. Anna Visser had found the fugitive assassin the same time MacLachlan had. He did not know Anna was on the Keys. As his finger tightened on his Glock to kill Camu, Anna shot her under the chin with Camu's own CZ. It was determined to be a suicide conveniently. A Key West based FBI agent investigated the murder of a foreigner traveling on a diplomatic passport.

She believed MacLachlan had killed her and set up the scene as a suicide. After being called off at the highest levels, they reached a state of accord. She said for MacLachlan to call her on his next trip down. They would get coffee or lunch.

He might call, he thought. But he hesitated. She was another beautiful professional married to her career. One who was rising fast and loving it. Which was what he already had. Did he need a second? Or was this type the most convenient. No ties? He did not think so.

With Kelly's help, he found a small cottage to rent while his house was being built.

The design and the construction bids came in. MacLachlan accepted both and purchased the land. The project was underway.

He reviewed the first set of designs and asked for a few changes. The architect agreed and MacLachlan approved a final set of plans.

They went to the contractor and found construction would start in two weeks.

The realtor from Sarasota called and said she had two offers on his property on Casey Key. He told her to accept the one which would close the soonest. He drove the Bronco up and loaded his few remaining guns and photos and kitchenware into the back of the Mustang. He got a car tow hitch from Budget and towed the muscle car and his items back to the Keys. He was out of Casey Key for the first time in his life.

He never looked back.

He told Will Grafton. Grafton did not tell him in

turn he had mitigated a potential disaster which likely would have caused MacLachlan's death. The world and the Russians thought the late Faheem had turned a Russian agent to conduct a hit in retribution for his kidnapping. National pride felt nobody but a Spetsnaz could be good enough to pull such an attack off. Even a rogue one.

Grafton did not tell him what the Russians had decided either. The wily spymaster felt even a little talk with MacLachlan about the attack in Russia was too much.

MacLachlan spoke with Anna. She said business was flourishing and Adele was fully operational and could almost run the office alone now.

This signaled to MacLachlan Anna was getting ready to take on some wet work assignments herself.

"Anna, don't go into Camu's business for God's sake. It is illegal and dangerous and one day, it will get you hurt or killed. I am being selfish. I cannot lose another person I love. Don't do it."

She played coy with him. He knew being an international assassin had always been her dream.

Adele called him later when Anna was out of town. She hinted Anna had gone to consummate a hit contract in France. France was too close to home. Adele had developed keen perception in the six months since he had seen her.

MacLachlan just hoped Anna would not draw her into her own collision course. What they did was illegal to begin with. He warned Adele as he had Anna and they discussed words like "accessory" and "collusion". Adele got it but was having too much fun to think about ramifications.

MacLachlan, in his most recent call with Adele, quipped he was thinking about becoming a fly-fishing monk and living a life of abstinence. Adele broke out in peals of laughter, telling him women worldwide would go into mourning over it.

"And, young lady, how would you know?" he asked.

"Well, I can assume for now. But I'm coming to visit you on a holiday to find out on my own!"

MacLachlan started to remind her he could be her father but decided not to remind her. She was simply gorgeous, after all. He quickly dismissed a whole series of thoughts to assuage his conscience. He changed the subject to fishing. Fishing prompted Adele to say she had another call coming in. "Yeah, right!" he thought.

"One day, I am going to find someone who loves to fish and will have to find another line to change to a safer subject."

With a bit of time to kill while the house construction was started, he decided to call Grafton about the instructing to which he had agreed.

"Good morning, Will. How are you?"

"Busy. But I wanted to talk to you about the instructing thing we planned."

"Exactly why I am calling. Things are settling down here, so I am reaching a point where I can get away and teach some classes. I have officially moved to the Keys. I'm just south of Marathon in a rental cottage now. Weather notwithstanding, I could be in the new place in two months. I can slip off to FLETC or up to your area any time."

"I was hoping you were ready. There's a class of

new non-FBI or DEA agents getting ready to start at the Federal Law Enforcement Training Center at Glynco, Georgia. Most are from the DOD investigative and intel services. Another specialty class is within a couple of weeks of wrapping up at Artesia, New Mexico."

"Can you get me the syllabuses for both, Will? I need a feel for what they are teaching now and will plan my remarks to complement it and be an appropriate wrap-up."

"Which is just what I want. My office is offering your capstone as a freebie on top of what they are already doing. It has gotten a lot of interest, so I want some classes done to keep the interest at a high level.

"The syllabuses are classified in some of the courses. The standard FLETC one is and this specialty one at Artesia is, too.

"I can send them to the Naval facility at Key West by courier. Can you pick them up there? I will trust you to have a secure storage place for them. Nothing is above Secret, as far as I know now. If so, I will arrange for you to keep them where I'm sending and read them there. Just keep any notes you take for your presentation unclassified or low classified, okay?" Grafton said.

"Think about trying to negotiate an office with a desk, computer and safe for me in Key West. I've only been far enough in there to keep my Jag there when I was down here looking for Solange Camu. They may be real tight for space," MacLachlan said.

"Will do, but don't go holding your breath for an office. Even a closet with a safe."

"Okay, Tooth Fairy. But I still believe in you."

"You got more damn chance of a penny under your pillow than an office at Truman Annex or somewhere else in Key West!"

"Humph! A penny hasn't cut it for a perfectly good baby tooth for at least a hundred years, Will."

"I'll let you know when the syllabuses are on the way. Once you get the house built, put in a safe room. You know the specs. I'll get a security specialist from one of the agencies to do an inspection and approval for up through TS."

"Deal! Bye."

"Bye, Slickmeister."

MacLachlan fixed a gourmet breakfast of cold cereal and hot coffee, then went by the site to see how things were progressing.

A team was there sinking the piers to support the stilts upon which the house would be built. It would be twelve feet off the ground. High enough to keep it dry during most hurricanes. MacLachlan knew a big one could destroy the Keys.

The infamous September 1935 hurricane hit the Keys as a Category 5, the highest. sustained winds of 185 miles per hour devastated the lower Keys. Gusts exceeded 200 miles per hour, taking out the railroad to Key West. Four hundred twenty-three people died.

Relative to MacLachlan's stilts on the new house, the Labor Day 1935 hurricane had a storm surge of approximately twenty feet. It swept over the islands, taking people and houses with it. Structures between Tavernier and Marathon were destroyed. Marathon, where he was building, was hit really hard. His stilts were below twenty feet by a few feet.

The design of his concrete block house had a so-called flat roof. It was surrounded by a five-foot wall. The only thing really flat was a twenty-by-twenty foot sunning space on the top. The roof itself had a very slight A shape which directed rainwater through scuppers strategically cut in the wall around the roof. Two of these would empty into rain barrels for irrigation use.

MacLachlan had the architect design these larger, at a foot square. He did not give a specific reason.

His reason was so they could be used as shooting ports if necessary. The architect would not have thought of such use in a thousand years. It was MacLachlan's first thought about them though. Initial power was run to the site to allow for power tool use.

He had the boat lift installed and a roof put on it. He immediately put the Hells Bay skiff on the lift and raised it. It beat launching it from a trailer. He would still trailer the boat over to Chokoloskee to fish the Ten Thousand Islands. The last time he had done it, he camped on one of the Park Service camping platforms. Kate had been with him.

---

WILL GRAFTON PULLED A COUP. He obtained a slightly larger than closet-sized office at a Navy facility in Key West. It had a computer and a safe rated up to Top Secret. MacLachlan, though he had an Intelligence Community access badge, would also be issued an entry badge and password for this particular facility. The entry badge would have an LE mark on it, allowing him to be armed. A windshield entry sticker for the Bronco and the Mustang and he would be good to go.

Grafton had done well by him. He always did.

MacLachlan got notification his package with the syllabuses had arrived and immediately drove the forty miles to his new office. He was not worried about the distance, knowing he would only be in the office infrequently.

He made a point of meeting the security staff and, as an inactive reserve colonel, paid a courtesy visit to thank the commanding officer.

MacLachlan spent several hours going over the syllabuses he needed to amend the notes from the Tactical Analyst School capstone week he ran a couple of years ago.

His notes were unclassified. He locked the classified syllabuses in his safe and drove back to Marathon. He called Grafton.

"Thanks for the office. Just spent several hours there. Will be ready for Artesia and Glynco. Just send me the time to show, duration of my instruction and contact person when you can."

"Mack, you can coordinate with Kate, if you want. She is officially coordinating the program."

"I have not heard from her in a while. Until I do, you are stuck with me."

"Hell, I've raised you like a son for thirty years. What's a little longer?" Grafton said.

Over the next month, MacLachlan flew to Artesia, New Mexico and drove the Mustang up to Glynco, Georgia. The money was not a prime mover for his participation. Staying active was. He now officially considered himself retired, though nobody seeing him on the street would pick him as a retiree.

By the time he got back from Georgia, the house near Marathon was ready to move into. Which meant he had some serious furniture shopping to do. He did not move a stick of furniture out of the now closed and paid Casey Key property.

Two weeks later, he had the house furnished, pictures and plaques hung, a new gun safe lifted in a by a small crane, and he even fitted out the dock box by the boat lift.

He could have had a housewarming party, but did not have anyone to invite.

Instead, he got his own invitation.

"What's up, Slickmeister?"

"I've been traveling a lot. For you. How are you, Will?"

"I'm okay. You are coming up here next week for a three-day capstone for a special group of jarhead analysts in Quantico, right?"

"Right."

"What day are you free to buy me lunch?"

"Thursday."

"Okay. Make it noon at the OK Corral Steak House in McLean. Bye."

*Typical Grafton call*, MacLachlan thought after being best friends with the spymaster for over thirty years. He grinned and finished his presentation for the analysts. His next step was to book a flight to Dulles. It would be good to see his old friend soon. A face-to-face had been a while ago.

MacLachlan delivered his talk at the Marine base. He drove the highly modified early 80's Bat

Jeep over to McLean and cruised the area around the restaurant. Nothing seemed amiss.

He was a little concerned a bodyguard had been ordered for Will Grafton. Grafton had taught MacLachlan what he lived himself. An out of the public eye, low key life. This was one of the reasons MacLachlan had sold the property of Casey Key. Though the Marathon home was almost as valuable, it did not *look* like it was. Perception is everything on the darkside.

There must be some threat extant on Grafton MacLachlan did not know about. It would take more than a pittance of collateral intelligence to even know who the elusive Grafton was or what he did. Which made MacLachlan worry more. The Chinese? Russians? Who? He would press Grafton at lunch.

———

EARLIER THE SAME DAY, a very large, powerful man, going slightly to fat received a call.

"Yeah?" he answered.

"This is Bennett. Your private detective."

"Yeah, yeah. I know who you are!"

"Are you in place near the target's office?"

"We are."

"I am following the target. He is in a beige Suburban with a chauffeur or bodyguard. The guy looks tough so he could be both. Start moving south-west of the office complex. I will keep you up to date on roads and progress. Once it's definite, I will drop off and go home. You can do whatever it is you want to do."

"Yeah, okay. We are rolling in the area now," the man who looked like a pro football player said. He and his associates were exactly what they looked like. Former pro ball players.

MACLACHLAN HAD HAD lunch with Grafton there before. Its location made it a prime eatery for the top of the US intel leadership and its intelligencia. MacLachlan knew his friend would have a technical security countermeasures team inspect and scan the property before the lunch ever occurred.

As per his normal surveillance detection procedures, his ride around the neighborhood a half hour before the meeting was followed by parking, facing outward, in as inconspicuous a spot as possible while still affording a clear view of comings and goings around the restaurant.

He parked the Jeep out of sight around a corner of the restaurant and walked to the front door. There were some columns at the entrance. They provided a good barrier and some amount of cover. He stood behind one in his dark suit, white shirt and dark Ray Bans.

"Humph!" he grunted to himself, "all I need is an earwig to look like a member of somebody's protective detail myself."

A car was coming into the parking lot too fast. It was a luxury hot hatch driven expertly by a beautiful redhead. One MacLachlan had not spoken with for a while or seen in person for a much longer while. She slid into a parking space and got out. Her outfit was almost the same uniform as his. Except she wore a skirt too short for government work and very high red heels. They would lift her to his six feet one inch. Her hair was down. The way he always liked it best.

She walked to the door, then spotted him. She walked over and gave him a very long hug, her head pressed into his chest.

MacLachlan spotted a beige Suburban entering the lot. Driver in front, tall thin black man in back.

His old boss had arrived.

Still behind the column, Kate whispered. "Remember when we last spoke?"

"I do."

"I was going to tell you something important and we got interrupted."

"I remember."

"Well, here it comes. I have soul-searched long and hard and come to a decision. I..."

Before she could speak, the driver door opened on the Suburban and Brooksie Strahan got out, dressed just like MacLachlan. Ever observant, he still missed MacLachlan in the shadows holding Kate.

A black Escalade simultaneously roared into the parking lot and slid to a screeching stop twenty-five feet from the Suburban.

As a window came down, MacLachlan shoved Kate to the pavement behind the column and cleared his coat. The muzzle of his new Walther PDP Compact was swinging towards the open window as he yelled, "Gun!"

Grafton was already out and Brooksie had walked him around the SUV towards the restaurant entrance.

He drew a Glock and saw MacLachlan drawing a bead on the Escalade.

Brooksie pushed Grafton to the ground behind the safety of the front wheel of the Suburban and raised his Glock.

Before he could get a sight picture, a large man in the rear driver side seat of the black Escalade opened up with a submachine gun. Simultaneously, MacLachlan sent three controlled pairs of Buffalo Bore 124 grain hollow points through the window where the shooter was exposed.

A couple had walked out of the restaurant. Stupidly, in view of a gunfight happening with them in the line of fire, the woman began videoing the incident with her phone.

The submachinegun shooter had screamed as MacLachlan's six rounds hit him.

MacLachlan swung the Walther to the left and broke the driver's window with two more so fast they sounded like a single shot.

The big SUV turned in as tight a circle as its length would allow, all four hundred twenty horsepower pulling the turn.

MacLachlan ran out into the parking lot past Brooksie and Grafton. He dropped his mag and did a combat reload, putting twelve of his fifteen rounds from the new magazine into the back window of the Escalade as it sped away, swerving erratically.

He turned to Brooksie.

"Cover and evacuate! I'll drive!" He yelled and jumped behind the wheel of the still-running vehicle. He slammed a third magazine into the Walther as he levered into Drive.

Brooksie lifted the unhurt Grafton in as if he no heavier than a child.

Grafton yelled. "Kate! Handle the cops and press! No names."

The door closed and the big beige vehicle sped off pedal planted firmly to the floor.

"Our big issue, Brooksie, is we are following the escape route of the shooters. But it's the only way I know back to the building," MacLachlan said to the big Aussie who was laying protectively over top of his new boss, gun out.

MacLachlan took the Suburban up to ninety, exactly twice the posted limit. He looked down and spotted a radio. There was a siren and lights control console attached.

He turned the flashing blue grill and rear window LED lights on and energized the siren. Traffic moved aside, sometimes with a little help from the air horn overpowering the siren.

Grabbing the mic off its hanger, he asked Brooksie "What's the call sign for us?"

"Delta-Four, Mack!"

"Delta-Four, Emergency!" he said into the mic. Radio control, he was not sure from where, came back on the speaker.

"Delta-Four. Location and emergency?"

MacLachlan gave him the road, distance from the restaurant and their direction of travel.

"We have had an assassination attempt. The principal and all government persons are okay. The shooters are in a black Escalade."

"They are tracking us by now on the vehicle's GPS tracker!" Brooksie yelled over the roar of the engine.

As MacLachlan rounded a curve he saw a traffic crash ahead and laid on the brakes. He could feel the brake pedal undulating up and down under his foot as the ABS tried to bring the fifty-six-hundred-pound vehicle to a stop.

MacLachlan clicked the mic.

"Control. Delta-Four. The shooters are wrecked in front of us. We have armed subjects exiting. We have to engage. Send help."

MacLachlan threw the door open. He quickly handed the backup .38 in his ankle holster to Grafton. Brooksie bailed out the passenger rear.

MacLachlan could not believe his eyes. These were the arena football players who had assaulted a woman in a DC bar almost a year and a half ago. Grafton intervened, put one in the hospital and the other several MacLachlan was looking at right now almost killed the older man.

MacLachlan had waited in the dark for them to leave interrogation and bear sprayed them in the eyes. He then carefully applied an aluminum baseball bat to their knees and elbows...and, maybe a kidney or two. He visited the assaulter at home when he left the hospital. Kate was with him as a decoy. She was dressed as the hottest hooker ever. He set the guy up in bed with his bodyguard. Both appeared to be asleep. They were actually unconscious. MacLachlan had photographed them and emailed photo to every sports reporter in the DC area. The man was not invited back to football when he recovered. The homophobic owner's lawyers found a clause in his contract and dumped him unceremoniously.

All of the men lost their careers. For the ones MacLachlan had beaten, it was because it was very difficult to play football with destroyed joints. Yet here they were with guns. Standing there getting ready to die.

As one raised what appeared to be a Mac-Ten, Brooksie shot twice and he fell, leaving a pink spray from the back of his head on the one undamaged window in the Escalade.

Another raised a shotgun.

MacLachlan was pissed.

He shot him in the chest four times and the forehead twice. A double "Mozambique" or failure to stop drill.

The driver was head down behind an airbag inflated from the crash into a Jersey barrier, then careening into a tree and spinning back to block the road.

The original shooter was dead from MacLachlan's shots at the parking lot.

"Control, Delta-Four. We are en route home. All shooters neutralized. We cannot hang around in case there is a backup team. Tell Fairfax PD to call for a medical examiner and some homicide detectives. Out."

Lights still on, MacLachlan drove around the wreck. He had to drive off the paved road and into undergrowth. He punched it when he hit pavement and headed back to headquarters at high speed.

"Will, did you recognize those guys?" MacLachlan asked.

"Weren't they the football players somebody virtually destroyed after they put me in the hospital?"

"Yep."

"Mack?"

"Yes, Will."

"Why in hell didn't you kill them to begin with?"

"I was out for justice, not blood. I mistakenly thought I had ended it and justice was served."

"I like this little S&W snub nose. Can I keep it?"

"I'll get you another one. I promise. The one in your hand is kinda special to me."

"Why?"

"It's the one Lexi had in Florida when she was murdered."

Brooksie knew all about the murder of Alexandria Campbell in Florida from his British Intelligence pal, Rory.

"Will?" MacLachlan said.

"What?"

"I told you Brooksie was going to be good."

"Yeah. He's gonna almost be another Slickmeister."

"Yep. But, better," MacLachlan said, chatting now at down to eighty miles per hour in traffic.

"Naw. Good. Real good. But there's only one Slickmeister."

Brooksie, listening, was not totally sure what they were saying. But he realized it was complimentary.

The guards at the complex saw them coming and opened the gates and bollards. They stood aside, M4s at the ready as the Suburban with MacLachlan behind the wheel. He came in hot.

Once they got in, an emergency management meeting was held. Kate was still at the restaurant dealing with witnesses, media, the police, and the FBI.

It was unanimously decided MacLachlan would lose his under the radar cover if identified. He was given a ride to a distant rendezvous where another agent delivered his Jeep.

His cabin was secured each time he left, so he did his reverse procedure of putting the Jeep in the storage facility with his suit and pistol. He donned khakis, boat shoes and a T-shirt with his Barbour waxed jacket over top due to the autumn weather.

He went to Florida. The new house. Home. It did not feel like a home yet. He hoped it eventually would.

On the plane, he thought about how odd it was for the arena football players to attack Grafton. MacLachlan himself was the one they should be seeking to get even with. But, then again, they had no idea who had blinded and attacked them in the pitch dark and ruined their lucrative careers. They must have gotten some inside help somewhere.

He wondered if the Dunkin Donuts clerk was still there dispensing coffee and donuts. He had used her as a credible alibi. An initial suspect in the beatings, she told the detectives he was at the donut shop across town when they said the beatings took place. He had chatted, flirted with her. He intentionally left her a big tip so she would remember him. He had looked at his watch and given a time aloud which was a half hour earlier than it really was.

Then, MacLachlan attacked the impenetrable question. The one he could not answer by himself. What important thing was Kate going to say starting with "I...?" It could have been anything. Anything at all. He did not have a clue.

--------

THE NEXT DAY Warrant Officer Sergey Bulanov, limped to the entrance of the Russian Embassy on Wisconsin Avenue. He would always have to use a cane since the recent incident at the pharmaceuticals' laboratory. A member of Spetsnaz Vympel, commonly called Vega by insiders, he was the new head of physical security at the Embassy.

He showed his credentials and went to his basement office. Pravda and the Washington Post waited on his desk.

He poured some hot water on a tea bag and let it steep.

A first page article on the American newspaper caught his eye. "Former Arena Football Players Attack Government Official."

It was not the headline which drew his attention. His English was good, but not perfect yet.

It was a photo taken by a civilian witness. It showed two men shooting at the attackers. Both were in dark suits and sunglasses. One was big and muscular. The other older and trim. From their shooting stance in a real gunfight, he knew they were professionals.

The newspaper referred to them as "unidentified protection detail members".

He did not have a clear facial shot of either, but the older man, probably Sergey's age, was most assuredly the man who had shot him and then saved his life with a tourniquet and popping a smoke bomb to get him help.

If he was on a US government protective detail, how could he be a rogue FSB agent? Or was he really a really deep FSB undercover agent. One on a new assignment after all?

Sergey wondered what he should do about this possible discovery. He might win a hero medal. Or, more likely, be castigated or worse for blowing the cover story the government had distributed far and wide.

It was a dilemma. He would have to think about whether he should report it. He removed the tea bag and sipped his tea. It warmed him after his cold, painful walk to the embassy.

# TAKE A LOOK AT: RETRIBUTION
## BY BRENT TOWNS

**EVERYTHING COMES AT A COST…**

**Author Brent Towns keeps the action coming thick and fast, lets you up for a breath and then drags you back in for more.**

After he is betrayed and shoots the two most powerful men in the Irish Mob, John "Reaper" Kane is forced into hiding. He thinks Retribution, Arizona, is the perfect hiding place, but he is wrong. Underneath the old, crusty surface of the dying town, hides the Montoya Cartel, for they use it as a funnel to ship their drugs across the border.

Trying to lay low in a town gripped with lawlessness is impossible for the ex-recon marine, especially after the local sheriff is brutally murdered by the Montoya Cartel's *sicario*, leaving an old friend, Deputy Sheriff Cara Billings, the only person standing between them and the town.

Things go from bad to worse when Kane is arrested by Cleaver, the deputy in the cartel's pocket, for shooting a local gang member.

Enter DEA Agent Luis Ferrero who has expressed to his bosses for a long time the need for a task force to fight the cartels on their own ground. He's about to get his wish, and to head up his team, he wants the Reaper.

***AVAILABLE NOW***

# ABOUT AUTHOR

**G. Wayne Tilman** is a full-time author. He retired from the Federal Bureau of Investigation several years ago. Prior to the FBI, he was a Marine, bank security director, deputy sheriff, investigator, and security contractor.

He holds baccalaureate and master's degrees from the University of Richmond and has been an adjunct faculty member there, as well as the University of Phoenix, St. Petersburg College and Florida Metropolitan University.

Some of his law enforcement subject matter expertise includes threat assessment, continuity of operations, security and executive protection, counter intelligence, international terrorism, and small arms. He has been an instructor in those subjects in a number of training academies, conferences and seminars. Mr. Tilman holds the internationally-recognized Certified Protection Professional board certification, generally accepted as the highest in the security profession. He also earned a US Coast Guard 50 Ton Inspected Vessel Master Captain's license.

G. Wayne Tilman's primary interests are family and writing. His avocations are bushcraft (survival/primitive camping), hiking, boating, kayaking, shooting sports, and travel.